DISCARDED

"I might need *you* . . ."

Willa hated the breathy notes in her voice. She wished she could be more forceful. More demanding.

She flattened her palm on Burk's skin. She could feel the soft hairs of his forearm, and the knots of muscle just beneath the skin.

Burk didn't say anything, but his sharp jawline flexed.

"It doesn't have to be anything complicated," Willa continued, feeling a flush creeping up her neck. "Just us. Here and now. Nothing but the present."

She sucked in a breath as Burk inched closer. "What are you saying?" he asked, his voice impossibly low.

"You and me," she replied, her insides shivering. "Let's put something else between us besides the past."

Burk leaned in so far that she was forced to lie back on the faded bedspread. His hands came to rest on either side of her head. His eyes stormed like a thousand blue waves. He moved her legs apart with his knees, and she gasped as he eased himself lower.

"Like this?" he asked. "Is this what you want between us?" He shifted so she could feel the thick hardness of him. She closed her eyes at the shower of sparks that ignited her flesh.

"Yes," she murmured. *"That."*

A Kiss to Build a Dream On

By

KIM AMOS

FOREVER

NEW YORK   BOSTON

This book is a work of fiction. Names, characters, places, and incidents are the product of the author's imagination or are used fictitiously. Any resemblance to actual events, locales, or persons, living or dead, is coincidental.

Copyright ©2015 by Lara Zielin

Excerpt from *And Then He Kissed Me* copyright ©2015 by Lara Zielin

All rights reserved. In accordance with the U.S. Copyright Act of 1976, the scanning, uploading, and electronic sharing of any part of this book without the permission of the publisher constitute unlawful piracy and theft of the author's intellectual property. If you would like to use material from the book (other than for review purposes), prior written permission must be obtained by contacting the publisher at permissions@hbgusa.com. Thank you for your support of the author's rights.

Forever
Hachette Book Group
1290 Avenue of the Americas
New York, NY 10104

www.HachetteBookGroup.com

Printed in the United States of America

First Edition: March 2015
10 9 8 7 6 5 4 3 2 1

OPM

Forever is an imprint of Grand Central Publishing.
The Forever name and logo are trademarks of Hachette Book Group, Inc.

The Hachette Speakers Bureau provides a wide range of authors for speaking events. To find out more, go to www.hachettespeakersbureau.com or call (866) 376-6591.

The publisher is not responsible for websites (or their content) that are not owned by the publisher.

ATTENTION CORPORATIONS AND ORGANIZATIONS:

Most Hachette Book Group books are available at quantity discounts with bulk purchase for educational, business, or sales promotional use. For information, please call or write:

Special Markets Department, Hachette Book Group
1290 Avenue of the Americas, New York, NY 10104
Telephone: 1-800-222-6747 Fax: 1-800-477-5925

*For Ellen Baker, who dragged this one
out of the recycling bin, too.*

Acknowledgments

White Pine, Minnesota, has been a place in my mind for years now. And Willa—well, she's been there a long time, too. Many drafts of her story have come and gone, and I'm grateful to the amazing people who helped her find her way into Burk's arms.

My agent, Susanna Einstein, has tirelessly read drafts and taken calls and believed in not only this book, but me as a storyteller. I owe her my sanity, which I think some days comes at the price of *hers*. Susanna's encouragement helped this book find a wonderful editor, Michele Bidelspach, who gave White Pine and its residents charm and depth and life. I am deeply grateful for all Michele's incredible, insightful work.

I owe a giant thank-you to friends who read drafts of this book early and often. Diana Rose, you not only inspired the character of Betty, but you didn't give up on the White Pine story, even when it was really clunky and bad. Thanks for reading some of those first (awful!) pages years ago. Kristy Demas, Rhonda Stapleton, and Ellen Baker, thanks, too, for your eyes on drafts of this book. And Margaret Yang, your friendship and beta reads have changed the whole landscape of my writing life. I owe you at least six key lime pies.

Colleen Newvine and Katie Vloet, you helped bring a little bit of the Axis to White Pine, for which I'm so grateful and so happy.

And finally, I wouldn't be writing many love stories at all if it weren't for my husband, Rob. You're the cheese in my hot dish, tying everything together.

A Kiss to Build
a Dream On

$\mathcal{P}$ROLOGUE

$\mathcal{W}$illa Masterson shifted her shopping bags from one hand to the other as she rode the elevator up to her sixtieth-floor apartment. *The highest you can go in this building*, she often thought to herself—but not today.

This afternoon, each additional second she spent ascending in the elevator's cramped, square space fostered a growing sensation that she was starving. Not literally, of course—she *had* just eaten a divine spice-crusted salmon with a ginger yogurt sauce for lunch—but instead feeling like she was hungry for affection. For intimacy.

Frankly, Willa knew, she needed to get *laid*.

The elevator stopped and the doors swooshed open. She stepped out, head up, determined to give her boyfriend, Lance, her brightest, happiest smile when she entered the apartment. It might not lead to sex, but at least it would stop her brain from pickling itself in lust-filled thoughts.

The long, carpeted hallway stretched before her. Somewhere, she could hear raised voices and slamming doors. Probably someone getting work done by noisy contractors. It happened all the time in the building.

Thinking about how much she needed a good romp between the sheets wasn't fair, she knew. Sex with Lance had never been melt-your-panties hot. It had never really even been that good. But it had, at one time, at least been *existent*. Sort of.

She clutched her bags, knowing she had countless female friends who longed for their husbands and partners to back off the bedroom antics a bit. Why couldn't she be one of them? Lance had been so persistent and convincing early on in their relationship that she'd agreed to moving in together and combining their lives after a few weeks. She'd done it, had kept taking her birth control pills dutifully, even though that one critical, physical piece between them was...broken. Or soft and limp, depending on your take.

Not that it was just the sex. Willa swallowed, knowing that whatever was—or wasn't—happening in the bedroom was actually a symptom of something else. Of she and Lance shopping too much and not talking enough perhaps. Of them traveling to exotic locations but never venturing beyond the hotel. Willa pictured the first edition book of poetry they'd bought for their coffee table, a lovely piece from the late 1800s with Moroccan leather and gilded pages. They'd spent thousands on the volume, but neither of them had ever read its contents.

Willa walked underneath the hallway's sparkling chandelier thinking that she and Lance weren't opening each other, either. A year into their relationship, and they were like that dusty book: untouched and unexplored. In mind and body both.

Perhaps it was time to acknowledge they weren't museum pieces—that they both needed handling. Maybe even by other people.

The thought didn't sting as much as bring her relief.

She exhaled and continued on—white crown molding above her and plush Berber carpet underneath her. The voices grew louder as Willa rounded the corner. She paused when she saw men in embroidered shirts swarming about. These weren't contractors; they were too clean for that. And they weren't police.

Had something happened to one of her neighbors? She wondered if Mrs. Faizon had finally passed away. The woman was at least a hundred.

Just then, a tall man with a buzz cut marched down the hallway toward her. He was carrying a finely framed work of art, and she was able to read the embroidering on his polo shirt.

Midtown Repossession.

Willa understood immediately that one of her wealthy neighbors had fallen on hard times. Her heart sank with compassion. Her corner of New York City might be wholly focused on status and wealth, and someone's loss often meant another's gain. But it never felt good to see people bumped out of the game entirely.

And then her eyes fell on the art, and her blood turned to ice.

The painting was *hers*: a sparse Andrew Wyeth watercolor she'd fallen in love with a few months ago. It had been hanging above the fireplace.

Dumbly, she cut through the cluster of repo men—one

of them swept past with her jewelry box, another with an original Eames chair she'd purchased at an estate sale—and stumbled into the apartment.

Her heels echoed on the polished wood floor. Her Persian carpets had been rolled up and carried out. Straight in front of her, sitting with his head in his hands on the single couch that remained, was Lance. Standing next to him was a police officer.

"What is happening?" Willa asked. She'd meant to shout it, she'd meant for her indignation to be loud enough to bounce off the now-empty white walls and startle everyone, but she'd barely been able to whisper. Lance looked up. His dark eyes were bloodshot. His face was puffy, as if he'd been crying.

"I lost it," he groaned. "I lost everything."

Willa blinked. This wasn't possible. Lance was an *exceptional* investor. They were so far in the black, he often said, that she could buy whatever she wanted every day for a hundred years and still not put a dent in their wealth.

"There's been some mistake," she replied. A distant part of her realized she was still holding on to her shopping bags. She set them down on the bare floor.

"I'm afraid not," the police officer replied. He glanced through wire-rim glasses at the notebook resting in his thick hands. "Charges are being filed, and I need you to come down to the station."

Fuzzy spots dimmed the edges of Willa's vision. "Charges?" How was losing your own money a criminal offense?

"We'd like you to give a statement," the officer said to Willa.

A statement about what? Dimly, she realized the officer's uniform was the same rich navy blue as the crisp edges of their bathroom towels. She wondered if those had been taken away, too.

"If you'll just come this way," the officer said. When Lance stood, Willa saw his hands didn't fall to his sides. He was *handcuffed*, for crying out loud.

Sudden fear made her jaw tremble. *What had he done?*

The officer led them to the freight elevator near the stairwell, where their things were being loaded. Cramped between her dining room chairs and a postmodern sculpture, Willa stared at Lance.

"What *happened*?" she asked him.

He only shook his head and repeated the same phrase he'd used in the apartment: "I lost it."

Her fear switched to frustration, which in turn kindled sparks of anger. It sharpened her thoughts to a razor's edge. She wanted to reach out and shake Lance, to insist he tell her everything, but the police officer was right there. Best to wait until the station, she reasoned. She wasn't about to add to the mess he'd created by forcing Lance to explain everything right this second.

Instead, she tried to calm her ragged breathing and her churning insides.

Not ten minutes ago she thought she needed to get laid.

Now she understood she needed to figure out what had been going on in her life—what had *really* been going on, that is—while she'd been running around Manhattan thinking everything was fine.

The elevator doors opened in a matter of moments. The ride to the bottom, she thought numbly, always seemed so much faster than going up.

CHAPTER ONE

Two months later
Wednesday, September 19, 11:21 a.m.

Willa Masterson tilted her head back and moaned. Underneath the table, her toes curled in her shoes. Her spine was on fire.

With a hot buttered biscuit in one hand and a steaming forkful of casserole in the other, Willa was as close to pleasure as she'd been in—well, months, really.

Opening her eyes and taking a deep breath, she tried to regain some of her composure. Customers in this crowded, wood-paneled space might begin staring if she didn't stop with the sounds already. Never mind that the food at the Paul Bunyan Diner could make *anyone's* insides heat up with a shivery, goose-bumpy thrill. At least the hot dish could anyway, which was what Minnesotans called a casserole—in this case, a spinach, mushroom, and sausage concoction that had her wanting a second bite before she'd finished swallowing the first.

Willa chewed slowly, trying to savor every moment of

her hot dish bliss. It was all she'd been eating since she'd arrived in White Pine two days ago. Part of it was out of necessity—there just weren't that many restaurants in town, and God knows she herself couldn't cook—but the truth was that Willa had yet to get her fill of the stuff. It was a wonder, really, considering that in Manhattan, there were five-star restaurants that could barely hold her attention for a single meal.

Lucky that the food is so good, Willa thought, taking in her surroundings. The décor was straight out of a pioneer exhibit she'd seen once at the New York Historical Society. The lace-edged curtains were yellowed with age, the fabric fraying. Peeling birch logs leaned into some of the corners, the wood tired and dusty. And the tin plates and lumberjack saws nailed to the walls were more primitive than rustic.

Willa stared over her gingham placemat and imagined ripping out the old booths—wood splintering and nails creaking—and replacing them with shiny chrome tables, the tops so reflective you could see your own face. She imagined painting the scuffed wooden floor a velvety black, and swapping out the sawed-off stump of a hostess station with a sleek podium. It would be the kind of place she could imagine in Manhattan, where all her friends would be angling for a dinner seat.

All her *former* friends, that is, since these days they'd probably rather sue her than have lunch with her.

Willa stared at her chipped coffee mug and wondered what they'd say if they could see her now, shoveling her face full of food at a two-bit diner in her hometown. They'd no doubt purse their perfect lips in barely contained laughter. Their wrinkle-free faces would stretch with mirth at the ramshackle house where she was staying, their manicured hands clapping together at the debacle her life had become.

She knew exactly how they'd react because she'd done it to others herself. She grimaced, remembering how Mercedes Whittaker's husband had dumped her for a much-younger woman. He'd left poor Mercedes nearly penniless in a brutal divorce, and when Mercedes had to move to Brooklyn, Willa had simply deleted the woman's phone number, as if they'd never been acquainted at all.

Willa swallowed a lump in her throat, regretting how awful she'd been and thinking of what a field day these women had—and were no doubt still having—with *her* wreck of an existence.

Not that her life was a mess exactly. She straightened in her seat, reminding herself that things could always be worse. Her dad had once told her that she had a solid brain for business, and a knack for getting things done. So what if she was back in Minnesota? She had a foolproof plan for her life here, and it was *going* to work.

But her gut clenched nonetheless. Part of her was beginning to wonder if she was navigating a new path to success as much as clinging to her only means of survival. Was she here because she wanted to be, or because she *had* to be?

The cowbell over the diner door clunked, and she set down her fork and biscuit, glad for the distraction. She'd expected the contractor twenty minutes ago, and she didn't like being made to wait. She was also miffed that they weren't meeting at her house. Didn't a contractor need to *look* at a project to assess what needed to be done?

Willa knew firsthand how exhaustive the to-do list was since she'd been staying in her childhood home for the past forty-eight hours. By day, she'd pull white sheets off old furniture and try to sweep up years of dust and dirt; by night, she'd lie awake in her childhood bed, breathing in the house's old air and listening for the scrabble of animal feet in the walls or, worse, close by her head. In the quiet darkness with the vermin closing in, she'd battle back tears—sometimes winning and sometimes sobbing until her ratty pillow was soaked with snot, wishing she felt more *victorious* already. She'd left Lance, after all. She'd started over. She was still standing, even if her former friends were rooting for her to fall on her face.

Instead, she'd stare at the ceiling, memorizing every crack and chip, thinking that her own life was cracked, too. She'd go red-faced with the realization of what a fool's life she'd been living in New York. Her friends had been fake, her relationship had been a joke, and her whole life had been covered with a veneer she was too frightened to shed. Until it shattered into pieces before she could stop it, and she was left with raw reality staring her in the face.

In those moments, her only comfort would be the house's persistent quiet. At least there was no one around to see her shame.

Because she'd been pacing the floorboards and staring at the walls in her misery for the past two days, Willa understood precisely what improvements needed to happen with her place. Even so, the contractor had insisted on meeting at the diner. By way of explanation, he said he knew he was up for the job—he'd been caring for the house since it had been abandoned nearly twelve years ago, after all—but he said he wanted to see Willa face-to-face, to determine if working together was going to be a good fit.

The New York Willa never would have put up with that kind of attitude. She would have snapped off her cell phone and found someone who would do exactly what she wanted, precisely when she wanted it. Spoiled New Yorkers could get away with so much. Like stealing their girlfriend's money to make bad investments, for example, not to mention screwing up the finances of every single one of their friends.

Willa was just turning to see if the contractor was, in fact, there, when a man slid into the booth across from her.

"Willa?" he asked.

She couldn't even reply. The air had gone from her lungs. The clinking, bustling sounds of the diner had receded to the edges of the earth. The world had gone still and silent as she stared into the eyes of Burk Olmstead. She'd know that stormy dark blue color anywhere.

B.C.'s Contracting was *Burk's* business. In a million years, she never would have guessed or expected it. But now that he was here, it made perfect sense. No wonder he wanted to meet face-to-face: He wanted to ensure it wouldn't be awkward for the two of them to work together.

Willa continued to stare, speechless, until the lines around Burk's eyes deepened in a confused crinkle. She realized he was waiting for her to confirm her identity.

It had been more than a decade, after all.

Willa forced herself to smile and hold out her hand. "Hello, Burk."

He grasped her fingers in a short, rough shake. The feel of his skin against hers sent an electric tingle through her body—a hundred times stronger than any pleasure the food had given her. She blinked, surprised at how easily it all came back. How her body could remember the touch of him, even all these years later.

He nodded at her. For an awkward moment, neither of them spoke. Willa waited for him to say something—anything—in a greeting: "It's nice to see you" or "it's been a while" or "what are you doing back?" But he remained stonily silent, the hard line of his jaw unmoving. His wide, muscular forearms rested on the table, perfectly still. His dark blue eyes never left her face. Nor did they betray any emotions. They were as hard and fixed as diamonds in a setting.

She hoped her own eyes were the same, but she doubted it. She was alarmed at how undone she felt at the sight of him—just like when they were teens.

Not that she was about to let herself get swept up in old memories.

"Would you like some coffee?" she asked finally. "Or some lunch? Sorry I started without you, but I'd been waiting a bit."

Burk shook his head, instead pulling a small, battered notebook from the front of his plaid shirt. "I'm running behind. We'd better get started."

Willa couldn't remember Burk ever being this gruff. Or this handsome, she thought, taking in the tumble of dark hair, thicker than she recalled, and the edge of his cheekbones, sharper than when they'd dated in high school. The shadow of stubble across his face made her pulse quicken.

Willa, by contrast, knew her recent past hadn't done her any favors. She'd put on weight from all the financial strain and legal battles related to Lance's botched finances. She tried not to think about how her newfound curves must look next to a plate of decimated hot dish.

Not that Burk appeared to notice. He tapped a pen against the notepad's spirals. "So you're finally going to fix the old place up, eh?"

His vowels were incredibly round. "So" and "going" sounded drawn out, as if he was adding extra O's to the words. Willa wondered if she'd talked like that at some point. She must have, but now it sounded like a foreign language.

"Yes, it's stood empty for a long time, as you know. It needs a lot of work."

"What do you want to start with?"

The brusque question was no doubt the result of Burk being time-strapped, but disappointment needled her nonetheless. Did he have to be so curt? She couldn't expect Burk to treat her any differently just because they had a past. But she suddenly felt as if a long-buried part of her *wanted* him to.

No. Absolutely not. She stared at his mouth, fighting off the memory of his lips against hers all those years ago. The warm, tender brush of them. The sweet touch of skin on skin.

Forget it. She was not going to allow her emotions to sidetrack her. She knew firsthand how disastrous it could be to want something that just wasn't there.

Besides, Burk was being terse, not to mention inefficient. If he'd met her at the house, they could have covered all his questions already. They could have walked around and talked about the things that needed taking care of first. If the purpose of the meeting was for them to figure out if they could work together, why was he asking about project priorities?

"As you know, there's a lot to be done," Willa answered carefully, reining in her emotions. "In addition to fixing up the obvious things—the roof, the floors, the windows—I also need to knock down some walls. And reroute some plumbing. Probably also put some additional appliances in the kitchen. A second stove maybe."

For a moment, Burk didn't answer. Willa wondered if his face had paled slightly, or if she was imagining it.

"That's quite an overhaul," he said finally.

"It needs to be. My goal is to turn it into a bed-and-breakfast. It's about time, don't you think? I'm positive this town is ready for a first-class place to stay." Willa didn't know why she sounded like she was trying to talk the entire diner into liking her idea.

Something dark flashed in the depths of Burk's stormy eyes. There was a time when Willa would have been able to read it—to know exactly what every expression or gesture meant—but that was long ago.

"We already have the Great Lakes Inn on the other side of town," Burk said. "And I'm not sure they're exactly bursting with customers. You sure you want to open a second motel when the first one can barely break even?"

Willa's insides flamed with frustration. "It's not a *motel*, it's a bed-and-breakfast. There's a huge difference. And I'm not going to have rotting bedspreads with lighthouses on them like that dump. I'm going to have down comforters and roaring fires and five-star food. Comfy couches and beautiful grounds and freshly baked cookies in the afternoon. Plus fresh juices and teas anytime you want them. Not to mention first-rate wines. All the things they have in B and B's out East."

Burk arched a dark eyebrow. For some reason, the motion sent a shiver through her.

"Sounds expensive," he said.

Willa squared her shoulders. "It will be elegant. *Lovely.*"

"Suit yourself," he said, his eyes returning to his notebook.

Willa had the distinct impression he wasn't convinced. Which was fine, she supposed. She needed a contractor, not a consultant.

"There are a few outdoor issues as well as indoor," she said, pressing forward with her project list. "Some rotted wood on the front porch, though I'm not sure—"

Burk held up his hand. "No need to go into any of that yet."

Willa blinked. She wasn't used to being shut down like this by anyone, much less Burk. In high school, he had once driven to the next town over for ice cream when it turned out that White Pine's own Lumberjack Grocery was out of rocky road, her favorite. She would have settled for vanilla, but Burk told her she deserved to have what she really wanted. When he came back with the rocky road, she kissed him so hard that they wound up entwined together for hours, and the ice cream had melted into a puddle on the counter.

"You under a deadline?" he asked, jarring her back to the here and now.

"Not strictly. Certainly the sooner the bett—"

"Well, I'm always on deadline. And I like to finish

projects quickly. If I take this on, I'll be at the site often.
No screwing around. If I'm in your way, that's just part
of it. I aim to get it done fast. And right. Will that be a
problem?"

Willa sat back, shocked by his tone. She suddenly
debated hitting the yellow pages, maybe trying to find
someone else to do the work. But if it had been Burk caring for the house all these years, then he'd know it better
than anyone. It would only make sense to keep him on
the job.

"No," she replied.

He scratched something on his notepad, then shoved
it back into his flannel pocket. When his eyes met hers
again, she thought she saw a softness there—a spark of
kindness. Her heart fluttered in anticipation. He was going to tell her how good it was to see her, and that it
made sense for them to collaborate on this project together. *Finally*.

Instead, he stood up. "We'll get started tomorrow.
Eight o'clock sharp. I was late today, but it's only because
my truck wouldn't start. That's the exception, not the
rule."

Willa pressed her lips together, more disappointed than
she wanted to admit at his gruff manner. It shouldn't matter to her whether Burk Olmstead was glad to see her.
She didn't need him to be *nice* to her, for heaven's sake.
All that mattered was that he was willing to work on the
house.

Or so she thought until he gave her a small smile. Instantly, her breath caught. She leaned forward, tensing
with an inexplicable desire to hear him say how glad he
was to have her back in White Pine again.

"You have melted cheese on your upper lip," he said instead.

Willa raked her napkin over her mouth, her cheeks flaming with embarrassment as he strode out of the diner. As she heard the cowbell clunk over the door, she suddenly wanted nothing more than to be back in New York, breathing in the dense air of the city as she threaded her way down packed sidewalks, past galleries and shops and restaurants where she could pop in and get sushi anytime she wanted. She rubbed her forehead, knowing that if she asked for an eel roll here, they'd probably send her down to the Birch River with a pole.

Taking a breath, Willa flattened her palms on the table's slick wood top. Two days in, and she already wanted to flee Minnesota. It wasn't a good sign, that was for sure, but New York was in the past. She was going to have to make White Pine work now. She was going to have to make her bed-and-breakfast work, for that matter.

She paid the bill, marveling at how little her meal cost and at how the waitress, Cindi, had dotted her *i* with a heart on the handwritten ticket.

People like Cindi-with-a-heart needed what she had to offer them, Willa reasoned. They were behind the times, and she had a New York aesthetic to bring to the town. People like Cindi would positively eat up the level of culture and sophistication she'd give them with her B and B.

Right. Because shacking up with a fumbling investor and then leaving town when you're on the edge of broke is so high-class, a voice inside her chided.

Willa swallowed. Her past wasn't blemish-free, that was for sure, but she wasn't going to let that stop her. And she wasn't about to let Burk Olmstead stand in her way, either.

He could give her attitude all day long and it wouldn't matter. He could yammer about the Great Lakes Inn and it wouldn't make an iota of difference.

Her job was to think of him as a contractor now, and nothing more.

She stepped out of the diner into the crisp sunshine and tilted her face to the sky. A breeze rustled the leaves of Main Street's trees. The smell from the nearby bakery floated on the air, warm and sweet.

Behind her was New York and all the mistakes in her life she couldn't fix. The embarrassment of it was right there, a tar pit of humiliation bubbling just under her skin. But she refused to crack. She blinked away the tears that sprang into her eyes. A herculean wave of embarrassment was trying to drown her in the idea that she was just a stupid, shallow socialite, and she'd lost everything as a result.

But she wouldn't go under just yet. Because ahead was the one thing she *could* fix: her house.

Or more precisely, Burk Olmstead could fix her house.

Briefly she wondered if she could trust herself alone with him for weeks on end, but then she shook off the thought and the all-over tingle that accompanied it. She exhaled to cool the heat in her body. The girl who had loved Burk Olmstead was long gone, and the boy who had loved her back had disappeared into an exterior as hard as concrete.

Which was just as it should be.

Houses needed lots of concrete, after all.

CHAPTER TWO

Wednesday, September 19, 11:57 a.m.

Burk Olmstead started up his battered red pickup and told himself that his hands were shaking from the vibration in the engine—not from seeing Willa Masterson again after all these years.

When she left twelve years ago, he'd longed for her to come back with a ferocity that bordered on insanity. But *now*—well, seeing her in White Pine again after all this time, he was anxious for her to turn around and head back the way she'd come.

Not that it was any big deal. After all, she barely even looked like herself anymore. Her blond hair was shorter and darker. Her clothes were crisp and tailored, so prim and proper compared to the wisps of T-shirts and shorts he remembered her wearing, the kind that would expose great swaths of her silky skin. In other words, she was a woman now, curvier and more solid in a way that had caught him completely off guard. And if he was honest, had him wanting to place his hand in the space where her hip met her waist—a contour that hadn't been there when they were kids.

He shook his head. Whatever she looked like today, it didn't matter. She wasn't the fiery, hotheaded blonde he once knew.

And once loved, he thought.

Except that was a long time ago. He was a different person now.

And clearly, so was she.

He drove down Main Street, keeping the hardware store on his left and the Birch River on his right. The sidewalks in front of all the stores were dappled with sun and shadow, the leaves on the nearby trees fluttering and dancing. The bright green of summer was yellowing as fall approached—the air was already turning cool, and the sky was that impossible, cloudless blue that would soon form the backdrop for fat orange pumpkins and stacks of yellow hay and baskets of red apples.

The American flag in front of Loon Call Antiques flapped above painted pots bursting with yellow and orange mums. When the snow started, the store would pull in its wooden benches. But for now, anyone could sit and watch the town's hustle and bustle. Not that it was much of a show, but Burk often liked to get a donut at the Rolling Pin, or a scoop of ice cream at the Dairy Dream, and weather permitting, sit on those rough old seats, listening to the whisper of the river or the splash of the small fountain in front of the library.

He loved the quiet comfort of this place, but Willa Masterson never had. Back in the day, she couldn't wait to leave White Pine, which made him wonder what in the world had happened to bring her back. And to think about opening a B and B to boot.

He frowned, still feeling the warmth on his skin where they'd shaken hands. When he was in high school, he thought he would burst into flames just being around her. Now here he was, fighting the same urges. His groin tightened, but he took deep breaths, forcing his muscles to relax.

He'd thought the days when Willa Masterson could have any effect on him were long gone. He'd thought he'd made sure of that. Which meant that if she was back in town and he was getting riled up again—well, he'd just have to work a little harder at putting the past away. He wasn't a sinewy kid in a secondhand leather jacket anymore, trying to get close to the most beautiful girl in high school. Not to mention the richest.

These days, he was fit and successful. Ladies liked a self-made man, which was good for Burk, who liked the ladies. He had it good, he knew. B.C.'s Contracting was doing well. Or if not well, then it was doing fine.

Most months anyway.

Burk shook his head. He was in the black now, and that was all that mattered. He looked great. He felt incredible. The list of things in the world that could mess up his game was short, and Willa Masterson was definitely not on it.

His phone buzzed on the seat next to him, and he glanced down at the text. *Dinner later?*

He fought a stab of disappointment when he didn't recognize the number. He'd hoped it was his sister, Anna, inviting him over for a family meal. Now he'd have to figure out whether the message was from the curvy brunette he'd met at the bowling alley the other night, or the raven-haired cashier at the lawn and garden store. Or that large-animal veterinarian whose skin had smelled like strawberries.

He swung a left at the library and drove up a small hill—out of the river valley and into White Pine's tree-lined neighborhoods—and wondered if he should just invite himself over to Anna's instead. He'd never say it out loud, but spending time with his sister and her family, especially his niece, Juniper, was the highlight of his week. Those dinners were worth it, even if he had to endure his sister fussing and clucking over him all the time, like he was a chick wandering too far away from the coop.

You work too much, she'd tell him when dinner was over and it was time to serve dessert. Inevitably, she'd set down an apple pie or a peach cobbler or still-warm chocolate chip cookies (he had to hand it to his sister, she could bake), along with a strong cup of coffee. Then, like it was a ritual, he'd sip the coffee—black—and try to explain how hard it was to keep a small company afloat. As the owner, you had to do *everything*.

"And that includes denying yourself dessert, too, apparently," Anna would reply, folding her arms across her chest and letting her dark blue eyes, the same color as his, take in the untouched treat.

He didn't know how to tell her he couldn't handle the excess. What were the words he could use to explain the system, the routine he'd developed once he'd realized no one was going to hand him anything in life? He and his sister had grown up in the same hardscrabble house, but they'd responded differently to identical conditions. She had softened, finding clever ways to indulge herself when she could—like baking delicious meals and desserts—whereas he'd scraped all the indulgences away in favor of ruthless pragmatism.

These days, he favored checklists and rules that formed the building blocks of the life he wanted, working as hard as he did because it felt right, like the harder he labored, the better he became. He could control more, do more, achieve more.

Plus, he was responsible for a crew of six. If he didn't pay them, no one did. When times were lean, like they had been recently, it was on Burk to make things right.

He inched the truck down Oak Street, thick tree branches arcing above him. A V of geese honked overhead, wings carrying them south, away from the inevitable Minnesota winter. *You're leaving too soon*, Burk wanted to call to them as the sun filtered through leaves that would soon explode with color. It was the best time to live in Minnesota if you asked him. He threw the truck in park and stepped out into the fresh, open air, filling his lungs with it.

This is where I belong, he thought, facing the house at 802 Oak Street. Willa's house, technically.

He studied the 1920s Arts-and-Crafts-style house as he had a thousand times before—sometimes from the street, and sometimes from up close, when he'd trim back the bushes or clean out the gutters or shovel snow in the winter.

The thick columns on the front, more square than round, rose up to meet a porch roof lined with teak slats. Above that, on the second story, windows filled with thick, wavy glass twinkled in the sun. The third floor was capped with a strong peak, angular and elegant at the same time. The whole house was like that, Burk thought, *angular and elegant*, which was why he loved it so much. He had admired it ever since Willa's family had lived there, when he used to climb up a trellis in the back and sneak into Willa's bed.

It was the only way boys like Burk got inside the Mastersons' house, or any house on Oak Street for that matter. Burk glanced at the stately Victorian next door, and the sturdy brick Tudor across the street. Growing up, his family had lived closer to the river, in tumbledown apartments that were perpetually damp. He could still remember the sandy, moldy smell that permeated the place, so omnipresent you'd swear it was pressed into the walls.

There was a time the Olmsteads didn't belong on Oak Street.

But things were different now. Burk had worked thousands of hours to make something of himself, to build a life and a business that earned him respect and a decent living. He wanted a home on Oak street—*this* home in particular.

He was the one who'd kept the place up after Willa's mom, Edna, had abandoned it. He'd hammered new boards into the porch. He'd torn down ivy winding its way into the old chimney. He'd hacked back the bushes so it didn't look so overgrown. Sure, she'd paid him as a caretaker, but he kept it up even after he'd grown his maintenance company into a contracting business. He'd kept it up even when he didn't get reimbursed for restaining the back deck or buying a new lawnmower when the ancient one in the garage finally expired.

When he was honest with himself, he'd admit that, initially, there was an idiotic, foolish part of him that had wanted the place to look perfect when Willa came home. At least in those first few years after she'd left.

There were days he'd find himself staring down the driveway or peering out of the third-floor windows, aching to see her walking toward him. Always he imagined her returning with an apology on her perfect lips, reaching for him with both remorse and hope. In his secret dream, he'd sweep her into his arms and crush her to him, the past forgotten and the future spread before them like a summer sky.

But the image in his mind's eye grew dim and distant as time marched on and Willa didn't come back. Eventually his mom got sick, and he kept up the house for her, imagining himself buying it for her one day. He'd talked to Anna about moving their mom onto Oak Street for the remainder of her life, letting her live in luxurious surroundings after all her years of poverty and backbreaking work. But Anna just shook her head, reminding him that a big, rambling house was no place for an old lady who couldn't climb stairs. Anna insisted on a nursing home for Mom, where she could be looked after and cared for. Which was precisely what happened, and where Mom was happy until she passed away three years ago.

Burk stared at a gap around the front window that needed caulk, figuring the house was big for him, too. But when he settled down with the right girl and had a family, it would be perfect. And until he found The One, he was having a very good time with all the possible candidates.

In the meantime, he would keep up the house because that was what hardworking people did when rich people like the Mastersons cast things aside. They were careless with valuable items (people, houses, it didn't matter), whereas Burk had the patience and resolve to prove that what the Mastersons left to rot could still become something meaningful, something worthwhile. It was a bitter thought, he knew. There was a shard of sadness in it, too, sharp enough to make him wonder if there wasn't part of him that still wished Willa had come home sooner, and that they'd been able to build their lives together. Right here in this very place.

But that was not to be. And now, in its current state, Burk knew he could get the house for a song. He'd not only restore the home, but make it more beautiful than it had been before. This house had been his dream for years, for so long it felt like he and the house were inextricably connected. It was his past, and it would be his future. Whether Willa was part of that dream didn't matter much anymore.

Burk had sent Edna a few letters about buying the house before she passed away. She'd reluctantly agreed to consider his offer, but then she died, and the title had passed to Willa.

It was a blow to his plans, to be sure. But if he knew anything about Willa Masterson, he knew an old house wouldn't hold her attention for long. And when she lost interest, he'd be there with his checkbook.

Besides, anyone could see this B and B idea was all wrong for Willa. He could recall weekends, back when they were together, when folks from Minneapolis would stream into White Pine to hunt for antiques on Main Street or at barn sales, and Willa would be flying in the opposite direction, into the heart of the city itself, to shop or eat at a new restaurant. The irony of the traffic pattern was never lost on Burk: City folks thought their answer was in the country, while Willa couldn't wait to get out of the country and into the urban jungle.

Sometimes Burk went with Willa on these city excursions, and it was because of her that he'd tried Korean bibimbap and seen an Andy Warhol painting at the Walker Art Center. Life with Willa was never dull—in fact, it was just the opposite, packed with enough curiosity and energy to make him dizzy. His chest tightened, remembering how differently he saw the world when Willa was around. He'd cover her smiling cheeks with kisses, plunge his hands into her wild hair, or run his lips along her golden skin, never curbing the emotions that came tumbling out of him with reckless abandon— happiness, passion, devotion. He'd been drunk with love, it seemed, so intoxicated that sometimes he was light-headed for days.

He shook his head. The memories were pale and far away now, which was how he was determined to keep them, even if Willa was back in town. Light-headedness wasn't a sensation he particularly liked anymore.

The truth was, Willa was never in one place for very long or interested in something past a certain point. Burk figured she'd pursue the B and B idea for a while until she grew bored of it. And then he'd persuade her to give the place up.

Besides, this wasn't going to be a cheap renovation. Not that money had ever been an issue for Willa's family, but if he played his cards right and emphasized everything that needed to be done (and the subsequent costs), he'd have her *begging* him to take the place off her hands.

Burk clenched his jaw, wondering how he was going to feel, working on his house with Willa directing the overhaul. He tried not to picture her full lips and shining eyes, the color of summer leaves. He pushed away the thought, wondering if having her around could be a blessing in disguise. Not because there was any attraction there, but because he could get the first stages of the rehab over with and *she'd* have to pay for them.

He and his crew would get paid for the big stuff that needed to get done regardless, then she'd be gone. He'd get her out of there before she did anything too crazy. Like knocking down walls and messing with the plumbing.

If by some chance she managed to do something he hated in the short time she was here, he could always change it back when she left.

Because she *would* leave. She always did.

And this time, he'd be ushering her out the door, instead of mourning her absence. Burk knew how to push her buttons, after all. He'd had experience getting her riled up, the same way she'd have him straining against his own skin, wanting her so badly his whole body ached. Oh man, they sure could get each other to *do* things back in the day. He tried not to think about how good some of those things had felt when they were together years ago. He closed his eyes against the warmth that suddenly spread through him.

For so long that warmth had been followed by pain, and he wasn't about to let himself forget that Willa Masterson had torn him apart.

More than he'd like to admit most days.

She'd let a crumbling home life drive her from White Pine, refusing to allow Burk to help her think things through or work things out. She'd rejected the idea that

Burk, the poor kid from the wrong side of the tracks, had anything to offer her, and she'd fled to the East Coast.

He and the house—they'd both been abandoned. Together.

He'd worked hard to forget her. He'd filled his life with enough women to create a library of pleasurable memories that didn't involve her. He wasn't about to let the curve ball of her reappearance throw him off balance.

He was focused on his goal instead: the house on Oak Street. *This* was his dream. It was his opportunity to prove that the things that other people thought were no good were actually incredibly worthwhile.

To reach it, he would send Willa packing. It was a favor, really. To her. To the town. And most of all, to himself.

He wasn't that lanky, hard-up kid anymore, and she wasn't the magnetic, unreachable girl who called the shots.

The house required months of work, but he'd have her gone in two weeks. He could all but guarantee it.

CHAPTER THREE

Wednesday, September 19, 3:36 p.m.

*L*ater that afternoon, Willa inhaled the scent of wood smoke from a distant bonfire as she strode across the high school practice field, quickening her step so she wouldn't be late. In New York, she'd never cared much for punctuality, but she knew she needed to start off on the right foot here. Burk had upset her whole morning, but she wasn't about to let that keep her from meeting an old high school friend who had messaged her on Facebook. She'd encouraged Willa to "stop by and say hi" today.

It was a casual request, but Willa could still feel a damp sweat starting on the back of her neck. She knew all too well that an invite to anything—even a casual drop-in—was more than she deserved. She hadn't exactly been Miss Congeniality in high school. And now she worried whether her past might be an obstacle as she tried to start her B and B. Would locals refuse to patronize her establishment because she'd been a ruthless snob more than a decade ago?

It would serve her right, she supposed, for the way she'd had her nose in the air all these years. Karma would make sure she'd show up today wearing her tailored jacket and flawless makeup, and everyone would see right past it, straight to her jumbled, wrinkled insides and fear-knotted muscles.

They'll know right away I'm a failure, she thought, sweating even more. She took a deep breath, telling herself there was nothing she could do about it. Not really. The time to be nice had been years ago, and it was too late for that. It was time to face the music playing *now*.

She stepped onto the red clay track where she had perfected her stride in the 800-meter run when she was a teenager. She blinked when she saw her name still painted on the side of the field house. It was back from when she'd set the high school record in the event, and it still stood.

A surge of pride made her feel both elated and ridiculous. If Lance could see her now, he'd probably caution her not to share her accomplishments any further. "If you trained for the Olympics at Choate, that's one thing. But setting a track record in a Midwestern town won't impress anyone."

He'd be right, of course. It was one of the things that she admired about him, the way he knew exactly how to navigate their social circle in New York. What to say, what to withhold, which invitations to reply to, which to blow off. He knew the game even better than Willa did, and that was what had drawn her to him. She'd respected Lance for his acumen, for his ambition. At least until his need for *more* had consumed him—and led to a series of bad investments.

Looking back, she could kick herself for not being the daughter her dad had raised, the one who checked bank balances regularly, who looked at the bottom line and didn't automatically trust when other people said her money was fine, just fine. She'd been a fool for months, trusting Lance blindly with her finances; and she'd lost nearly everything as a result.

But no more.

She lifted her chin in spite of her pounding pulse, and kept walking. Her fortune had started in White Pine with her dad's sound investments, and it would be rebuilt here, too. Literally, in fact, starting with her childhood home.

Her one asset. She could sell it, she knew, but her dad had taught her to cultivate an income, not pursue a short-term windfall.

"Make your assets work *for* you," he'd told her.

When it had dawned on her that a *house* could make money—that it could generate revenue like all good investments—she had two choices. Either she could rent it out to tenants, or fix it up and turn it into a B and B. She'd chosen the latter, mostly because she herself needed a place to stay (she couldn't very well rent out a house that she needed to live in). Plus she liked the aesthetic of a B and B. She loved the idea of creating a space where people could enjoy themselves.

And all it would take was a top-to-bottom renovation.

She blinked against the image of Burk Olmstead that was suddenly in her mind. His sharp jaw, his dark hair. As her feet carried her across the red clay, she realized that Burk had cheered for her during track meets on this very same field, his voice ringing in her ears above everyone else's. Her cheeks heated at the memory of his hands on her body when they were young.

We were just kids, she thought. *We didn't even know what we were doing.* And yet there was a magical sweetness about their relationship she'd never forgotten. He might be a jerk now, but back in the day, he had been the prom king to her prom queen, tipping her plastic crown sideways to get her to smile. *My king*, she'd called him, giggling when he'd put the plastic scepter in the front of his pants. He was always ribbing her, cracking jokes, and getting her snobby, stuck-up self laughing until her sides hurt.

That is, until her dad passed away late into her senior year. Oddly, her desire for Burk had only increased when her dad was gone. Burk had loved her, had been there for her when no one else had, holding her so she wouldn't be consumed by the bottomless pit of her own grief.

Willa trembled at the memories she'd locked away for so long. Their bodies pressed together in the back of Burk's old Chevy. Willa's bed at night, when he'd climb the trellis and sneak in. Later, after her mom fled the house, he came in the front door. They'd spent whole nights together, and she could remember his fingers trailing down her skin, both of them shivering with excitement and maybe a little bit of fear.

You never forget your first time. *And sometimes those memories get you all hot and bothered while you walk across a field*, Willa thought.

She shook her head, wanting to tuck her memories away. After all, it wasn't exactly an ideal time. Her dad had passed, her mom had taken off, and her story with

Burk hadn't ended happily ever after. She wasn't exactly brimming with warm feelings for that period.

Instead, she focused on the other side of the track. Her high school classmate Audrey Tanner was standing near a cluster of aluminum bleachers. It had been twelve years since they'd seen each other, but they'd recently gotten back in touch on Facebook. Out of all the friend requests Willa had sent to her old classmates when she knew she'd be coming back to White Pine, Audrey's had been one of the few that had been accepted.

"You made it!" Audrey said as Willa approached. Audrey's white teeth flashed, and her thick brown ponytail bounced. Willa relaxed slightly when the note of sarcasm she'd half expected to hear in Audrey's voice wasn't there.

"It's so good to see you," Willa replied as the two women embraced. Willa couldn't remember them ever hugging in high school, but here they were, clutching each other as if they'd been best friends. Willa was so used to the brief, showy hugs of her friends in New York that she was surprised to find herself squeezing Audrey for real. She told herself it was because she was trying to show Audrey she wasn't an ice queen anymore, but part of her wondered if she was actually, genuinely desperate for a few crumbs of affection.

It didn't help that the close hug meant Willa could feel Audrey's lean, muscled figure underneath her work-out clothes. She pushed down a stab of envy. Audrey was the high school girls' track coach now, and had almost the same body as she did when she and Willa had run together all those years ago. As the two women separated, Willa pulled her jacket more tightly around her torso. Her figure was decidedly *not* the same.

"It's so insane that you're here," Audrey said, her molasses brown eyes fixed on Willa's. "I can't believe you actually moved back. How are you settling in?"

Willa hedged, suddenly wondering how to answer. *The coffee here is swill and I'd kill for real espresso. Burk Olmstead is my contractor and it took my breath away to see him again. Sometimes at night I think it's too quiet and I can hear my own pulse.* Instead, she gave Audrey her biggest Miss Dairy Pageant smile. If she was going to build a new life in White Pine, she needed to convince everyone that she—the former prom queen, track star, and pageant winner—not only belonged here, but *loved* it.

"It's wonderful. I am beyond excited to get my B and B up and running. It's going to be just like having one of those romantic East Coast establishments right here in White Pine."

She hated the tinny sound of her own voice, how high-pitched it seemed as she worked to cover up her fear of being here. Of failing again. Of being in White Pine only because she had no other choice.

Audrey's smile didn't falter. "If you need anything, be sure to let me know. And of course, you'll have to come to Knots and Bolts. Everyone will want to see you."

"Knots and what?" Willa asked, wondering if Audrey was setting her up for something involving ropes. Just then, a swarm of girls came pouring out of the high school. They gathered around Audrey, who gave Willa a hold-on-a-minute gesture.

"Hurdlers, you'll go get set up over on the other side of the track," Audrey said, glancing at the battered notebook she'd picked up off a metal bench. "I want you to do five drills apiece and time one another. Sprinters, you stay on this side with me, we're going to do a different exercise. The entire team is all going to start with a one-mile warm-up, except the distance runners, who are going to do three more miles on top of that first mile. Distance runners, do your first mile on the track with the rest of us, then I want you to race over to Lumberjack Grocery and back. Got it?"

Audrey clapped her hands and the girls took off on the track. "Remember, it's four laps to a mile!" she called after them.

Willa watched, impressed at Audrey's newfound authority. In high school, Audrey was so much mousier. She wore thick glasses and got good grades and didn't say much. If it wasn't for track, Willa knew their paths never would have crossed. In fact, there were times senior year when Willa was bitterly jealous of Audrey's natural speed and athleticism.

"So Knots and Bolts," Audrey was saying, tucking an errant piece of her glossy brown hair behind an ear. "It's the local fabric store run by Betty Lindholm, you remember her? She has a lovely back room and there's a group of us that get together for a recipe exchange on Thursday afternoons. You should come by tomorrow."

Willa forced her Miss Dairy smile bigger. "Oh, that sounds great," she said, though her brain was reeling. Betty Lindholm was a name she hadn't heard in years, and had forgotten about entirely. Shame surged deep within her, and she glanced down at her hands, pretending to inspect a cuticle. She wasn't sure she was ready to face Betty. And standing here with Audrey Tanner was awkward enough already. Memories she'd kept buried were beginning to dig their way out, and she wasn't sure she wanted to see what poked through.

Suddenly, there were sharp cries from the track. A runner was down on the ground, clutching her ankle.

"Oh, hells bells," Audrey muttered, taking off. Willa raced after, trying to keep up and not look like she was struggling for every breath, which in fact she was.

"What happened?" Audrey asked when they arrived at the panting redhead, who couldn't take her pale blue eyes off her foot.

"I tripped over a starting block," she said, gesturing to a scattered pile of them. "I just wasn't watching."

"What were the starting blocks doing over *here*?" Audrey asked, kneeling down to probe the ankle tenderly. Her voice was calm, but Willa could see her neck was corded with emotion.

"W-We just dropped them off until we finished the mile," replied a stocky brunette standing nearby. Her eyes were shining with regret. "I know this isn't where they go. I'm so sorry."

Audrey's brown eyes locked on Willa's. "Thirty girls and I'm the only one supervising them. It's madness."

Willa's heart constricted at the strain visible in Audrey's face. Strain and something else. Powerlessness perhaps.

Suddenly, memories surged in her mind's eye: Willa and Audrey at cross-country meets, both of them in shorts and tank tops getting ready to run. Instead of supporting her teammate, Willa would hiss insults at the lanky, spectacled girl when the coach had wandered away.

Audrey Tanner was good. She was fast. And Willa, who'd been given everything she'd ever wanted, couldn't contain her jealousy that she didn't have Audrey's talent.

Willa's eyes smarted. She didn't want to remember

this stuff. She wanted to bury it underneath polite Facebook messages and her new B and B plans. She wanted to shut the past away, and pretend it had never happened. But she was beginning to think she couldn't do that and make her B and B work. How could she be around all these people and expect them to support her new business if she didn't acknowledge she'd wronged them?

"Injuries make me queasy, too," a freckled girl next to her whispered. Willa could only nod in reply.

Audrey elevated the injured ankle slightly. "Emily, go get the nurse and I'll stay here with Layla. Everyone else, get back to your practices. Show's over."

The crowd parted, leaving Willa with Audrey and the injured girl, Layla.

"I'm so sorry," Audrey muttered. "I should have been watching this more closely. I would have seen the starting blocks if I'd paid attention."

"It's not your fault, Ms. Tanner," Layla replied. "I don't think it's that bad. I'll be back at practice tomorrow, I bet."

Audrey glanced back over to Willa. "Budget cuts. I used to have an assistant coach and an equipment manager. Now, it's just me." She sighed. "I feel like I'm letting these girls down. I just can't do it all, you know?"

Willa nodded, but the truth was, she *didn't* know. She had no clue. Growing up, she'd been pampered and sheltered, which only got worse when she turned eighteen and suddenly had access to a fat trust fund. Added to that were inheritances as her parents had passed. Which meant that, in New York, her biggest source of stress involved figuring out what to wear when she volunteered at the Bishop Gallery, a small and exclusive art museum.

And even *volunteer* was too gritty a word for what she did, which was mostly drink espresso and flip through Christie's catalogs.

"I can help," Willa blurted out suddenly. Both Layla and Audrey looked up.

For a moment, they all looked at one another. *Shut up now*, part of her brain commanded.

Her mouth was uttering words she could barely comprehend. "I mean, I'm out of practice, obviously, but I can help you. I ran track, remember?" She swallowed nervously. *No doubt* Audrey remembered.

Audrey studied Willa's face.

As the silent seconds ticked by, Willa was overcome by the urge to take it all back. She should have just let well enough alone. But something in her wanted to help, maybe even wanted to atone for the past in White Pine by lending a hand. Frankly, it would also be nice to be part of something that involved a *team* again. Willa knew she'd been a bitch to her track mates back in the day, but underneath everything, running had made her happy.

"We have practice three days a week," Audrey said slowly. "You're going to have to . . . jog a bit."

Willa squared her shoulders. "I can run just fine. And I can coach some girls over hurdles and make sure there's not crap in the middle of the track if that's what you need."

"We can't pay you."

"I'm *volunteering*."

Audrey exhaled. In that breath, Willa knew that Audrey likely doubted her ability to coach anything, much less a gaggle of girls. No wonder. Standing here in her tailored jacket and jewelry, Willa knew she looked out of place. She could feel the heat of embarrassment mottling the base of her neck. She felt so much shame, about both the past and the present.

And she had to admit: She might not let herself volunteer, either.

A breeze picked up on the other side of the field, swaying the tops of enormous pines along its grassy edge. Audrey watched the dance of the boughs for a moment before taking a breath.

"Thank you," she finally acquiesced. "That's very kind. Next practice is tomorrow, three thirty sharp. Afterwards, we can head over to Knots and Bolts for the recipe exchange."

Willa didn't know whether to be happy or horrified. *What had she just signed up for?* It had been years since she'd run track. Good grief, if she needed to atone for the sins of the past, there was probably a better way.

Except she hadn't been able to *find* a better way. Hell, she had barely been able to scrape together *this* way. She had no friends, very little money, no college degree, and only one thing of value—a falling-down house—that could generate any kind of income.

Six months ago, Willa would have pitied the small existence of everyone in White Pine. People like Audrey who worked hard and made smart choices. People who had lives and friends and steady jobs. Now she was beginning to realize she'd had it all backward. That she was the one who had been living the joke of the existence—not them.

"This will work, Audrey, I'll make sure of it," she said, and knew she meant more than just volunteering. She meant *everything*.

Audrey nodded, and returned her gaze to Layla's injured ankle. Off in the distance, Willa saw a flutter of white and realized the nurse was approaching from the brick school building. She'd be here in moments. That meant there was no time to figure out what Audrey had meant when she'd mentioned the recipe exchange.

What *was* a recipe exchange, for starters? And was Willa really going to have to face more high school classmates at Knots and Bolts?

The answer was looking like a resounding yes. Willa told herself she'd better get used to it. She shifted uncomfortably in the afternoon sunlight.

The good people of White Pine didn't need her—but boy, it was looking more and more like she was going to need them.

Chapter Four

Thursday, September 20, 7:58 a.m.

Willa's eyes flew open. She sat up straight and glanced at the alarm clock: seven fifty-eight. She'd overslept. And now, there was a furious pounding on the door.

Burk was already here.

"Coming!" Willa hollered, and rolled off the ancient brass bed, the worn mattress squeaking in protest. Getting new furniture was high on the list of things to do, but it would have to wait until the walls were replastered and painted and the floors refinished and—

Wham! Wham! Wham!

Burk was going to break down the door. "I said I'm coming!" Willa yelled, shoving her feet into slippers and shrugging into her robe. She fumbled with the robe's belt as she flew down the staircase, the warped wood nearly tripping her and sending her face first into the banister.

Wham! Wham! Wha—

Willa yanked open the door furiously. "I said I was coming!" She drew herself to her full height, glaring at Burk, whose enormous frame was back-lit by the golden sun climbing in the sky. As a halo of rich morning light ignited Burk's chiseled form, she suddenly wondered if she was still dreaming. Even in a flannel work shirt, his broad shoulders and rippled muscles made him appear like a Roman god. His ebony hair was like coal set aflame. His skin, tan from all the outdoor work, was suddenly bronze perfection. Her heart hammered involuntarily at the overpowering sight of him.

Burk stopped, mid-pound, and dropped his fist. For a moment, they both stared at each other.

After all the noise, it was suddenly, eerily quiet.

Willa's chest heaved from racing to the door, her robe falling slightly open. She watched Burk's eyes slide from her flushed face to her breasts, which she could feel brushing against the fabric of her nightgown with every breath. Her nipples were tight and hard against the cotton, and she suddenly pictured Burk's mouth on them, kissing and sucking with wild abandon. The thought sent flames along her skin, even in the cool morning.

Burk snapped his eyes back to Willa's face, but it was too late. They both knew what he'd been staring at. Willa quickly began belting her robe around her body, both mortified and thrilled at what he'd seen and what she'd felt. It didn't help that she fumbled with the material, thanks to a trembling in her fingers that hadn't been there a moment ago.

When she looked back up at Burk, she wondered if she'd find his stony expression unmoved. Just like yesterday. Instead, he was gazing right at her, a small smile creeping into the corners of his mouth. *He was laughing at her.*

Just like that, her embarrassment flipped to anger. Who did this guy think he was, pounding on her door, staring at her tits, and then *grinning* about it all?

"Good *goddamn* morning to you, too, Burk," she said angrily.

"Rise and shine," he said, his grin widening.

Willa barely held back from slamming the door in his face. Instead, she shot him the fiercest glare she could, and stormed off toward the kitchen.

She swore she could hear him swallowing back laughter as he followed her inside.

* * *

Willa made sure her robe was secured tightly as she brewed coffee and pulled down her favorite mug—a chipped ceramic behemoth that had been her mom's. It was one of the few things she'd salvaged from the New York apartment and brought to White Pine.

When she wanted to remember the best parts of her mom, it was through this mug. Like how her mom would use it to fix Willa warm soup for fighting off the flu, or bring her hot tea as they sat outside in the sharp springtime air, both of them shivering but desperate to enjoy the outdoors after a long winter.

Willa also couldn't recall her mom serving anything to Uncle Max from the old mug, which was another bonus. Especially since Uncle Max turned out to be more than just a family friend (the "uncle" was honorary, not literal).

Her dad's coffin had barely been lowered into the ground when her mom raced off to Minneapolis to spend more and more time with Max.

Willa's throat tightened, even though she'd paid an Upper East Side shrink thousands of dollars to try and make it so her eyes wouldn't smart every time she remembered the crushing ache of her mom's abandonment. Her eighteen-year-old self had feared she'd driven her mom away and that the one person who was left— Burk—would leave her, too. The therapist had helped her see that her mom's bad decisions weren't Willa's fault, and by the end, Willa had forgiven Edna, even flying into Minneapolis for the funeral a few years ago.

Still, it didn't help that being in this old kitchen made the memories that much sharper and more vivid. Willa pulled the mug closer, wanting suddenly to pad off into the living room alone, to study the ceramic and see if there was some clue in the glaze, something that would make all the pain of the past make sense. Because whatever peace she'd made with Edna didn't take away from those first brutal months after her dad's death.

Willa was suddenly afraid to look at Burk, afraid she'd focus on his strong workman's fingers and recall the way he'd run them through her hair, over and over, soothing her battered heart and mind after the funeral. "It'll be okay, I'm here," he'd say. And she'd weep, wanting to believe him but feeling cold dread sink into her bones nevertheless. She'd tremble with fear, wondering what she'd do if he took off as well.

So she hurt *him* instead. She winced with the memory of how awful she'd been.

The coffeemaker gurgled, and Willa started. She

shoved aside the old memories and grabbed cream from
the fridge. She tried not to think about how she could
still feel Burk's eyes on her. She prayed he couldn't
tell what she'd been thinking, because the last thing she
needed was him knowing she was reliving their relationship in her mind's eye. Not that she'd ever know by the
way he leaned in the door frame, casual as could be,
not to mention as *silent* as could be. His mouth was a
hard line as he took in her movements. His strong neck
was unmoving, and she saw with odd satisfaction that
it was the same warm brown color it had been in high
school from shirtless days in the sun. She could recall
putting her lips to his salty skin when he finished mow-
ing a neighbor's lawn or trimming hedges or weeding
flowerbeds.

A shiver prickled her flesh, and Willa peeked down,
making sure every part of her was still tucked neatly into
her robe. It was. But she couldn't help wondering—had
Burk registered anything when he'd stared at her, when
they'd faced off at the front door? The thought of his eyes
on her breasts sent a scarlet heat burning through her. She
blinked, alarmed by how much she enjoyed the idea of
Burk hungering for her.

You don't want your contractor leering at you, she reminded herself. This was business. Professional. Willa set
a spoon in the old porcelain sink, hoping Burk didn't see
how flustered she was.

This was ridiculous. She felt like she was in high
school all over again, with Burk Olmstead suddenly oc-
cupying her every thought.

To her relief, the coffeemaker beeped and she poured
a mug for herself. She didn't offer any to Burk. *Two*

can play rude, she thought, resting against the peeling linoleum counter and taking a sip. She arched an eyebrow at him, daring him to ask for some.

Of course, he didn't. He just stayed in the doorway, never taking his dark blue eyes off her. *They're like a tumultuous ocean*, she used to tell him. Like waves crashing against the rocks.

Suddenly her *heart* felt like it was crashing against the rocks, too. Every beat was like water slamming against stone, over and over. Her chest quite nearly ached. Burk's proximity was starting to unnerve her.

Thankfully, he spoke, interrupting her thoughts. "I think we should tour the house this morning, and I can gauge what specifically needs to get done. I'm not going to lie, though—I don't think it will be a short list."

Willa nodded, even though his tone was downright ominous. Were things really that bad? She hoped not. Her dad had run the White Pine Bank and Trust for years, and he'd built a fortune over his lifetime. It was a fortune that had passed to Willa, and a fortune that Lance had squandered. Still, she'd salvaged enough of what little was left for some house repairs. When her now-very-small pile of cash ran out, however, there was no more to be had. She needed to be careful. And get her B and B up and running as soon as possible.

"All right. Where should we start?"

Burk pulled out the notebook from his shirt pocket again. Willa noticed how strong—how big—his hands were. They must have doubled in size from high school. She tried not to think about how they'd feel against her skin.

He joined her at the linoleum counter. She could smell

him, even over the coffee—a mix of citrus and pine and fresh-cut wood. She set down her cup with a thump, suddenly aware of how close he was. Their bodies could actually touch if they each scooted in a few inches.

He showed her the scratches on his notepad, written in his blocky, angular hand. "I already have a project list started here. Obvious stuff I can see just by looking at the place. It's in order, from basement to roof, and subcoded by cost. The most expensive projects are in red. Midlevel projects are in blue. And relatively inexpensive projects are in green."

Willa squinted at the pad, wondering if the whole thing was alphabetized to boot. "That's a lot of red."

"There's going to be more. I haven't been inside in a while. Your mom left me a key, but I haven't seen that much up close yet."

Willa chewed her lip. She'd anticipated the house would need some work, but she hadn't planned on it needing a total overhaul. Her stomach clenched with worry. *Please let what I have be enough to cover it all*, she prayed silently.

"You should change," Burk said, closing the notepad. "We need to get started."

Willa bristled. She'd change if and when she wanted. "I'm fine," she insisted. "Let's go."

Burk glanced at her slippers, as if questioning her footwear, but didn't say anything else. Instead, he headed toward the basement, Willa following.

"See the crack there?" he said, standing on the cement floor at the bottom of the stairs and pointing to a wall behind the ancient washing machine. "That's a foundation issue. We're going to have to dig out around it and see how things have shifted before we can fix it. It's serious. And it'll be expensive."

"I have no idea what you're looking at," Willa protested. In the dim light, all she could see were cobwebs and dust.

Burk switched on a flashlight. Of course he would have one at the ready. His beam illuminated a small crack, around six inches long.

"That?" Willa asked. "You're calling that little line a serious issue?"

"It's foundational," Burk replied, his tone sharp. As if that explained it.

"If you say so."

Burk rapped his knuckles on top of the water heater. "Have you showered yet?"

"What, today?"

"No. In general. Since you've been here."

"No, Burk, I've been here for *three days* without cleaning myself. Of course I've showered."

"And it's been hot?"

Willa hesitated. "Well, not hot, no. It's more like lukewa—"

"New water heater, then." He shifted the flashlight to his back pocket while he wrote it down. Willa was starting to hate that notebook.

"There's some old knob-and-tube wiring down here. It's not up to code. I gotta call in a buddy to do that. So you're looking at another couple grand there in electrical."

He flipped the page of the notebook. The list went on.

"New insulation is a must; you're letting in cold air underneath the floors above. It's inefficient."

"I can live with inefficient," Willa said.

Burk shook his head. "No. You can't live with it. It's critical."

Willa tilted her head. "Insulation? Is critical?"

Burk just kept writing. He wouldn't meet her gaze. Her gut tightened in response. Surely he wasn't inflating the seriousness of all this, was he? Burk was a lot of things, but he wasn't crooked. He wouldn't swindle her.

Would he?

He might if he was still mad, Willa thought. If he was still furious for the way she'd abandoned him twelve years ago without a phone call or a note and started over—Poof! Just like that!—in New York.

Words she'd never said were suddenly bubbling in her throat. In the basement's musty darkness, she suddenly wanted to grab him and explain to him why she'd fled. Burk knew the basics, of course—her dad's death, her mom's absence, Willa's loneliness—but did he really understand how afraid Willa was that she'd lose him, too?

Burk had a job lined up with a landscaping company after graduation, and told her he wasn't going anywhere, even as all their friends were getting ready for college. But a needling doubt had Willa questioning everything as summer waned. As her classmates began to disperse for school, Willa convinced herself that she had to leave as well. She had to get out before Burk left her first. *Because he would. Everyone did.* Or so she believed at the time. And once he took off, she'd have no one.

So she fled to New York, reinventing herself as a socialite and cutting herself off from the boy she loved, and from the town where the life she'd known had crumbled.

Would it make any difference to say all this now? She opened her mouth to try, but the timing was all wrong.

Burk was focused on the repairs, and he barreled ahead with his list.

"New paint and caulk down here," he continued, oblivious. His blue eyes swept from floor to ceiling. "And I recommend a new washer and dryer."

Willa shook her head. Questions about the past faded amid the demands of the present. "Does it matter if I don't want a new washer and dryer?" she asked, eyeing his notebook. "Because you just keep writing, Shakespeare."

Burk stopped. "I'm outlining everything. You don't want a new washer? Fine, I won't install one."

"That's right, you won't."

Burk straightened. "Don't shoot the messenger. It's an old house. Your mom left it a long time ago, and you didn't do anything with it. It's just been sitting here for twelve years. If it costs money to fix as a result, that's no one's fault but your family's."

Ouch. Willa wanted to fire back, but she couldn't deny he was right. She couldn't blame Burk if everything needed to get overhauled. He'd been a caretaker, not an owner.

The people who should have cared about the house— Willa and her mom, namely—never had. So now it was up to Willa. The weight of the responsibility pressed down on her in the basement's close space. The memories of her family, and of Burk if she was being truthful, were practically mixed into the plaster and paint of this old place. She'd have to face them the same as she faced the rotting wood and leaky pipes.

With a deep breath, she met Burk's gaze. "You're right," she said, "let's keep going." The repairs had to get done, no matter what had led to them.

They worked their way back upstairs. New windows were needed everywhere. The kitchen had to be ripped down to studs. Floors had to be sanded. New outlets had to be put in. The ceiling had to be replastered. The bathroom pipes had to be refitted. And that was just the basics—it didn't even begin to cover the changes Willa wanted in order to turn the place into a thriving B and B.

On and on Burk went, pointing his flashlight at things and writing it all down. Not to mention frowning over the costs. "That's gonna be a steep one," he'd mutter, scribbling furiously.

At the end of it all, Willa's head hurt and her eyes smarted from studying all the minute details everywhere. She was exhausted, and more than a little bit worried. At this rate, she wondered if she should just raze the house and start anew. It would probably be cheaper.

When it was all over, she slumped in a chair at the kitchen table, her head in her hands. Burk puttered on the front porch, making sure he didn't miss anything.

Dear God, she thought, *the man takes thorough to a new level.* His notes were meticulous. His ideas were articulate. It was as if he'd spent weeks preplanning some of these fixes. How to redo the built-in bookshelves in the living room, for example. What kind of flooring would be best in the kitchen, or how to maximize space in the reading room on the first floor.

She heard the front door close and the thump of his work boots as he came back inside. The warped floorboards creaked as he made his way to the kitchen.

"Can I join you?" he asked, gesturing to a metal chair next to her, the one with its upholstery ripped. Clumpy yellow stuffing leaked out of the tear.

"Of course," she replied, trying to smile. She didn't want Burk to see the repairs weighing on her.

He eased his body next to her. She could smell the fresh air on him, and resisted the urge to sidle closer.

"You sure you want to do this?" he asked, folding his massive hands on the table. Willa stared at the depths of his blue eyes, thinking about how to answer. She noted the flecks of green there, like dark pine needles floating in a deep stream. There was something else, too—a hardness she hadn't expected. When they were together, he'd been the one to shake his hips and sing to her like Elvis, making her guffaw with laughter. She was the one who needed to loosen up, not him. Now stress tightened the muscles around his neck. She could see the strain just underneath the skin. She suddenly pictured her fingers on his flesh, working out all the knots and tension.

Because it would be helpful to him, that is. Not because of anything...else.

"I—I don't know," she answered, erasing the picture of the imaginary massage. "It's a lot."

"You could always sell," he said. "If it was me, that's what I'd consider. Make it someone else's problem."

"But it's *my* problem," Willa said, wondering where she'd go if it wasn't here. How would she make money? She had no friends. No college degree. And no career prospects.

"Doesn't have to be all yours," Burk shrugged. "House like this, even with all its needs, could still go. Market's soft, but you might find someone."

"Oh," Willa replied, wondering why Burk sounded like he didn't want the job. It would probably pay for his kids' college. If he had kids.

She sat back, very much aware that she didn't know anything about him these days. Was he married? All these years, and she still selfishly thought of Burk as hers in some way. It never occurred to her that he'd find someone else, though of course, that would only be natural.

"A big project like this would take time," she said. "It might keep you away from...Mrs. Olmstead."

Burk paused. "There is no Mrs. Olmstead."

Relief flooded her. It shouldn't have mattered. But it suddenly did.

"This is no small thing," Burk said, barreling ahead. "If you want to sell, now's the time. I would even discuss that option with you."

Willa felt her eyes widen. "You? Want to buy this house?"

"I'd consider it. I'd make you a fair offer. I've been taking care of it all these years, after all."

Willa studied him. If she sold, she could take the profits of the house, mix them with the little bit of money she had left, and...what? Start over somewhere else maybe. And do...something. She didn't know what. But maybe she could think of a new plan. Even if it meant shirking her dad's financial advice.

"What do you think is a reasonable price?" she asked.

"I would say one twenty-five. In this town, that's solid. Respectable. And this place needs a lot of fixes."

"One hundred twenty-five thousand?" she asked, her voice tight with incredulity.

"Yes."

She drew her brows together. "Are you kidding me? In New York, that would buy a closet. With a rat's nest in it.

And no bathroom. This house is more than three thousand square feet. It sits on nearly an acre of land."

"We're not in New York. This is White Pine, Minnesota. And a house just down the street with no problems and no issues just sold for one forty. So I'm telling you, one twenty-five is a very fair price."

Willa shook her head. She could remember a day of shopping for clothes where she'd spent close to what Burk was offering for an entire *home*. It made no sense. That couldn't possibly be right, could it?

"No. That's too low. I wouldn't take any less than five hundred."

Burk's mouth made a little O. "Are you kidding me? A half million dollars for this dump?"

"No less," Willa said, sitting up straighter. "And while we're at it, you seem like you're inflating a lot of the repairs here. I think maybe I need a second opinion on this job."

Burk's face reddened. "That's not necessary." He seemed to be struggling for words. "My crew—they'll do a good job here. They want this project."

Willa wondered what Burk wasn't saying. Was there something more going on here? "A good contractor finds a way to work with their clients," Willa said, "not against them."

"I *am* a good contractor."

"We'll see." She knew she sounded like a bitch, but she also knew she needed to keep costs down, too. And the best way to do that was to have Burk think she could give the project away to anyone else at a moment's notice. "We'll revisit estimates as they come up. I also want to be able to pick out kitchen cabinets, as well as floors and paint. I don't want you doing any of that."

Burk scoffed. "I don't care about kitchen cabinets."

Willa stared at him. "You know, I realize I don't deserve a warm homecoming from you. But this whole grumpy contractor routine is really grating."

There was a flash of something behind his eyes. Hurt? Surprise? "I never thought I'd see you again," he replied stiffly.

"Disappointed?" She forced a playful smile onto her lips, even though her heart was racing. It wasn't fair to bait him like this, she knew. For crying out loud, she'd fled. She'd *hurt* him. No matter that her hands were clenched together with regret under the table. No matter that New York had failed her, Willa had failed *herself* even, but Burk Olmstead had never once failed her. Not ever. And now she'd just tempted him to say *yes*, that he was disappointed she was back around. It was a terrible move, especially since, deep in her bones, she wanted him to say no—to confess that he was delighted to have her back around again. Never mind that Burk would never use the word *delighted*.

Burk inched closer to her. She could feel his body heat, could feel something inside her twist at his nearness. Even sitting, he towered over her, and she had to tip her head back a little. If she inclined his head toward hers just slightly, she realized, their lips might meet.

"I'm not disappointed you're back," he said, his voice low, "but I don't think you're suddenly going to like White Pine."

According to the way her neck hairs stood on end and the way her skin prickled deliciously at the heat of his breath, she liked being in White Pine very much. Or at least her body did, as long as it was this close to Burk.

He pushed away from the table and stood, the gap of air between them suddenly cold. Willa shivered.

"I'll be up on the roof if you need me. I'll call my crew later in the afternoon to get started on some plastering." His clinical tone had her muscles tightening with both frustration and disappointment. And then he smiled, big and catlike. Willa wondered what that was about, until she looked down and realized her robe had fallen open again. Her nipples were pebbled against her nightgown, and he had certainly gotten another big eyeful of them.

As she heard his boots on the shingles above, Willa steeled her resolve. Burk Olmstead wasn't going to tell her whether or not this new house—or this new life in White Pine for that matter—was a good idea. It was too late for that.

She was going to make it work. She had no other choice.

CHAPTER FIVE

Thursday, September 20, 11:47 a.m.

*B*urk nearly fell off the ladder.

Twice.

Damn Willa Masterson and that stupid nightgown and those emerald eyes of hers, he thought. She'd followed him around the house all morning tousled from sleep and looking like the most delectable thing he'd seen in days.

No, weeks.

It almost made him feel badly for how he'd made sure to point out every flaw in the house during the tour. He'd inflated the seriousness of each issue, which was unprofessional to say the least. He'd left Willa with the impression that the whole thing could come toppling down at any moment, and he'd clouded her bright eyes with doubt. But it had been necessary.

And it had almost worked.

At least until it had backfired spectacularly. He'd pushed too far, and now he had her questioning whether or not she should get other estimates. He'd just have to keep the costs in check, is all. Especially if it meant giving his crew some work for the next few weeks.

Besides, Willa was already debating whether to sell. Granted, her price was ludicrous, but a few more days of this, and Burk might be able to talk her down. Once she realized what a project this house was going to be, she'd abandon the whole endeavor.

Or at least, he hoped she would. Then he could buy it for himself and transform it the way he'd imagined for the past twelve years.

Truth be told, though, the Willa he remembered wasn't so easily swayed. It was part of what he had loved about her—how she barreled through her life confidently. He smiled, thinking about the time she'd convinced the high school administration to start a newspaper. She'd prevailed upon the IT manager, Mr. Quaid, to load publishing software onto a handful of school computers, and she'd cajoled the bespeckled drama teacher, Mr. Wolcott, into supervising the publication.

On her own she'd figured out how to write headlines, decks, and stories. Even more impressively, she'd had kids thinking it was cool to be flipping through the paper as they ate their lunch in the cafeteria. Later, when she passed the role of editor along to a different student, she'd said she only wanted the paper so that the school would write about her track wins. In secret, though, she'd confessed to Burk that she had loved starting the paper and being its editor. "I can't believe I started something that will be here after I'm gone," she'd whispered to him, her beautiful face shining with enough excitement to make his chest ache.

That version of Willa knew what she wanted and went for it. It was part of what had drawn him to her in the first place.

These days, however, she seemed less secure. Something about this situation wasn't right. She had concerns, and he could see them etched in her face. If he could better understand them, perhaps he could find an angle to exploit.

That wasn't the only thing he wanted to exploit, he realized, remembering the way her full, round breasts had brushed against her nightgown, and how her skin had been rosy with morning freshness.

He nearly groaned at how curvy and womanly her shape was now.

Burk remembered Willa being all plains and angles in high school. Now he could imagine getting lost in the sweet, soft space between her shoulders, along the lines of her collarbone, in the tender skin of her thighs, and then moving upward to—

The hammer slipped and came down directly on his thumb. Pain flared.

"Dammit," he swore, so loudly that a pair of cardinals took flight from a nearby tree—a streak of scarlet angry enough to match his mood.

Get a hold of yourself, Burk.

He sat back on his heels, forcing his breathing to slow and his mind to stop racing. He reminded himself he didn't find success by accident. He ran out and chased after it, day after day, week after week, job after job. He found it because he was focused. *Disciplined.*

Keep your eye on the prize, his mom used to say to him. Usually after working a double shift at the bakery, her clothes dusted with sugar and flour and her skin smelling like bread.

For his mom, the prize was keeping him and his sister, Anna, clothed and fed. And hiding any extra money from his dad, who would just drink it away if he found it. *When* he found it, more like it. The apartment wasn't that big. There were only so many places to stash an old Coke can with the lid cut off, fat with change and rattling like an old car.

His mom might have lost the fight for the Coke can, but she had won the bigger battle. She'd taught her kids resilience. Especially Burk. And his prize was this house. The pleasure of working on it, of knowing that he, not Willa, would reap the benefits from all the improvements.

She'd throw up her hands eventually and scamper away. Just like she had in the past. And when she did, he'd have the house all to himself.

Burk picked the hammer back up and tried to picture the brunette from the bowling alley. He was meeting her later tonight. *Lori*. That was probably it. Or was that the name of the leggy blonde he'd met at the gym? He tried to imagine bowling alley girl's dark hair, her olive skin. But all he could see were Willa's nipples, the color of ripening strawberries.

I just have to work harder, Burk thought. At forgetting Willa. At focusing on the house. At getting more done. At keeping his crew employed. At thinking about the woman with the pale skin and dark eyes who'd just moved into his apartment building.

He grabbed a handful of nails and brought the hammer down again and again, until sweat broke out on his forehead and soaked his flannel collar.

When he was exhausted, when it was lunchtime and his stomach was growling, he simply hauled up another pile of shingles and redoubled his efforts.

* * *

Willa stared at the pile of decorating magazines open on the kitchen table, trying to ignore the sound of hammering on the roof. She gritted her teeth, concentrating on the pictures, but like the cacophony that surrounded her, the images grated on her every nerve. *Nothing was right.*

All of the rooms she saw on the glossy pages were too polished, too perfect. The furniture was too minimal, the walls too white. She'd loved this look in her New York apartment—the gray tones, the silver accents, the dark hardwood floors—but she just couldn't picture it working in her old family home.

"Like trying to put lipstick on a pig," Lance might say, though even that wasn't quite right. It was more like the house needed a homey touch she just couldn't identify—something beyond the leather books stacked just so, or the fresh-picked flowers arranged in sleek vases.

The only problem was, Willa didn't *do* homey.

She paced along the faded floorboards—past the sagging, flowered sofa in the living room and around the battered claw-footed table in the dining room—wracking her brain for how to fix her decorating problem. What would she have done at the Bishop Gallery? She tried to think of the house like an exhibit she needed to curate. Her thoughts didn't get very far with all the hammering, however. The ideas and sounds blurred together in her mind. She couldn't take it anymore. She had to get out of the house.

She grabbed her purse and marched toward the car, wondering how she was going to survive months of this. It would only get worse when Burk moved to the inside projects, and then there would be dust and paint and plaster chips covering everything, in addition to the noise. And when he was done, what then? She had no idea how to decorate anything. A bed-and-breakfast might be a revenue stream, it was true, but first you had to know how to run one.

She had to make this liability into an asset, to quote her dad—just like her one-time friends the Davenports had. They'd started a couple B and B's, mostly in Maine and Vermont. As far as she knew, they were doing well for themselves. Not pre-Lance levels of money, but they could afford vacations in Paris and could put *No Vacancy* on the front door whenever they felt like they needed a break.

It was an appealing lifestyle that beat out a desk job with a boss and boring meetings and no paid vacation. Sure, Willa would need to figure out a few B and B logistics like how to cook all the meals, change the sheets, clean the bathrooms, and God only knew what else. But she could handle it.

The rising tension in her shoulders wanted to convince her otherwise. *Easy does it*, she told herself. *Do not panic.* It was all going to work out somehow. She was a fast learner and could teach herself what she didn't know. And it would be worth it when her dream B and B was up and running, and guests were stepping over the threshold with bright eyes saying things like, "Breathtaking!" and "Stunning!"

Willa stabbed her key in the ignition and peeled off,

letting the speed and freedom of her new vehicle clear her thoughts. She never drove in New York, where taxis and walking and the occasional hired car were more than sufficient, but here, the wide roads and open spaces gave her a thrill she didn't even know she wanted.

She could hear mud spattering the underside of her car and wondered at her vehicle choice: a Volvo. A practical car for an impractical girl.

Formerly impractical, she reminded herself.

She was smart. Savvy. And determined to rebuild her life after Lance had squandered so much of it away, making reckless investments he thought would bring money in fast.

So what if it meant she had to cook some breakfasts and clean some sheets? With a little luck and hard work, she'd earn back her stolen fortune, plus build a thriving business in the interim.

Speaking of thriving businesses, Willa figured she should visit Knots and Bolts downtown before the crew gathered there tonight. Her new B and B would need custom drapes and possibly custom linens, and it made sense to talk to Betty Lindholm about it. Maybe sending some business her way this afternoon would help clear the air later that evening. She could have a chat with Betty, then come home and change before track practice and the recipe exchange.

Easy, breezy.

Right?

Willa's heart fluttered behind her breastbone. *Hardly.* Seeing Betty Lindholm meant more than just a conversation about custom fabrics. It meant Willa would have to face someone she'd been awful to in high school.

Not awful, Willa thought determinedly. Just…honest. That is, if you could say that making fun of someone's facial features was *honest*.

Willa suppressed a groan and tried to remind herself that she was the prom queen. She was the pageant winner, and she was the one who'd moved to New York to live the glamorous life—which she *had*. At least for a while. And now she was back, determined to start over as a successful B and B owner in her hometown.

The idea of talking to Betty Lindholm again should *not* make her skin prickle.

Only, it did.

Willa realized the sensation was more shame, akin to what she'd felt with Audrey. It crawled along her body and pinched her nerves.

The sun peeked out from behind spongy white clouds as she drove toward downtown. She tried to concentrate on the warm fall rays instead of her shivers of dread.

CHAPTER SIX

Thursday, September 20, 2:15 p.m.

Willa stepped into the dim, cramped store space and paused to let her eyes adjust. "Hello?" she called tentatively, wondering if she'd misread the *Open* sign.

She walked forward a few paces. The inside of Knots and Bolts was a dizzying array of fabrics crammed together so closely there was hardly room to maneuver. She fingered a yard of silk and could imagine the store substituting for a fortune-teller's booth at the circus. It was all colors and drapes and confusion—the perfect environment for the right soothsayer (or salesman) to get you to believe just about anything.

Willa glanced at a polka-dot fabric where the polka dots were actually dogs' faces. *Purple* dogs' faces. She turned away.

Beyond all the ribbons and fabrics was a small doorway leading to a back room. The door was cracked, and Willa spotted a shadow of movement.

"Be right there," someone called.

It was Betty. Even all these years later, Willa still recognized her voice.

Willa could picture Betty's curly blond hair, her round face, and her wide eyes. *And her jutting teeth.*

For so many years, Willa had called her *Bucky* Lindholm. And that wasn't even the worst of it. Willa had made references to beavers all the time around Betty. *How's your beaver? Oh, you like beavers? What do beavers eat again? That's right, wood.*

Willa swallowed, suddenly overcome with regret. She could try and play it down all she wanted, but she had been horrible to Betty. She had used the poor girl to perfect the art of clever cattiness. In New York, the skill had transferred seamlessly. Only instead of overtly making fun of people's faces, she'd lace her conversations with droll condescension, placing her put-downs *just so*, asserting her power not with terrible names but with sarcasm and wit.

Willa had modeled the behavior for her friends. They, in turn, adopted the skill flawlessly when it came time to use it against her. When Lance lost everything, she was suddenly the brunt of all the jokes. She was the pariah, standing outside a group of people who had secretly wanted to see her fall.

And what a spectacular plunge she had given them.

Willa turned back toward the front door. Her whole body ached with remorse. How had she behaved so cruelly for so long?

She grabbed a nearby handful of seersucker cotton, wondering why she couldn't have realized the error of her ways without the humiliation of financial ruin. It had taken a terrible fall to make her see that her life, and the lives of the people around her, had become a series of blade edges, each one sharper than the next. They sliced into one another every time they moved or changed direction. Coming up or going down, you got cut.

Willa released the fabric, feeling slightly sick. She could stand here feeling sorry for herself all she wanted, but it was beginning to dawn on her that *seeing* the error of your ways and *atoning* for it were two different things.

Her past had consequences. She couldn't just start over in White Pine—or anywhere, for that matter—without facing them.

Eventually, she would have to face the people she'd hurt.

People like Betty Lindholm, for starters.

She took a deep breath, trying to calm her nerves. She could do this. She was genuinely sorry. That had to count for something. Right?

She heard more movement from the back room. Her throat tightened.

There was no reason to rush her encounter with Betty. She had a few more hours before the Knots and Bolts gathering. What would be the harm in postponing the inevitable for just a little while longer?

She headed for the door, squeezing past bolts of cloth, seemingly as endless as ocean waves. Her purse got stuck on the end of a thick roll of shimmering satin, and she had to yank it free. The door was nearly in reach. She needed to get out.

Almost there, she thought.

"Hello? Can I help you?" Betty called to her retreating back.

Willa closed her eyes against a tide of anguish. She almost answered, but at the last moment, she simply ignored the query, and stepped out the door.

* * *

Willa felt the sun on her cheeks first: They were already burning with embarrassment, and the golden afternoon light seemed to add insult to injury.

Her sensible heels clicked on the cobbled sidewalk as she fled to her Volvo, locking herself inside. She buried her face in her hands, feeling the scarlet heat of dishonor on her skin. Tears pooled, but she wouldn't let them fall. She *couldn't*. She might feel terrible for the way she'd behaved in the past, but sobbing wouldn't change a thing. The people who *should* be crying were Audrey and Betty, and here they were holding down good jobs and being productive members of their communities.

It certainly was more than Willa had been able to do.

She sat up and took a deep breath. As awful as she felt, she knew she couldn't sit in a Volvo dwelling on it. Come what may, she was going to see Betty later, and crying on Main Street wouldn't make that encounter any less difficult. While she could, she needed to get back to her layouts, her designs, and figure out how one even *ran* a B and B.

Focusing on the here and now, Willa steadied herself. It was time to head back to Oak Street. She placed the key in the ignition, but nothing happened. The engine wouldn't turn.

She jiggled the key, made sure she was in park, and tried again.

Silence.

Willa jumped when a set of knuckles met her window. They rapped once—twice. "You okay?"

Willa looked up to find Burk's blue eyes blazing with concern on the other side of the glass. Her hammering heart froze in her chest. What was he doing here?

"You need something?" he asked.

I'm fine, she mouthed, ignoring him to focus on the problem at hand. He wasn't going to show up while she was parked on Main Street and act like he hadn't been a total jerk that morning. No way.

She pressed on the gas, turned the key a number of times, and then exhaled sharply. Something was really amiss with the engine. She wondered briefly if it was the transmission. That was a word she'd heard her dad use when things went badly with cars. *Transmission*.

"Let me in," Burk demanded from the other side of the glass. He went around to the passenger door and tried to open it. It was locked, and Willa stayed still.

"Willa," he said. He took a breath. "Please."

As if she were watching someone else's hand, Willa stared at her fingers on the unlock button. The switch flicked. The locks lifted.

And then Burk slid into the vehicle. His smell was everywhere at once in the small space. Fresh pine and an undercurrent of salty sweat, which didn't turn her off at all, but instead had the opposite effect. A tingle started in the base of her spine and didn't let up.

"What's the problem with the car?" he asked.

She worked to steady herself. "Nothing. Why are you here?"

"I was down at the hardware store getting some things.

I saw you, and you looked like you were having trouble."

"I think it's the transmission," she said. "I'm sure I can get it going again in a moment. I'm fine. I appreciate your concern."

Something tugged at the corner of his lips. "The transmission? That's a pretty serious problem."

"I'll handle it."

Burk leaned over, his arm coming to rest on the back of her seat. Willa froze, realizing that she could press herself into the crook of his shoulder with no difficulty whatsoever.

"Dash light says you're out of gas."

"Excuse me?"

"Right there." Burk pointed to a tiny orange light next to the speedometer. "That little pump? Means you're out. Probably why the car won't start."

She stared at him. Surely it couldn't be as simple as that. "So it's not the transmission?"

Burk's whole mouth quirked with amusement before he managed to pin it back. "No, it's not."

Willa's face reddened. He must think she was a complete idiot.

"Let me go get you some gas," he said. "I'll be right back."

"What, now?"

"Sure, it's close by."

He moved to exit the car. "Wait! It's fine. Please. Let me do it. I need to get reacquainted with the gas pump anyway."

Burk looked unsure. A little V formed between his brows. Willa caught herself staring at it, remembering the same crease on Burk's much-younger face. "Come on," he said, interrupting her thoughts, "I'm happy to do this."

"No. It's what I get for being a New Yorker for so long. I haven't driven in ages."

"All right," he relented. "But how'd you get around in New York, then, if you didn't drive?" *He's asking the question like he's genuinely interested*, Willa thought, though she didn't let herself believe it.

"Mostly cabs and such. Sometimes the subway, but I tried to avoid it because it's dirty. A lot of the time you can just walk if you want."

"Sounds pretty nice. Why'd you leave?"

Willa shook her head, wondering why in the world Burk was in her car, asking after her like he cared. This morning, he'd acted like he couldn't care less.

"My circumstances...changed. That's all."

His blue eyes held her and wouldn't let go. "Changed so much you're back in White Pine out of gas?"

"The B and B is my priority now. I need custom drapes and linens, and I was visiting Betty Lindholm at Knots and Bolts for exactly that reason." She made her voice deliberately light. *Just a visit with Betty like we're old friends.*

"Did something happen in there?"

He asked the question as if he already knew Willa's reception in White Pine wasn't going to be a warm one. And why wouldn't he? This was a small town. The way Willa had spread hurt like fairy dust—well, people were bound to talk about it. Both then and now.

Willa studied him, suddenly wanting to confess how awful she felt about the past. If anyone understood how she'd acted in high school, it was Burk. She'd even treated *him* badly, at least at first. She'd wanted to dismiss him, telling him that she would never date someone *who wore those clothes*. But his gaze was always so intense. It seemed to pierce her skin, going straight into her platelets and nerves and marrow. It was as if his eyes were telling her that, deep down, they were just the same: an assemblage of cells and parts that would work together. If she'd let them.

When she'd finally opened her heart to him, it had been a relief, in a way. She had found someone she could be herself with.

Which meant Burk got a front-row seat to all her bad behavior. They'd fought about it in high school, even, with Burk telling her she was beautiful and smart and that if she'd let other people see her true self, it would be better than being on the offensive all the time. She never listened, of course, but maybe he'd actually understand what she was going through now.

"Do you remember how I used to make fun of Betty?" she asked hesitantly. "I was pretty mean to Audrey Tanner, too. And now they've invited me to their recipe exchange, whatever that is."

Burk nodded. "I can see where that would be awkward."

Willa waited for him to continue, but he seemed to be done.

"Do you talk to them much?" Willa asked after a moment, wondering if Burk might have some useful intel.

"Mostly I talk to my sister. You remember Anna? She's in the group. Thursday afternoons they bring dishes. Anna is a good baker." He studied Willa. "Maybe you should be more nervous about your food."

"The past is what's gnawing at me. I have a lot to— account for."

"Seems to me you should think more about the recipes."

"Because food is the way to win people over around here?"

Burk shook his head. "Because you were always so bad at anything in the kitchen. Remember the roast?"

Willa laughed in spite of her concern, recalling how she'd tried to cook a Valentine's Day dinner for him their senior year. She'd purchased a *roast*, for crying out loud, like it was the 1950s and she was Betty Homemaker. It had been so badly scorched, she'd set off the house's fire alarm. Burk had to take her out for pizza instead.

She smiled at him. "You had to save the day. As usual."

"You call getting pizza saving the day?"

More like loving me when I wasn't lovable years ago and offering to get me gas just now, she wanted to say. Instead she just nodded.

"Huh," Burk said, his eyes not leaving her face. "Where I come from, I think they just call that being there for each other."

There was an awkward silence. Willa broke his gaze and stared at her nails. Acutely she recalled worrying about being a burden to Burk. That he'd wake up one day and realize she was selfish and spoiled and a boring lump of a grief-stricken person, and he'd just abandon her.

It was part of the reason she'd left first.

"Look," Burk said, his voice suddenly softer, "you've been away a long time. A lot of water has passed under that bridge. Betty is a good person. So is Audrey. If you've been invited to the Knots and Bolts group, I say go for it. The way your kitchen skills go, the free food might come in handy."

"I still can't even make pancakes," Willa admitted.

"You could barely fry an egg."

"At this rate I might have to bring tap water," Willa said, laughing.

To her surprise, Burk smiled back. "If it's from you, it'll be great." He reached out, covering her hand with his enormous one.

And just like that, the energy in the car shifted. It went from warm and friendly to hot and lightning-struck. The storm clouds gathered in Willa's nerves, the electric charge of desire setting her hair on end.

She saw a dangerous darkness in Burk's eyes—the one she remembered so well from high school. The look he'd get just before he'd kiss her, before he'd put his hands on her.

And suddenly, she was welcoming the past back.

In fact, she wanted the past very, very badly.

CHAPTER SEVEN

Thursday, September 20, 2:40 p.m.

This was going all wrong.

Burk hadn't meant to touch her. He hadn't meant to be moved by her sadness, the way her lips pulled downward in a delicate frown. And he certainly didn't mean for the hot lava of lust to come roaring through his guts, pushing him to touch her, to comfort her with a small gesture. But now here he was, holding her hand and wanting for all the world to put his *other* hand on her.

Being in the car with Willa was suddenly, enormously complicated when, in fact, it had started out just the opposite. He'd come out of the hardware store and seen Willa struggling with her car and knew it was a perfect opportunity to drop a few more hints that moving to White Pine was a bad idea. That maybe she didn't belong here. He'd slid into the car thinking she was putty in his hands. He just hadn't banked on how he'd be putty in *hers*.

His thumb involuntarily grazed her knuckles. She bit her lip, as if his touch was tying up her insides. This tiny thing, touching her knuckles like that, looked like it might undo her. Imagine, then, what more could accomplish. He stared at her, wanting to put his lips on her lids, to kiss away the worry in her eyes.

Except that was impossible.

The past was the past, and he intended to keep it that way. He'd worked too hard to do anything else.

"I should go," he managed. He glanced at the clock on the dashboard. It was nearly three o'clock. He had just enough time to pack up his tools, get home, and clean up before meeting his dark-haired date at Ray's for happy hour. *Lacey.* He was nearly sure that was her name.

"Of—of course," Willa said, her voice unbearably husky. But she didn't pull her hand away from his. And she left her lips open, parted just so, exactly like she'd do in high school when she wanted just one more kiss.

Those lips could launch ships, he thought. No one had kissed like Willa, not in all the years they'd been apart. Only one girl had ever come close—Brittany Langley, who had waitressed at the Paul Bunyan Diner. They'd been together for more than a year, a record for Burk. But when she'd squawked about wanting to live together, wanting a ring and a family, he'd balked. Not long after, she'd moved up to Minneapolis to work at a new pub opening near Lake Calhoun.

Willa glanced down, as if she could see the hot hardness pressing against the seam of his jeans. When she found his eyes again, there was no mistaking the naked want there.

Tell her the house needs too many repairs, he thought.

Tell her it's going to cost too much money and take too long and she should just sell it. To him.

But the words wouldn't come. They were lost somewhere between his brain and his throat, and he couldn't get at them. So instead he leaned forward. The leather squeaked. With one hand still covering Willa's, he put his other hand on the base of her neck, at the place where her hair met her skin. It was delightfully warm, unbelievably soft. He swallowed a groan and pulled her toward him. Just one kiss, he thought, just to remind himself what it felt like.

Willa's breath mingled with his. Their lips were a whisper apart. He could already taste her, the warm sweetness he could remember on her lips and between her legs.

This time he couldn't catch his groan before it escaped. He put his mouth on hers, finally taking what he wanted, and she melted into him.

Whatever Willa wanted to be, whatever she thought she was, her true self was in her kiss. She was willing, playful, and just the right amount of demanding. Sparks ignited behind his closed eyes as their tongues reached for each other achingly. They mingled, tentatively at first, getting reacquainted. Oh, but he still knew this mouth. It came back to him in a flood of hot memories, their bodies tangled and sweaty, so hard to tell where one of them began and the other one ended.

Willa pressed toward him in the car's close quarters, a sound in the back of her throat like a plea. He answered her by taking her mouth captive, his tongue penetrating and plunging.

She kissed like she hadn't been touched in years. She opened for him hungrily, so passionate and wanting that he was nearly crushing her, trying to fill her need. He wanted to give her everything his body—and hers—would allow. Soon they were breathless, breaking apart so they could regain their bearings.

"Burk," she murmured as he let his mouth slip from hers to her delectable neck, "don't stop..."

At the word *stop*, he froze, the heat sucked from the moment. She wanted him to go on, but that was exactly the problem. He was acting like they were back in high school, and she was begging him to stay the night in her bed. What was he doing, jeopardizing all his dreams by regressing into a teenager again? He hadn't labored all this time just to lose his vision to lust.

He had to get Willa out of the way, not draw her closer.

Tearing himself from her warmth, he straightened in the car seat. He almost couldn't bear to look at Willa, whose lips were parted and kiss-swollen. Her green eyes were lidded with desire. Her short hair was mussed, and she looked impossibly beautiful. And confused.

"I should really go."

She blinked. "Now?"

"Sorry," he managed, trying to ignore the twist of regret in his chest. There was so much of him that wanted to stay, he worried he might not actually make it out of the car.

But no, he would go. Burk was good at denying himself things.

"What's wrong?" Willa asked. He could hear her trying to stay calm.

"I'll be at the house tomorrow," he said, his hand on the door.

"Burk—"

"I mean to be a professional," he said, cutting her off. "I have a job to do at your home. I'm a contractor, you're a client. I'll keep it that way. This won't happen again."

He stepped out into the afternoon sunshine, leaving Willa looking unsatisfied and confused in the front of her Volvo.

And hurt, too. There was no mistaking the pain in her eyes as she watched him go. He ignored it. A mean and small part of him thought that it served her right to see how it felt to get abandoned right in the middle of something.

He shook his head. Except that wasn't how he wanted to operate. He didn't want revenge. All he wanted was the house.

He tried to refocus his thoughts there instead. He imagined all the curves and surfaces he could enjoy once he lived there. Counters, bookshelves, floors.

They wouldn't satisfy the ache he currently had in his groin.

But they'd do. Eventually.

* * *

Willa punched the passenger seat of the Volvo.

Twice.

Who did Burk think he was, ogling her in the kitchen this morning and making out with her this afternoon and then *walking away*? She glared at the blue sky through the windshield and wished she could hurl clouds into the atmosphere, darkening the day to match her emotions.

Not to mention she was still parked on Main Street without any gas in her tank.

She let out a muted cry of frustration.

Damn Burk Olmstead! She'd been in town for what seemed like five minutes, and here he was, pushing all her buttons and making her feel like a teenager again.

Not that it had been bad. For a few moments there, it had been perfect. Her skin still prickled from his kiss. His touch. How incredible his mouth had felt on hers. How much desire had simmered inside her.

After the desert of Lance's affection, Burk felt like an oasis of passion. She wanted to revel in him, and let her hunger for human contact—oh, who was she kidding, for contact with *him*—to be sated. And, God help her, she would have taken it much, *much* further if Burk hadn't switched himself off like a goddamn robot.

She whacked the steering wheel with her palms until she realized how she must look, parked on Main Street having a fit. She took a deep breath. Glancing at the clock on the dash, she groaned. It was just after three o'clock. Her afternoon plans were shot, and now she had to get herself together and hustle down to the high school track. Practice was starting soon.

A few more inhales and exhales helped, but the crash course in meditation didn't entirely stop her fingers from shaking, or dampen the desire she still felt coursing through her body.

Willa stepped out of the car. The afternoon was crisp and bright all around her. She'd walk to the track, no problem. It wasn't that far. Surely Audrey could help her get gas back into her tank before the Knots and Bolts gathering.

Willa turned right, toward the fountain in front of the library. Crimson and gold leaves floated in the water at its base. She could remember its gurgle and splash during summer months from when she was little. Her dad would give her pennies to throw into the water, and she'd wish for ponies and Barbies and enough gumballs to fill her closet.

If she had a wish now, she'd ask for the ability to erase her past. To start over fresh in White Pine, without the cloak of bad behavior smothering her.

Quickening her pace, she caught glimpses of the Birch River between the squat, brick buildings. The bells in the steeple of the Lutheran church at the far end of Main Street tolled for the half hour. The fall air rippled with the sound. Three thirty. She was going to be late. Nevertheless, at a small bridge she paused, watching the sun glitter on the dark water. Its rushing current created the whispered background Willa had never forgotten, even in New York. It was always there, like a quiet murmuring: *shhh, shhh*.

Willa resumed walking toward the track field with determined steps, knowing she had to make her foray back into White Pine work. The house, Audrey, Betty, the recipe exchange—all of it. Because she had no place else to go. If she failed here, she failed *period*. The thought made her chest hurt, but she refused to dwell on it. She'd simply do whatever it took to make White Pine her home. If it meant an apology to Betty, she'd offer one. If it meant learning how to cook to be part of a recipe exchange, fine. And if she had to run laps on a track with some girls, she'd do that, too.

Suddenly Willa looked down, realizing she hadn't been back to the house to change for track practice. The gas crisis and the encounter with Burk had wiped her afternoon to-do list from her head entirely. Her wedge heels weren't going to accommodate running long distances, and her woven wool pants were lovely but they weren't the kind of thing you wanted to sweat in.

She bit her lip, worried, until she figured she'd just borrow some clothes from the school. Surely they had something she could wear. Willa tried not to think about how the borrowed clothes might smell, or how she might look in them. She was not going to give up on her promise to help Audrey. The high school appeared in the distance, and she lengthened her strides, ready to do whatever it took—on the field and off.

CHAPTER EIGHT

Thursday, September 20, 4:06 p.m.

Willa began to have second thoughts when Audrey shoved a pair of scratchy old gray sweatpants, an oversized hoodie, and a busted-up pair of sneakers at her.

"Here, it's all I could find. Meet on the field when you're changed."

She took off at a clip, ponytail bouncing, leaving Willa alone in the high school locker rooms. The smell that permeated the space was the same smell Willa could remember from long ago—sweat and musty showers and chlorine from the nearby pool.

Willa stripped off her wool slacks and jacket slowly, wondering what in the world she was doing. The clothes Audrey handed her smelled like old socks. They were the most unflattering gray she'd ever seen. What would the girls think when they saw her in this? Willa wondered. With her out-of-shape butt jiggling and her lungs wheezing—she could only imagine.

They are going to laugh at me, she figured. The same way Willa would have laughed if she had seen this version of herself six months ago.

Willa could feel her brows knitting together, and she knew she must look worried. She supposed she was. She took a deep breath, trying to relax her face.

She buried the idea that helping Audrey and the track team was a mistake. So what if this wasn't the kind of volunteering she was used to? She tried not to think about the Bishop Gallery, with its fresh white walls and clean, dark floors. There was hot Jasmine tea and an even hotter intern, Raoul, who once told Willa that her eyes were as vivid as a Chagall painting.

Willa pulled on her dingy gray sweatpants, figuring the Bishop Gallery employees had all flattered her because she was one of their biggest donors. They'd also let her curate exhibits or weigh in on where and how to hang pieces. She loved rearranging things and making the space complement the art *just so*. She'd gaze with pride at the pieces she'd positioned, even while her feet tapped impatiently in her designer shoes, wondering if she wasn't capable of more. The artists all around her had such vision, such a voice. *Surely I have one, too*, Willa had thought, while wondering what in the world she'd say if even she could figure out a platform.

It was a moot point anyway.

She'd stopped her donations and visits to the gallery when Lance lost her cash. Lance had made a series of terrible, short-term investments with her money and with others'. Since he was a financial manager, that wasn't so bad in and of itself (investments often had a risk quotient, after all), but then he'd taken more from the accounts to try and make up for the losses. He wasn't authorized to touch the additional funds, but he did it anyway. And of course, he never stemmed the financial hemorrhaging.

Part of what he'd squandered was the retirement fund belonging to the Bishop Gallery's wealthy landlord. Willa was so mortified, she never returned to the space. It was hard to go anywhere, in fact, without people glaring at her or hissing insults about her and Lance.

Never mind that Willa had lost out, too. Never mind that she was listed as a plaintiff on the civil suit against Lance. In spite of her innocence, she had still been linked with his crime—at least socially.

Willa stood, clad head to toe in her scratchy gray clothes, and headed toward the track, working to ignore the past the same way she was ignoring her smelly outfit. Volunteering with Audrey had to end better than her stint at the Bishop, she figured. At least she couldn't leave White Pine High humiliated and broke. She was already both.

She strode out onto the field with her chin up. That is, until a fall wind whipped her dark blond hair into her face and she couldn't see. She tucked the errant strands behind an ear, just as Audrey trotted up. "Most of the girls are still warming up. Why don't you join the group on the track. Get a couple laps in, and then lead them in some stretches. Make sure none of them trip on any equipment."

Audrey smiled, but Willa couldn't return it. A couple laps? If Willa remembered correctly, that was at least a *half mile*. And unless she was hailing a cab in the city, she hadn't run more than a few steps in years. Still, she nodded. "Sure thing," she replied, forcing her feet to take her over to the cluster of long-legged girls on the red clay track.

They stared at her unabashedly as she joined them. Their wide eyes traveled from her battered shoes to her dumpy sweatpants to her disheveled hair. Willa reminded herself she'd sparred with New York's elite—she could handle these girls.

"I'm Willa," she said, "and I'm helping Ms. Tanner out for a bit. Let's all do two laps around the track, and then we'll stretch and go from there." She supposed she sounded authoritative enough, because the girls nodded and took off. There was nothing to do but follow them.

She was going to have to run.

A few yards in, her breath became ragged. Halfway around the track and the girls were already lapping her. "You can do it, Willa!" one of them shouted. It was Emily, the one who'd stayed with the injured girl, Layla, the other day. "Tha-anks," Willa huffed, her face burning with embarrassment. *Who was coaching who?*

A quarter mile in, and Willa was still running while the rest of the girls were finished. They stared at her as she shuffled past. She could quit now, she supposed, but how would that look to all of them? How would they listen to anything she said if she didn't complete what she set out to do?

You didn't get to quit just because you were slow, she knew. She could hear her old track coach, Mr. Iverson, shouting at her through his bristled mustache. "Everyone does *all* the work! No one gets a pass around here, Masterson."

"Ca-alf st-retches," she wheezed at the girls. "Qua-ads, too! I'm a-a-almost do-one." The girls did as she said.

Willa wound her way slowly down the track, putting one foot in front of the others as her muscles ached and her lungs burned and the sweat poured off her face.

When the half mile was finally over with, Willa was never so relieved to have something behind her. She rested her hands on her knees, trying to catch her breath, while the girls chatted and stretched. Some of them called "Good job!"—which only made Willa want to keep running, away from the track and her bone-deep humiliation. These girls must think she was a joke.

She squeezed her eyes closed, knowing if that was the case, then she didn't have much time to rectify their opinion. She had to assert her authority, and soon.

"All right, ladies," she said when she felt like her throat was no longer on fire. "Let's get our hamstrings—"

Nausea twisted her gut. She tried to press it down, but it was roiling and churning. "Our ham—" she tried again, but it was no use.

She turned, but it was too late.

The girls squealed in horror as she emptied the contents of her stomach on the red clay track.

* * *

Willa approached the back doorway of Knots and Bolts in her oversized track pants and hoodie, smelling like gas and sweat, and panting heavily. Her mouth was still sour from vomiting on the track, and she wanted nothing more than to just go home already. She'd tried to tell Audrey there was no way she could meet the Knots and Bolts group tonight, but Audrey had insisted she come. "Oh, you're fine," Audrey had said after practice, handing

Willa a bottle of water. "No one cares about looks around here."

Easy for you to say, Willa thought, taking in Audrey's trim figure in her track pants and fitted T-shirt. Willa figured Audrey could roll out of bed with barely any sleep and a massive hangover and *still* look better than Willa on her best day.

Willa shoved her shaking hands inside the sweatshirt's front pouch, hoping no one would notice her nerves. Which was too kind a word, really, for the humiliation that was shredding whatever scrap of dignity she had left after practice.

She swallowed back a cry of frustration. Back in New York, she spent time fixing herself up just to make a run to the corner market. She was used to looking her best. Now she'd barely had a moment to catch her breath, much less change or reapply her makeup, before meeting a whole new group of women who had every reason not to like her. A few steps ahead, Audrey's glossy brown ponytail bounced with unbounded enthusiasm as she opened Knots and Bolts' painted back door. Willa clenched her jaw. All that running around, and the woman had barely broken a sweat today.

Willa followed Audrey inside, entering a cozy space with warm light and vases of sunflowers and spider lilies placed here and there. It would have been lovely, inviting even, except for how the conversation that had been taking place didn't just die when she showed up—it fell off a kind of vocal cliff, fading and fading, until it hit the ground and crumpled into surprised silence.

Four women stared at her. For a moment, none of them moved.

Willa's feet twitched, telling her to *run and get out of there now*. Her shoulders wanted to hunch, her spine wanted to curl. But instead she took a breath and held her ground. Besides, she was sore enough that she might never run anywhere ever again, so she might as well stay put.

Audrey cleared her throat. "As I mentioned, Willa Masterson is back in town and I thought we could help her feel welcome."

Willa met the flat gazes of the women seated at the bright red table in front of her. There was Burk's dark-haired sister, Anna Palowski, as well as Stephanie Munson, a freckled woman Willa remembered being a cheerleader. And of course, Betty Lindholm.

"The recipe exchange sounded too good to miss," Willa said, smiling too brightly. "God knows I could use some help in the kitchen." She let out a laugh that was more high-pitched than she would have liked. In New York, it would have signaled weakness.

Audrey smiled back. "We're happy to have you."

Clearly not everyone shared Audrey's enthusiasm. Especially not Betty, who looked like she was clenching her fists—maybe to keep herself from punching Willa.

"What a great space," Willa said, distracting herself by launching into overzealous guest mode. She gazed at the large table in the middle of the room and the woven carpet underneath. The room was wider than she would have guessed the back room of Knots and Bolts would be, with space for a small love seat toward the rear, and lots of windows all around. Off to the right was a small kitchenette, where the smell of chocolate brownies was drifting into the room. It wasn't Willa's style, but it was definitely cozy. Comfortable.

"Come on in, make yourself at home," Audrey said, leading her toward the table where the other ladies were seated. There was an assortment of odd chairs to choose from—some painted, some with fabric seats, some just cheap plastic. The eclectic mix of it all was oddly charming. Willa chose an old oak seat with armrests, and eased herself next to Betty.

Keep your enemies close, as her dad used to say.

"Willa and I were just at track practice," Audrey said. "Willa's volunteering, and helping out a ton."

Willa winced. That was too kind. The reality was that she'd been awful, gasping and panting and trying to be useful to the girls, but feeling more of a joke instead. She could all but feel them smirking at her as she bumped into hurdles or fumbled with the stopwatch. Plus, her muscles were going to be sore for days. And she might *never* stop sweating.

"Your record still stands on the field," Stephanie said, her red hair glinting in the warm light. "That must make you feel proud after all these years."

It should, except it didn't. Willa realized that she hadn't really *done* anything since setting that record. She'd moved to New York, thinking her life would be so much better, so much more important. But here she was, twelve years later, back in her hometown and talking about what she'd done as a teenager.

"Can I get you some coffee?" Audrey asked, bringing her a cup before she could refuse. The Minnesotan way.

The hot liquid was going to have her sweating even more, and she needed water badly. But instead she smiled and sipped at the bitter drink. "Thanks."

The conversation petered out. They were all just *staring* at her.

Betty finally gave a little cough. "You back for good?" she asked in a way that made it clear she hoped Willa wasn't.

She thought about how to answer. In New York she would have laughed while she oozed venom. But this wasn't New York, and Willa needed to make White Pine work. She tried on another pageant smile—one she hoped said, *Look, I'm not a threat! I'm nice now!*—but that felt fake, too. So instead she just went for the truth.

"I'd like to think so. I'm opening a bed-and-breakfast here. In the house where I grew up."

Okay, partial truth. No way was she going to tell them about Lance and losing her money and her house being her only remaining plan.

For a second Betty just stared at her. Willa had time to study how age had softened her looks. Betty's teeth were just fine now, though Willa wondered if Betty might still haul off and bite her like a beaver, for old times' sake.

Instead Betty just shrugged. "We've got the Great Lakes Inn. Not sure why we need another place."

Before Willa could answer, Burk's sister, Anna, spoke up from across the table. "Burk's doing the work for you on the house?"

Willa tried not to blush at the recent memories of Burk and the Volvo. "He is. We walked through the project list this morning."

Something dark flashed across Anna's face, and Willa wondered what she'd said wrong. Twelve years ago, Burk had treated Anna like a pesky little sister but Willa had adored Anna and fawned over her. Anna would follow Willa and Burk around, asking to look in Willa's purse or wanting to try on Willa's headband. Willa had always indulged her, sometimes even bringing her lip gloss or a downy stuffed animal she no longer wanted. Now Willa wondered if that little girl had grown up to despise the way she'd broken Burk's heart all those years ago. Not that Willa could blame her.

"I bet it was a surprise being around Burk again," Stephanie Munson said, not unkindly.

"Burk's a good contractor," Willa said, trying to shift the conversation. "The house needs a lot of work."

"Well, you can come on down to Knots and Bolts if you need to get away from the construction," Audrey said. "We have our recipe exchange every Thursday afternoon, of course, but the place is open during normal business hours. And sometimes during not-normal business hours. If there's an emergency."

Willa fidgeted with her coffee cup. Did this mean they were going let her stay in their group?

"Betty keeps the key in the geranium pot if you ever need to get in and we're not around," Stephanie said. Betty shot her a searing glare from across the table.

"Except I'm almost always here," Betty said pointedly. "It being my store and all."

"That's such good news," Willa said, surprised at how much she meant it. Maybe this was all going to be easier than she'd anticipated. She faced Betty, remembering her unfinished errand from earlier, and how she'd fled before Betty could see her. Willa's regret was still there, a hot flame inside her chest, but she couldn't help wondering if there was a chance the past would get swept to the side. They'd all see how hard she was trying, and everyone would simply forgive her and move on.

"It's great to have an excuse to be at Knots and Bolts,"

Willa told her, pushing past her mortification, "especially because I'm going to need some upholstery and curtains for the B and B. I was hoping I could enlist your services."

Betty narrowed her eyes. "Probably not."

"Excuse me?"

"I could sell you some fabric, but I'm busy with a different business on the side. With blood. And skeletons. And *death*."

Willa shifted, suddenly nervous.

"Oh, stop," Audrey interjected. "It's not that macabre. It's Halloween items. Betty sells them year round—online."

Willa let out a breath she didn't realize she was holding.

"Helps me stay busy in between customers at the shop," Betty said. "I've thought about doing it full-time. Knots and Bolts does pretty well, and I don't really want to close up, but I like the idea of being able to do my work anywhere. The freedom of not having a storefront."

"Don't you dare close," Stephanie said. "My four-year-old twins are no joke. I love them, but this place is a haven for me. I need it to be open."

"No kidding," Audrey said. "Especially when Betty stocks the good stuff."

She reached into a nearby cabinet and grabbed a bottle of Irish cream liqueur, pouring some into her coffee. Everyone passed the bottle and partook, including Willa, who added an extra splash to calm her nerves.

"Well, I just come to show off," Anna said, striding toward the kitchenette. "You guys know my brownies are the best in town."

Willa could hear her pulling a pan out of the oven, and the heady smell of baking chocolate wafted into the room.

"So what about it, Willa?" Betty asked as Anna set a plate of warm brownies onto the table. "You plan on contributing to this recipe exchange, or just showing up to get served?"

It was a direct barb, but Willa couldn't argue. She knew she was pretty much useless in a recipe exchange. She couldn't do jack in the kitchen, but that didn't mean she was going to give up on being part of this group. If they were cracking the door to her, she'd push it open and make sure she got all the way through.

"I am really good with a corkscrew," Willa said, lifting her chin, "and I took a world-class collection of wine with me when I left my asshole of an ex. I'm dying to share it."

For a second, Betty didn't say anything. "Then welcome to the recipe exchange, I guess," she offered flatly, looking away.

"Here, here," Audrey said, raising her spiked coffee in a toast.

It was a start, Willa thought, and she'd take it. Somehow her heart was already lighter as the thick mugs clinked together.

CHAPTER NINE

*A*nna set the apple pie in front of Burk unceremoniously.

"I don't think I—" he started but her sharp glance stopped him from saying any more. He picked up a fork. Tonight it looked like he was having dessert, whether he wanted it or not.

Out in the family room, Anna's husband, Sam, played with their two-year-old daughter, Juniper. It was a bad sign that Sam hadn't stayed in the kitchen after dinner. The man loved pie almost as much as his family, and he was a much-needed buffer when Anna had that glint in her eye that meant trouble. She was sporting it right now, in fact.

Burk speared the still-warm dessert wondering what Anna wanted to speak with him about.

As if on cue, Anna sat next to him at the worn oak table. "Willa Masterson came into Knots and Bolts yesterday."

Well, Burk thought, *there it is.*

He set down his fork. "You don't say."

It was all he could do to keep his emotions locked underneath his skin. Jesus, just the mention of her name and he was getting riled up. What had gotten into him? He had to be careful. His sister could read him better than anyone. Better than himself, some days.

Anna pulled her steaming cup of tea closer. Soft light reflected on the tile backsplash in the adjoining kitchen—Burk had installed it—and everything looked so warm and comfortable. It was a shame they were squandering all the coziness by talking about Willa. Burk glanced at the living room, wishing he were out there now, playing airplane or horsey with Juniper, watching her golden hair bounce and her big eyes shine.

"She joined the recipe exchange," Anna said, pulling Burk's attention back to the kitchen, "and she mentioned you're the one fixing up the house." She spoke the words calmly, but Burk could see the twin spots of color on her cheeks glowing like bonfires. She had some *thoughts* about all this.

"Of course I'm fixing it up," Burk said. "I've been taking care of it this long, haven't I?"

"You should have refused the project because that's the house *you* want. How are you over there fixing it up for her, when it's *your* dream?"

Burk thought about how to answer. In the other room, Sam was playing "Won't Get Fooled Again" by The Who for Juniper. Sam always said every kid should grow up with a classic rock education. Juniper squealed with delight as Sam played air guitar. *Good man*, Burk thought.

"Someone is going to work on that house," he said finally. "It might as well be me. And my crew. I don't see what the problem is."

Anna arched a dark brow. "The *problem* is, this is going to eat at you, day in and day out, if she takes over a house that's supposed to be yours. Why don't you just cut the nonsense and try to buy it from her?"

"I did. Yesterday. She wanted a half million for it. I can't afford that, and she's bent on turning it into a high-end bed-and-breakfast."

"So tell her that's ridiculous. Tell her that's the last thing White Pine needs."

Burk shook his head, thinking about yesterday in the car. "I'm trying. It's just—I'm not—it's not that easy."

"Like hell it isn't."

Burk almost smiled. No one talked to him like that. Crew members said "yes sir" and "no sir." Clients were nice because he vetted them and threw out the ones who weren't. Only Anna could get in his face like this, and talk to him like they were still kids.

"Burk, are you even listening?"

Anna's blue eyes were storming with irritation.

"Sorry," Burk said, "your pie puts me into a trancelike state. It's just that good."

For a moment, Anna softened. The way to her heart wasn't her food—it was compliments *about* her food. Too bad the thaw didn't last long.

"Look, I'm not interested in Willa getting hurt here. She was like a sister to me when you guys were dating, and I respect that she's trying to run a small business. It's just that she could open up a B and B anywhere. And this is a house you've cared for, for years. I think you should fight harder for it."

Irritation needled him. He *was* fighting, dammit. The problem was that Willa kept throwing him off his game. Her curves, her lips, her inability to put gas in her car. Cripes. He was frustrated for finding it all so *appealing*, when he knew better. He knew she was bad news.

"I'll figure it out."

Anna studied him for a few moments. He felt as though his thoughts were carved into her kitchen table, plain as day to read. "Are you going to ask her out?"

Burk nearly choked. "What? Of course not. Have you lost your mind?"

"Well, it's not working out with anyone else, so I thought maybe you'd try to rekindle things with Willa."

Out in the living room, "Baba O'Riley" was playing. Juniper babbled "teenage wasteland." It came out "neeeam beebaaa."

"It's working fine with plenty of women," Burk said. "I don't know what you're talking about."

"So last night's date? Bowling alley girl? That went..."

"Fine," Burk growled, not wanting to tell his sister that he'd taken bowling girl back to his place, only to have her storm out when not one but *two* different bras had slipped out from the pillow underneath her head as they were making out on the couch.

The blurry memory of how they'd gotten there came back to him in a rush, and he'd almost smiled remembering the pair of doe-eyed twins with unbelievable flexibility who'd been over earlier in the week. But he couldn't very well explain any of that to his date. "That's *classless*," bowling girl said, her tone biting.

He couldn't even argue with her. She was right.

"I'm glad it was a swell evening," Anna said, a smug smile playing on her lips as she watched his face. "And before that, it was another home run, right? With the woman who realized you'd taken out her best friend the week before?"

Burk frowned. It didn't seem right that Anna could sit here and give him a hard time about dating. Especially not when she had found Sam so easily, when they were seniors in college. "I met him in a Russian history class," Anna used to joke, "and I was so bored, I stared at Sam to keep myself awake." They'd gotten married right after graduation, and had Juniper a few years later. Here his baby sister was, happy and so clearly in love with her husband—and acting like Burk was somehow less just because he hadn't found someone yet.

It wasn't for trying. He had dates all the time. But he also had his business and his routine, and he wasn't about to foul those up for a complicated relationship that wouldn't go anywhere. Anna should know this better than anyone, Burk thought. She'd been the one with the best view of his heartbreak after Willa left, after all. She knew how determined he was not to let it happen again.

"We can't all be as lucky as you and Sam," Burk snapped. He could feel his stomach hardening all over again, the old pain from Willa's departure weighing like a cold stone in his gut. Twelve years in, and he was still feeling the effects of the first one.

"Hey, easy there," Anna said, "I just was curious if you and Willa—"

"My relationship with Willa is in the past," Burk interrupted. "I intend to keep it that way." He was shifting into contractor mode. Impersonal. Direct. He hated doing it with his sister, hated the hurt expression that flashed across her face, but he wasn't about to let her stick her nose into his love life. Or lack of it. It had taken years for his hurt to scar over, and now that it had, he wasn't about to risk opening that wound all over again.

Anna scooted back from the table. "More pie?" she asked, not looking at him.

Two pieces of pie were unheard of for him. But Burk accepted anyway, feeling small and mean. He'd been too harsh—he knew it—but he couldn't tell her he was sorry. If he looked at her too long, he was worried his sister would be able to tell he'd kissed Willa. That was the problem with siblings. You needed them at the same time you wanted them to get lost.

Burk concentrated on his pie, forcing it down, while strains of The Who's "I Don't Even Know Myself" played in the family room.

Somehow, he felt like that was fitting.

CHAPTER TEN

*W*illa crossed her arms, staring at the small coffee table in her dining room. The room was still dingy, the plaster cracked and flaking, the floors scuffed and dull. The table itself was a holdover from her mom's old junk. But there was something about it she couldn't quite put her finger on.

It was as if the table was the link between her high-end decorating magazines and the reality of life in White Pine. Or at least, it could be the link if she could figure out how to paint it.

She thought about a light blue, the color of an afternoon sky, with the edges roughed out so it still had a worn feel. It would be shabby-esque, but then Willa could place bright glass bowls filled with lemons on top—and it would work. *She knew it.* The only problem was, she had no idea how to paint anything, much less a piece of furniture. She bit her lip. When it came down to it, she wasn't

even sure where to buy paint. Did they have that at the
grocery store?

No. Of course not. It would be the hardware store,
wouldn't it?

She blushed, even though she was alone in the house.
Her inability to know how to do simple things mortified
her. How could someone grow up to be so clueless? She
felt small and stupid, and wondered suddenly how she
was going to make it on her own, in White Pine, without
more help. What would happen when winter came? She
tried to picture herself shoveling snow off the front porch,
or scraping ice from her car windows, or lighting a fire
if the power went out, and she couldn't do it. She didn't
know how to do *any* of those things.

Yet. She would learn. If Scarlett O'Hara could make
dresses from curtains and run a whole plantation, Willa
could certainly figure out how to scrape some ice.

"That table giving you a hard time?"

Willa jumped, letting out a little yelp of surprise.

"Oh, hey, sorry," Burk said, holding up his hands. "I
didn't mean to scare you. It just looked like you were giving that table the stink eye. Thought maybe I should break
up the fight."

Willa's heart raced, but she wasn't sure it was from
being startled. It might be Burk himself, who was standing there in a white T-shirt and jeans, his flannel shirt
discarded on this unseasonably warm September day.
So much more of him was showing, from his knotted
biceps to his thick forearms. She could see the rise and
fall of his strong chest through the T-shirt fabric. The
white cotton was in stark contrast to his stubbled chin
and dark hair. Good God. She was reminded again how

his body had been nice in high school, but nothing like this.

"You—you scared me," Willa said, trying to get a hold of herself. After all, Burk had barely spoken to her since their short make-out session in the Volvo the week before. She was angry with herself for how totally undone she'd let herself get after a few good kisses. But she was furious with *him* for starting something and then walking away in the middle of it. Like she was a switch he could just turn off.

"You need a hand moving that out of here?" Burk asked, glancing at the table. "I can help before I get started on the ceilings upstairs."

She followed his gaze. The safe thing would be to just put the table out on the curb and hope someone drove by and took it. Then she could flip through her magazines and find something else. Something new.

But suddenly Willa didn't want something else. She wanted *this* table. And she wanted it blue.

"No," she said, "I don't need you to move it. I need a hand figuring out how to paint it."

Burk grinned. "Paint? You're telling me you—Willa Masterson—are going to paint a table?"

Willa put her hands on her hips, not liking his tone. "No. The only thing I'm telling you is that I need help figuring out *how*."

Burk's expression didn't change. Damn him for looking so good, even when he was wearing a shit-eating grin.

"You? *You* are going to paint?"

Willa's temper flared. "Why is that so funny?"

"It's just that you're not really the house project type."

"Which is why I need your help, Einstein. What part of this aren't you getting?"

Burk was still grinning, like the whole thing was going to send him into peals of laughter at any moment. Willa wanted to slap the expression off his face, but she forced herself to stay put, to keep breathing calmly.

"All right," Burk said, his tone still amused. "Later I guess I could take you down to the hardware store. But I don't want to spend hours on this, if it's going to be one of those things you start and then just walk away from. Like your jewelry project."

Willa fumed. It would be just like Burk to bring up something she'd done in high school and throw it back in her face. Granted, she *had* been really overzealous about making her own jewelry. She was convinced it was going to propel her to fame—all the Hollywood stars would wear her pieces. She bought the supplies—beads, clasps, wire—and then had no idea how to put them all together. It was Burk who sat with her, hour after hour, and helped with the designs.

Of course, she got bored with the whole thing after making two necklaces, a bracelet, and an anklet. It's a wonder she even made that many pieces. And while she managed to sell the anklet to some freshman girl she'd practically begged to pull out her purse, it hadn't exactly been a successful endeavor.

So, fine, jewelry making hadn't been her calling. But it wasn't fair for Burk to judge her by her past. The table would be different.

"That was a long time ago," Willa said defensively.

"But you asking me for help for another one of your projects is right here in the present, isn't it?"

Willa felt like she'd been punched. The past was like a living thing, stalking her wherever she went, ready to mortify her at a moment's notice.

Asking him for help had been a huge mistake. She should have just taken the table down to Knots and Bolts. Maybe Audrey or Anna could show her how the painting process worked. Of course, Betty would probably hoot like a barn owl when she found out Willa didn't even know where to buy paint, meaning Willa should probably do a Google search about all this on her phone, and figure it out for herself.

She straightened. She didn't need Burk's charity. She didn't need Burk, period.

"You know what? Forget it. I got this. You'd better get started upstairs."

Burk opened his mouth like he was going to argue some more, then closed it. A tense moment passed. Then his nostrils flared as he took a deep breath. "Look, I'm sorry if I was rude just then. I'll help you paint that table. I can show you how right now." His voice was even, steady.

Willa narrowed her eyes. "Excuse me?"

"Let me help you."

"No."

A muscle in Burk's jaw clenched. "Five seconds ago you wanted my help. Now you don't?"

"Because you were a jerk about it! I'll find someone else."

Burk had that look again, like he was engaged in a battle of wills—with himself. She must have hurt him even more than she realized if he had to battle back anger just to be *around* her, even after all these years. "I'm sorry if

I offended you," he said quietly. "I just don't remember these projects working out so well."

"They didn't in the past," Willa agreed, "but people can change." She felt like suddenly she was talking about more than just the table. She hadn't done right by Burk in the past. But she could do better by him now, if he'd let her.

It seemed like a weighty thought, somehow about much more than paint and wood. Willa tried to stay focused. *Table, table, table*, she thought.

"Come on," Burk said. "We'll head down to the hardware store and pick out paint. I'll get a couple other things we'll need, and we can get started this morning. It won't take long."

Part of Willa wanted to stay stubborn and just refuse on principle. But here was Burk, agreeing to help, and she couldn't deny that it was him she wanted. For the project, that is.

"If we do this, you have to swear that you won't laugh at me at any point in the process," Willa said.

Burk held up three fingers. "Scout's honor."

"You weren't a Scout."

"I buy my weight in Scout popcorn every year. That's close enough."

Willa cracked a smile. "All right," she said finally, "let's do this."

"We can take my truck," Burk said, steering her toward the front door. Willa tried not to notice his hand on the small of her back—gently pressing, a rudder guiding her direction. What would life have been like, she wondered, if she'd let him keep his hand there since high school? Not literally, of course, but what if she'd let him help steer her course instead of running away from him?

She squeezed her eyes closed against the tide of memories that came rolling back, and the tear in her life that started when her dad died. She'd felt like she couldn't stop it, so she just kept ripping until she'd made a clean break with everything. Including Burk.

In the back of her mind, she pictured Lance and wondered suddenly if she'd chosen him because he looked like another pain-free option. After all, they were more like friends who had conducted a few failed experiments in the bedroom than actual lovers. Before he'd made all those reckless financial decisions, he'd been an advisor, a collaborator. But never the cornerstone of her heart. Willa pressed her elbows into her side, wondering suddenly if she'd loved anyone—really, truly loved them—since Burk.

"You okay?" Burk asked as they buckled themselves into the old truck.

If Burk knew what was on her mind, he'd probably just laugh at her confusion. She'd brought it on herself, after all. He'd probably tell her she was right to question her past and feel guilty. She *had* been foolish. She *had* been selfish. She *had* ripped his heart out when she'd tried to save her own.

So instead, Willa gave him her best Miss Dairy smile as they pulled away from the curb. "Never better."

CHAPTER ELEVEN

Wednesday, September 26, 10:10 a.m.

Burk steered the truck into town knowing he'd been too hard on Willa, just like he'd been too hard on Anna a few days before. He had to find a way to back off and be nicer, even though "nice" wasn't really in his wheelhouse. Being determined, professional, hardworking—those things were no problem for him. Nice was a little harder, unless it was directed toward Juniper, who was so tiny and wide-eyed it was impossible not to want to hand her the whole world wrapped up with a bow. But if he expected his plan to work, then he needed to start catching more flies with honey.

Which meant that showing Willa how to paint furniture was actually a brilliant idea. He should have thought of it himself, really. Because when Willa started crying at the first broken nail or paint splotch on her designer jeans, he'd use it to remind her that this wasn't the way of life she really wanted. It would be more proof that this house wasn't for her.

The truck coasted down the gentle hill toward the river, then turned right onto Main Street. The sun was just cresting over the tops of the buildings, warming the red brick and glittering on the Birch River. Over-stuffed scarecrows and fat, orange pumpkins graced the windows of the downtown shops. Burk glimpsed a sign advertising hay rides, and figured it must be Red Updike, who owned a farm a few miles outside of town. Every year, Red made a corn maze. Last season, he'd carved a path through the rattling stalks in the shape of the *Millennium Falcon* from *Star Wars*. Burk had walked through that maze. Twice.

A flap of a black coat caught his eye, and he glimpsed Randall Sondheim ducking into the Rolling Pin Bakery for his weekly donut. The pastor of the local Lutheran church had moved to White Pine a few years ago from the cold, flat plains of Minnesota's Iron Range. He was devout and stony—but he allowed himself a donut once every Wednesday.

Burk liked him enormously.

Next to him, Willa yawned. "I forgot to make the coffee this morning. You think the Paul Bunyan Diner will give me some to go?"

Burk could smell the scents from the Rolling Pin even through the closed windows. His stomach growled. "They probably would, but the Rolling Pin has better coffee. We should go there."

Without waiting for an answer, Burk pulled up behind Sondheim's sturdy Buick. "Come on," he said, "the first cruller is on me."

* * *

Willa tried not to think about how Burk's shoulder was brushing against hers as they stood in line at the Rolling Pin. She could feel the corded hardness, even through their jackets. And even over all the yeasty baking she could still smell Burk—like an evergreen forest with a twist of orange. She licked her lips, suddenly wanting to taste him as much as she could smell him.

To stop herself from reaching out and doing something ridiculous, she concentrated on the Rolling Pin's sparkling display case filled with crullers and frosted donuts and turnovers. The store's cheery green walls were paired perfectly with the white metal tables and retro art on the walls. A 1950s girl in a bathing suit smiled brightly from a framed poster, saying, *A good baker will rise to the occasion!*

In contrast to all the lively surroundings was the rounded back of the grumpy-looking man in front of them. "Usual," was all he'd said to the aproned woman behind the counter. He didn't say thank you, even when the woman began ringing him up.

"What was the place here before?" Willa asked, trying to remember back to the Main Street of her youth.

"Neilson Shoes," Burk said, smiling sadly. Willa tried not to stare at the curve of his lips. "Ed Neilson closed his doors a couple years ago, when people started buying so much of their footwear online. Or going to Minneapolis for a better selection."

"Poor Ed." Willa could remember the tall, thin man who always gave her a cherry sucker when she'd come in with her mom. Times sure had changed for shoe salesmen—a dying breed.

"Actually, he's all right," Burk said. "Retired to a

house on a small lake, about a half hour south of here. Good man. I still see him from time to time."

Willa smiled, liking how Burk knew what happened to the former shoe salesman. That was White Pine for you, though—people checked in on one another. Sometimes out of caring, sometimes out of gossip. But they always checked.

She realized suddenly that she was staring at Burk, specifically at the tiny freckle underneath his right eye, which she'd placed her lips on a thousand times. He was staring back, watching her watch him. Her pulse quickened involuntarily. Damn Burk and the way he could just look at her and set her off-kilter. In all the years she'd been with Lance, he'd never been able to undo her with a glance.

Burk's mouth quirked, as if he knew the effect he was having.

Good God, the man was *smoldering*.

To Willa's dismay, he broke the stare in order to address the grumpy, black-clad customer as he brushed past. "Hello, Pastor," Burk said.

The man stopped. "Mr. Olmstead. Fine day."

"Certainly is," Burk replied, reminding Willa how the weather was always a topic of conversation in Minnesota. He motioned to her. "This is a client of mine, Willa Masterson. Willa, this is Pastor Randall Sondheim."

Willa barely had time to be hurt that Burk had said "client" in lieu of "friend" or "former classmate" or any number of things that would be preferable. She should know that making out in a car with Burk wouldn't elevate her status in his eyes, but that didn't change the fact that she *wanted* it to. Before she could think much more about it, the man turned his sharp eyes on her. "You live here?"

It was an abrupt question. No "good to meet you" or "fine day for a donut." Willa thought about how to answer. "I've lived in New York for the past few years. But I'm back to open up a bed-and-breakfast here in town."

The pastor grunted. Then, abruptly finished with the conversation, he gave them a curt nod and went back out into the September morning.

"That was enjoyable," Willa said dryly.

Burk looked genuinely pleased. "I appreciate a man of few words. Not to mention a man of routine."

"Routine?" Willa asked, and Burk explained how the pastor allowed himself only one donut each week—on Wednesday.

"Sounds too regimented if you ask me," she replied. "Isn't a pastor supposed to be, you know, warmer? Friendlier?"

"I'd rather have that than a slick televangelist who just wants my money."

"Fair enough." She was just getting ready to order her coffee and cruller when her cell phone buzzed. A text. She pulled it out of her pocket, thinking it might be Audrey or even an order confirmation for the new bedding she'd found online, when the blood drained from her face.

It was Lance.

She hadn't spoken to him in weeks. Not since she'd dumped him and decided to add her name to the lawsuit against him.

Now, he texted her seven simple words.

Please, I need help. Can we talk?

Willa stared at the screen, her mouth dry. She should turn off the phone, eat her pastry, and ignore him.

Except for the fact that, apart from her, all he had was a lawyer in a cheap suit.

Which served him right, but—

Willa took a breath.

The truth of the matter was that if Lance had committed his crime while working for a big investing firm, they'd have gotten a team of lawyers on the case and worked to deny his wrongdoing at every turn, or at least worked to get most of the charges dropped. But as it stood, Lance was his own small company at the time of the fraud. He was fielding this mess on his own. Yes, he'd created it, but he also wasn't *fighting* it. He'd pled guilty in both the criminal suit and the civil action against him. The money might be gone, but he was willing to work to pay it back. For the rest of his life.

He'd be lucky to get a job at McDonald's after all this, so no one would ever see a cent of the missing money. But at least he was willing to try, to own his mistakes.

She could feel Burk's eyes on her, waiting for her to place her order, but breakfast was suddenly the last thing on her mind. "Excuse me," she whispered, and stepped outside the bakery, back into the crisp morning light.

Her hands shook as she held the cell.

Please, I need help. Can we talk?

God help her, she wanted to look down her nose at Lance and hate him with every fiber of her soul, but the truth was she couldn't. She wasn't a thief, but she certainly could understand what it was like to get so swept up into a way of life, into a warped state of mind, that you could lose track of what really mattered.

Willa clutched her phone, remembering how charming Lance had been when they'd first met. Debonair, even. He had the rigidity of an aristocrat, but then he'd bring her knuckles to his lips in an old-fashioned greeting, and everything would soften. She hadn't forgiven him for stealing her money, it was true. But shouldn't she *try* not to hold his mistakes against him, as long as he was attempting to make things right?

After all, wasn't she back in her hometown hoping other people would forgive her the sins of her past, too?

Please, I need help. Can we talk?

Willa chewed her lip, thinking about how to reply. She chose one word:

Fine.

She expected Lance to ask when he could call, but instead he started texting back in a furious blaze of words. Apparently, he was ready to talk now.

I messed everything up. I hurt you. I wish I could undo the past.

Willa's whole body tensed. She didn't want to have this conversation now. Not with Burk a few feet away.

Talk later, Willa texted back, glancing nervously over her shoulder.

NO. I need to see you. I need your HELP.

Willa stared at her phone, wondering if she was imagining Lance wanting to come see her. Lance shouldn't—*couldn't*—leave New York. He'd violate the terms of his bond.

She texted back. *You need to stay put.*

Please. Just let me see you.

Her heart raced.

No. Talk later.

*You're the only one who understands. I know you'll lis-
ten and help me.*

Willa was just typing *NO* into her phone again when it
rang. Lance's name came up. She held the phone in her
hand as confusion took root inside her.

How much could Lance have changed if he was begging for her help and threatening to leave New York? Her
head suddenly hurt. She turned off her phone, silencing
the ringer.

What in the world was going on?

Willa took a deep breath, trying to clear her head.
She'd talk to Lance later, when she had more time. When
she was ready, his demands be darned.

For now, she put the phone into the pocket of her coat
and turned to go inside. As she did, she caught Burk staring at her, watching with his stormy eyes narrowed. He
broke his gaze away before she stepped back into the bakery, pretending to be studying something else, but she
knew he'd been watching. And probably wondering who
she was communicating with.

Well, let him wonder, Willa thought. She didn't owe
him an explanation. And in fact, he owed her. A cruller,
that is.

She returned to the counter of the Rolling Pin, ready to
collect.

CHAPTER TWELVE

Wednesday, September 26, 2:45 p.m.

For Willa, the most challenging part of painting a table turned out not to be holding the brush or avoiding paint splotches, but keeping her eyes on the wood and not on Burk.

Unless it's Burk's wood, her brain quipped.

She felt the tips of her ears burn at the thought. She tried not to stare as Burk repositioned his shoulder to get a better angle with his brush. His intense focus had her heart pounding—she could remember when he looked at *her* that way—and she worried that her thundering chest was audible in the quiet room.

The muscles of his calves and thighs strained against his jeans as he held his position steady, moving the paintbrush at an agonizingly slow rate. Willa saw the wet bristles glisten along the table's edge. She tightened the grip around her own brush, thinking it would be so lovely if the paintbrush were Burk's mouth, and his muscles were holding him in place so he could kiss her precisely where—

"Do you think you want a gloss on the finish?" Burk asked, interrupting her thoughts. Willa started. All around her, the taupe drop cloth puddled in waves, protecting the living room floor where they were working, but she'd hardly needed it. She hadn't yet spilled a drop.

"Sorry, what's that?" she asked, trying to get her brain back into the here and now.

Burk shifted so he could get at a tricky corner of a scalloped edge. The movement brought him inches closer, and she resisted the urge to press herself into the contours of his body.

"We got a flat paint," he said, "but I wonder if you want a gloss. To make it shine."

Willa tore her eyes away from Burk's form to study the table. It was certainly blue. And they had painted it together, with Willa learning as she went.

Burk had showed her how to sand down the finish, then apply a white primer evenly, using a roller for the wide spaces and a small brush for the trickier edges. She couldn't remember the last time she'd used her hands so much. It was exhilarating. Her confidence grew with every stroke. Plus, it was already midafternoon, which meant Burk had spent the whole day helping her instead of working alongside his crew, and he didn't even seem to mind.

When they'd started adding the blue color on top of the primer, the result was a painted table, just like Willa wanted. And she was certainly proud.

The only problem was, it didn't match the table in her mind.

Frankly, it was boring.

"It kind of needs to be the opposite of glossy," Willa replied. "Not shiny but kind of . . . rustic."

"Rustic?"

"Maybe you could show me how to make it look a little more distressed?"

"Distressed?"

"You keep repeating me," she said, laughing. "Should I say more words? Hydrant. Terrier. Polish sausage."

"Not funny," he replied, but the edges of his eyes crinkled with amusement.

"But you know what I mean, right? The effect I'm after?"

"You'd better explain it."

He leaned back on his heels, as if he was actually interested.

Willa stood. "Hold on," she said, rushing to the kitchen. She rummaged around under a pile of magazines on the counter until she found what she was after, and returned to Burk.

"Here," she said, unfolding the piece of construction paper that had been glued and taped with myriad pieces of decorating magazines. No one magazine had been able to point her toward the right design for her bed-and-breakfast, but by buying magazines she'd never thought she'd touch—*Midwestern Living*, for example—and slapping pieces of them together with the books already in her collection, she was getting warmer.

She pointed to a picture of a table in the middle of her collage. "I don't know how it works, but do you see how this table has the edges kind of roughed out? It looks a little worn. Like maybe it sat in a garage for a while."

"A nice garage," Burk said, studying the collage, "with fruit bowls and designer couches, apparently. Can we talk about that garage instead?"

Willa laughed, smacking him on the arm. She'd meant it to be playful, but her fingers tingled where they connected with his body. She struggled to stay focused. "You see what I mean, though. Right?"

Burk nodded, still studying the page. Willa was suddenly aware of how near they were, both of them kneeling on the hardwood floor together. The afternoon light filtered in through the old glass and kindled dust motes like tiny stars. She reached out, her arm brushing his once again. Another tingle spread through her. She noticed there were flecks of paint on his skin. She envisioned herself giving him a bath, washing them away.

"Here," she said, forcing the image out of her mind and tracing the detail on the page, "the edges look sanded or something."

Burk didn't pull away. "I think you're right," he said. "Sanding the edges might help. There might be other techniques, too. I'm not an expert here. At least not in the more...delicate side of all this."

"If I can figure it out, will you help me?"

Burk turned then, looking her full in the face. The small pocket of space between them seemed to constrict even more. The air was charged, as if there was a current running through it. Willa could all but hear the hum in her brain, a vibration that was thrilling her deepest parts. "This piece you did, this collage. Is it how you envision things?"

Willa tried to concentrate on the question, even though she was suddenly, unbearably warm. She tore her eyes from Burk's to glance at the collage. It featured an open, homey space with cream walls and leather couches the color of an old penny. Stacks of books were placed here and there, as if any topic you wanted to read about would be within reach. The coffee table in this picture was yellow, not blue like hers, but the effect was the same. Its worn look gave all the newness a comfy feel, as if to say this was a room for using and living in—not just for staring at.

"It's a good start," Willa confessed. "I was thinking I'd like to have some of the same touches in the B and B."

Burk nodded, but didn't take his eyes off Willa. A long moment passed, during which she wanted desperately to reach for him, to take his strong face in her hands and to apologize already. To tell him how sorry she was for the past. For the way she'd been a stupid, selfish teenager and had wounded him.

Her heart pounded. She wondered what it would be like to start anew with Burk. Not in a relationship, necessarily, but to have something else between them besides the past. Maybe even just great sex, she thought, glancing at the thick muscles of his arms, taking in the strength of his large hands. She wondered at the hairs of his forearms, dark but soft, and how they'd feel against her skin.

God, it would be fun. She bit her lip. All this pent-up frustration would have somewhere to go. She and Burk could wash away the pain of the past with the pleasure of the present.

"I like this room," Burk said quietly. A sudden hoarseness in his voice thrilled her. He tapped a strong finger on the collage's page. "I'll help you with your projects if you can do a little background work on the how. You figure out the techniques, what supplies we need, I'll help you make it happen."

Willa's heart surged. She was downright delighted, happier than she'd been in ages. She'd found something she could do, could learn. "Thank you!" she cried, throwing her arms around his neck before she could think twice. His arms entwined her instinctively.

As soon as their bodies were linked, the blood rushed to her head in a roar. The warmth of his skin was going to melt her; his breath on her cheek was going to erode her; the pieces of his hair threaded between her fingers were going to end her circulation. Her body was going to cease to function, and she'd be locked in this moment. Forever.

She inhaled the scent of him and found she didn't mind.

"Willa," he growled. She couldn't tell if he wanted her off him, or wanted her pressed harder against him.

He pulled back to look at her and she saw the dark desire etched into his face again. *He's going to kiss me*, Willa thought.

And this time I won't let him flip a switch and walk away.

She was ready for it—ready for him—when the doorbell clanged and startled them both. They broke apart as the moment shattered. Their bodies distanced themselves, and Willa was instantly cold, missing the warmth of him.

Burk mumbled something and picked his paintbrush back up. Willa stood, smoothing the front of her work clothes, and walked to the door with as much dignity as she could muster. *I will kill whoever this is*, she thought. *I will strangle them and dump their body in the Birch River.*

She pulled open the door with a scowl, but it didn't

last long. Because on her front porch was Audrey Tanner, smiling, her dark ponytail swinging.

"I know it's not a practice day," she said, her white teeth flashing, "but I have some new drills I want to run past you. Can I buy you a coffee and pick your brain?"

Willa wanted to stamp her feet, to kick a wall, to punch a window. She wanted her moment back! She wanted Burk's arms around her and a whole afternoon of possibility stretched out before them. Oh, if only she could get rid of Audrey.

But Audrey didn't deserve that. And if Willa knew anything at all, she knew she couldn't get the past back. She could never change the way she'd hurt Burk, not even by throwing herself at him in the here and now. She stared at Audrey, realizing it was probably best to step away from Burk and the table—for now.

"All right," she said. She cast a glance at Burk, to see if he was at all tuned in to her decision, but he had already gone back to painting. He was focused on the blue wood as if nothing at all had happened between them.

Blue wood and blue balls, she thought dryly. He should be thanking her, really, for giving him one and not the other.

CHAPTER THIRTEEN

Thursday, September 27, 5:28 p.m.

*W*illa sprawled in a chair at Knots and Bolts, gulping water between ragged breaths. *Never again*, she vowed, closing her eyes against the memories of the track and the athletic girls and their impossible speed, all while she struggled to keep her out-of-shape ass moving.

This was ridiculous. She was a terrible assistant on the field, and she wasn't helping anyone. All her "volunteering" did was ensure she showed up to the Thursday recipe exchange sweaty and tired.

Next to her, Betty smirked. "Looks like it went great," she said as she sewed the wool tooth of an old witch's head. Vintage Halloween gear. A good online seller apparently.

Willa groaned and Audrey let out an exasperated sigh.

"Willa," Audrey said, "it wasn't that bad. You're being a baby."

"I am not," she replied, her voice whiny.

Next to her, Stephanie giggled, placing a freckled hand over her pretty mouth.

Okay, maybe she was being a baby. A little. But still. It was her second week, and the practices weren't getting easier. Willa had nearly collapsed during the mile warm-up around the track. It only got worse when Audrey had asked her to keep an eye on the sprinters, while she coached the hurdlers.

There was no way Willa could just stand there while that frizzy-haired blonde ran with her arms entirely too low. So Willa raced over to tell her to keep her hands up by her boobs, not by her pockets. And then of course there was the caramel-skinned girl who stared at the ground while she ran, and not at the finish line. So Willa dashed to her side, to explain how seeing her goal was going to help her get there faster. Back and forth she raced, from girl to girl, from starting line to finish line, trying to help and encourage. She could barely remember names or faces, but she could hear her old coach's voice in her brain, and she was compelled to pass along the advice.

"Willa was great," Audrey said to the group, "I don't know why she's pretending she wasn't."

"Because I wasn't," Willa grumbled. "I'm fat and out of shape." She crossed her arms, glad at least that Anna wasn't at the recipe exchange and couldn't see her mortification up close. It was a bummer that Juniper was sick, but if it kept Anna from blabbing to Burk what a mess Willa was every time she came to the recipe exchange, maybe that wasn't so bad.

"Willa, don't say you're fat," Audrey scolded. "You're not."

"She's a little fat," Betty offered.

"She's just not used to the workouts. Give it another week, and this will feel like old hat."

"I don't like old hats," Willa pouted.

Betty grinned, looking back and forth between the women like it was a tennis match.

Audrey crossed her arms over her fleece track jacket. "Is this about something else? Like the fact that you and Burk Olmstead looked pretty cozy when I showed up yesterday? Did I happen to *interrupt* something?"

Betty's wide-set eyes got big with interest. "You don't say."

"No, she *doesn't* say," Willa replied, striding off to the kitchenette for a snack. She rummaged until she found a piece of casserole and a fork. She brought it back out and slunk back into her chair at the red table. Audrey and Betty just stared.

"What?"

"You're blushing," Audrey said.

"Am not," Willa replied, spearing the casserole with her fork. But she could feel the heat in her cheeks, and it had nothing to do with the recent workout.

"I'm surprised he's helping you in that house," Betty said plainly. "I thought he'd hate you for the bitchy way you left him after graduation."

It was a good thing Willa hadn't taken a bite of the casserole yet. She wouldn't have been able to swallow it. Instead, she took a deep, steadying breath.

"I did hurt him. I was awful to him."

Betty narrowed her eyes. "Karma's a bitch."

Willa started. Betty had every right to be angry with her, it was true. After the first Knots and Bolts meeting, part of Willa had hoped they could just sweep the past aside, but that clearly wasn't the case. Betty hadn't forgotten it, and Willa needed to face it.

Now is the time, Willa thought. She had to own up to her past. And either Betty would accept that, or Willa had to find a different hangout besides Knots and Bolts.

Willa scooted her chair closer to Betty's. She could see the other woman lean back, uncomfortable. Nevertheless she pressed ahead.

"Betty, it occurs to me that I've shown up here and invaded your space and I've done all that without actually telling you how sorry I am. For how I treated you in high school." Willa looked at Audrey. "You, too, Audrey. I was terrible to you both. And I'm sorry."

"Oh, it's in the past," Audrey started, waving her hands like she didn't want to talk about it anymore, "and no one—"

"But it's *not* in the past," Willa interrupted. "That's the whole point. We can't put it into the past unless we address it in the present. Unless *I* address it anyway, and say, 'I was a bitch, and there's no excuse for the way I treated you.' So here I am, saying it to you both. I am sorry. Truly sorry. I have spent a lot of my life being shallow and awful. I don't want to be that way anymore."

Audrey's face was turning pink. "Willa, no—"

"Yes. Please let me own this apology. I just hope you can forgive me."

Audrey blew out a puff of air. "Well, as long as you've said you're sorry, then I need to say something, too." She played with the ends of her ponytail. "I knew these track practices would be hard for you. But part of me wanted to see you wheeze."

Willa could feel her eyes widen. Mortification and amusement flooded her all at once.

"But you're doing really well with the girls," Audrey continued. "That part wasn't bullshit. Anyway, as far as I'm concerned, we're even." She walked over to Willa's chair and leaned over to give her a hug. It was strong and honest—and Willa hugged her back.

The two women looked to Betty, who had set down her sewing. Her hands were shaking, and Willa braced herself for what was coming. Betty would yell at her and kick her out of Knots and Bolts and that would be that. And Willa wouldn't blame her. Not one bit.

"I spent a good part of my life believing I was an ugly, beaver-faced girl," Betty began, "all thanks to you, Willa. I didn't try out for any of the high school plays, because who would cast 'the beaver who loved wood'? And I didn't always sleep well, worried that you were going to find me the next day and make my life even worse."

Willa listened, her heart shattering with pity and regret.

"My grades weren't very strong, on account of how I didn't sleep much. But I managed to get into community college, and would you believe it, once I was away from you, my life got better. I did the costumes for some local theater productions. I got my teeth fixed. And you know what? I forgot about you. I really did. Until you came back anyway. To be honest, I wish you'd stayed away. You were not a good person to me, Willa Masterson. Not to any of us."

Willa nodded. It was true. She couldn't say that she'd react any differently if her nemesis came back, either.

"Why are you even back?" Betty asked finally, her

eyes sharp. "You say you want to open a B and B, but why now? Why here?"

Willa swallowed. No one had asked her that yet. People had listened to her plans, but no one wanted to know the driving force behind them. She thought about lying, but she knew if she did, she'd lose any chance to reconcile with Betty. Ever.

"I lost everything in New York," she said, trying to keep the warble out of her voice. "The man I was dating made some terrible investments with my money. The only thing I had left was the house back in White Pine. I had nowhere else to go. This was the only place I could think of to start over."

Betty's mouth opened slightly before she snapped it shut.

"Oh, Willa," Audrey breathed, "I'm so sorry."

Willa shook her head. "Don't be. I wasn't being smart, and I should have known better than to trust one person with everything. In a way, this has been a wake-up call for me. For the better."

Betty studied her. "Well, here's another wake-up call. If you ever—and I mean *ever*—treat me now the way you did in high school, I will kick you out of Knots and Bolts forever. You can have a second chance, but not a third. Understand?"

Willa nodded.

Betty's eyes softened slightly. "All right, listen, it's been a long time, and I have to give you a little credit here. So let's just say we'll put the past behind us for now. And I don't want any reason to pull it out and look at it again. Deal?"

Willa found she couldn't speak. Her throat wasn't

working. So instead, she held her hand out to Betty, who shook it.

"Well, that's better!" Audrey said, and Willa wondered if this was what it felt like to have friends. Real friends, who forgave the worst parts of you and tried to see the good parts. If there were any. Willa closed her eyes briefly and hoped there were—for her.

"There's a catch, though," Betty said after a moment. "No bullshit here. This group shares its secrets with each other, and that means we want all the details about you. Well, you and Burk anyway. You don't get to play coy with us."

Betty tucked a stray piece of her curly, corn yellow hair behind an ear, seemingly pleased with herself. Willa looked to Audrey, whose brown eyes were glinting with amusement, and to Stephanie, whose freckles stretched as she grinned. No help there.

Willa gathered her thoughts. It was doubly good Anna wasn't here tonight. "All right," Willa said, "but I don't know what to tell you about Burk exactly. It's confusing."

"Confusing how?" Audrey asked, pulling out the coffee liqueur. Willa was never so grateful to see a bottle of booze in her whole life. She wondered if she could just forgo the coffee and drink the hooch straight.

"Wait," Stephanie said, standing. "Before you answer that, I can't let you sit here and eat that hot dish cold. Let me go and warm it up for you." She pulled the casserole away from Willa.

"I went a decade without eating that in New York," Willa said. "Now I can't get enough of it."

"They don't have hot dish in New York?" Betty asked.

Willa laughed. "No, they don't. Or if they do, it's some

so-called 'refined' version. A reduction of something or other, on a bed of braised blah, with a leek and fennel hoohah."

"Leek and fennel hoohah? You don't say."

Stephanie put the now-warm hot dish in front of Willa. "Well, let New York have their version. We'll keep ours. Try that and tell me what you think."

Willa speared the mixture of hamburger, green beans, cheese, and tater tots. She closed her eyes at the burst of richness and comfort that filled her mouth. These were the odds and ends of the fridge, mixed together to make something better than the sum of its parts. This is the stuff you ate with your friends, your family. This was a meal that told you that you were cared for.

"Oh God," Willa said on the verge of another food orgasm. "This is amazing."

"This one is Betty's specialty," Audrey said. "But Stephanie makes a good one, too—a hot dish that's a little like a mac and cheese, only it has these delicious fingerling potatoes in it."

"Don't sell yourself short," Betty said. "Audrey makes a hot dish with sausage and egg and a flaky crust over the top. Won third place at the county fair last year."

Willa swallowed. "When can I try them? *All* of them?"

Audrey laughed. "We'll make hot dishes the focus of next week's recipe exchange—how's that?"

Willa nodded eagerly, digging into her hot dish with renewed vigor.

"You'd better bring extra wine," Betty cautioned, "since you can't cook yet."

Willa considered it. "If I can paint a table, I bet I can make a hot dish."

Stephanie stared at her. "You painted a table?"

Willa grinned. "With Burk Olmstead."

The ladies scooted their chairs in closer. "All right," Betty said, "tell us."

Between bites of hot dish, Willa brought them up to speed. And like a good hot dish, she threw everything in—all the details she could remember. When she was done, she didn't know if what she'd presented was any good, but one thing was certain: From the looks on Betty and Stephanie and Audrey's faces, it was a brand-new dish indeed.

CHAPTER FOURTEEN

Friday, September 28, 8:19 p.m.

*B*urk took a deep pull from his beer bottle, wondering why he couldn't stop thinking about a stupid picture. Ever since Willa had shown him that collage of the room earlier in the week, he hadn't been able to forget it. The colors. The furniture. The way her fingers had slid over the image, highlighting the parts she wanted him to notice.

It's just a photo. *Get over it already.*

Except it wasn't just an image. It was images. Plural. Willa hadn't been satisfied with one decorating magazine. No, she'd had to cut a pile of them up and make something even better than what they offered individually. There was a gnawing in his gut about that image that he just couldn't shake.

And he wasn't sure he liked the feeling.

He shifted on the barstool, while strains of an old Johnny Cash song filled the dark corners of The Wheelhouse. His favorite bar was beginning to get crowded on this Friday night, as folks came in for the cheap beer, good food, and a dance or two. Behind the bar, his buddy Dave flipped the top off another beer and slid it to him. Burk nodded his thanks. Dave always knew when he needed another. Good bartenders always did.

Burk tapped the bottle's amber glass and tried to concentrate on his settings: the crack of the pool balls from the table in the corner, the buzz of the neon Pabst sign above the bar, the burning stare of the leggy redhead over by the jukebox. But his surroundings were like a sepia picture in comparison to the bright memory of Willa in his mind: her dark blond hair tousled as she sanded her table, her perfect lips pressed together in concentration as she painted, her soft skin brushing against his as they studied the decorating collage together.

Damn that stupid collage. Burk shook his head. The room she'd showed him had been a searing revelation, burning into his brain in painful detail. It was the decor he'd always wanted inside the house he always wanted. Only he'd never been able to *envision* it. He'd gotten as far as the flooring, the shelves, the granite countertops, and the penny tile in the bathroom. But he had no idea how to tie it all together. In fact, he probably would have thrown his old plaid couches and La-Z-Boy into the living room and called it a day.

But when Willa explained her ideas, when she pointed to that picture she'd made, it had all come together. Willa had reached into the recesses of his subconscious and pulled out something he didn't even *know* how to conjure. She'd brushed color and detail onto his plain canvas, completing the picture in his mind.

The room was ideal. It was perfect. And now that Burk

had seen it, he wanted more of the same. He wanted Willa to look at every other room and bring his desires to light. Desires he didn't know he had. She could finish what he'd started, and make his house a *home*.

It complicated things to say the least.

Just when Burk had finally been able to imagine his house without Willa in it, here she was, inserting herself into his desires all over again.

He grunted, taking another swig of beer. *His house.* The idea was beginning to wear thin. Too thin maybe. He hadn't done a very good job of convincing Willa to sell him the title, or go back to New York to her glamorous, un-Minnesotan life. More alarming than that, he wasn't so sure he minded her being around.

With her green eyes glittering up at him and her fresh, clean smell all around, he had downright enjoyed painting that table with her. And if he was honest, he'd wanted to do more than just paint the table. He'd wanted to spread her across it and undress her slowly, taking in her new-found curves. He'd wanted to tangle his fingers in her hair and press his mouth against hers, hearing her moan and whimper like she used to in high school, meeting his hot need with her own. He wanted to spread her soft thighs with his knee and settle between her, laving her skin with his tongue, especially between her—

"Excuse me, is this seat taken?"

Burk started, nearly tipping over his beer. He looked up to find the redhead from the jukebox suddenly standing at the barstool next to him. Up close, her mouth looked hard, her body even harder. All sinew and bone. Burk wanted to buy her a sandwich. Instead, he gestured to the stool. "Be my guest."

She settled in, crossing one lean leg over the other. Her black tank top dipped dangerously low as she turned to face him. "You from around here?"

"Born and raised," Burk replied. On a normal night, he'd already have a beer in front of her, and *he* would have asked the first question, not her.

"What'll you have?" he asked, glimpsing the pale top of one breast over a strip of hot pink bra.

"Whatever you're buying," she replied. Too loudly. Trying too hard, Burk thought. He caught Dave's eye and got her a beer.

"And how about you?" Burk asked, taking in her flinty cheekbones, her straight red hair. "From around here?"

"Over in New Prave," she replied. "I'm a nurse there."

It was a town a few miles southwest of White Pine, with fewer shops and no river and miles of farmland marooning it. If she was a nurse, she didn't work at a hospital. New Prave didn't have one.

For the first time in years, the idea of another one-night stand with a stranger left a sour taste in Burk's mouth. It was suddenly tiring, this endless parade of women through his door. He imagined curling into bed and resting—sleeping instead of fucking for once—and how good it would feel to ease the bone-weary ache in his body.

Ready to tell the stranger he was turning in, Burk looked into the woman's eyes and noticed they were pale like dried moss. Green—sort of. Not like Willa's, but maybe in the same family.

Desire for Willa surged just under his skin. It flooded him, and he stiffened with its intensity. The raw, primal need for Willa was so overpowering that he was suddenly willing to do anything to redirect it. He was ready to give anyone—anyone at all—his time and attention to keep his longing for Willa at bay.

Wanting her was too dangerous. There was too much risk, and God knew he'd already lost enough.

He leaned closer to the redhead. She smiled at him, revealing small, uneven teeth.

"I bet you're a good dancer," he said. "We should hit the floor later."

"Dancing's not all I'm good at," she purred in reply.

Burk stared at her mouth to avoid her eyes. If he could stay focused on her lips and not see the hint of green in her irises, it might be enough to forget Willa.

For one night anyway.

* * *

A glass of merlot in hand, Willa strolled around her home, not minding that she was inside on a Friday night. She had Tupperware containers full of food, thanks to the previous evening's recipe exchange, and she had a new pile of decorating magazines to peruse.

With an online eighties radio station playing her favorite (albeit corny) hits from that era, she walked through the dining room—where peeling chintz wallpaper hung like broken sails—and into the living room, where her bright blue table sat in stark contrast to the dull trim and flooring.

Willa had spent the past few days figuring out how to rough the edges of the table, discovering that if she painted a dark color underneath as a base, then chipped off some of the blue, the distressed effect would come through. She wasn't sure how Burk would feel at her revelation, since it would mean they'd have to paint the table over again, but the fact that she'd figured out how to do it made her eyes gleam. Plus, she was pretty sure she'd need to learn how to use a palm sander—whatever that was— and she was dying to try it.

Everywhere in the house, Willa was suddenly looking at things and wondering if she could repurpose them. The dusty old hutch stored in the basement. The ancient dresser in her bedroom. The brass bed in the guest room. The baker's rack in the kitchen.

She sipped her wine and wondered how her mom would feel if she could see how Willa was reusing all the old pieces in the home. At the end of her life, Edna had softened—even apologizing to Willa—so there was a chance she might have grinned and said, "Go for it."

Willa could picture her mom's thin hands, so brittle and wrinkled the last time she'd seen them five years ago. They'd covered Willa's own with a dry rustle. Her old woman's voice had been shaky when Edna told her she loved her. That she wished she could have been there for her more, especially after Willa's dad had died. She confessed she'd fled to Minneapolis and into the arms of Max because she didn't know how to be without a man.

In the end, Edna had asked to be buried not in White Pine next to Harold or in Saint Paul, next to Max, but in a small family plot in Minneapolis. It was a decision Willa had respected enormously.

She closed her eyes, hoping her mom was looking down on her right now. Maybe she was the one, Willa mused, who was sending her decorating ideas every minute. Good ideas, too. In her mind, she was mixing old and new in the perfect balance. She could all but see the results in her mind's eye.

Either way, whether it was a little bit of Edna or her own innate talent—or both—Willa couldn't stop the ideas from flowing. Which was a good thing since rehabbed furniture would save money. She'd already had to give Burk a chunk of change for the roofing, the plastering, and some lumber to fix rotting boards on the siding, back deck, and front porch. But beyond all the repairs and decorating were the supplies she'd need for her guests. New dishes plentiful enough to feed a group of up to ten every morning. A load of new towels and bed linens. An industrial washer and dryer in the basement so she could wash them all. Or perhaps enough for a small salary so she could *pay* someone to wash them all.

Money was tight, and getting tighter. At this rate, she might need to go to the bank for a small loan. Not that that should be a problem. Her dad had owned the bank, after all. He had been adored there and she couldn't imagine they would refuse the daughter of Harold Masterson money if she needed it.

But even with the financial concerns darkening a corner of her mind, she could see the B and B coming together, and the progress made her elated. She hadn't felt this excited about anything since moving to New York twelve years ago.

And it was all thanks to Burk, really. Not only was he commanding a crew on the big projects, but he'd taken her to the hardware store and helped her pick out paint. He'd given her lessons in sandpaper coarseness. He'd sat here in this very room and helped her paint every surface of the table.

And he'd nearly kissed her again.

Willa took her merlot back to the kitchen, trying not to think about how close she and Burk had been—again— earlier in the week. When she'd told Betty, Stephanie, and Audrey about it, they'd both sworn up and down that Burk still had feelings for her.

Willa sighed. If only that were true. The reality was, Burk probably just had a handful of old, residual emotions being dredged up now that she was back in town. Knowing the new Burk, he'd probably experience a few sparks of feeling, and then douse them with his flat pragmatism.

In a way, Willa wished for the same stiff sensibility in herself. Her tousled hair would never move him to action—whereas the messiness of *his* ebony locks had the air catching in her lungs. He could see her fingers on a hammer or wrench and it wouldn't stir a single thing in his heart—whereas Willa would find herself wishing she was one of those tools in *his* hands.

She shook her head and stared out the window above the kitchen sink. Burk was such an all-consuming idea in her brain lately. She very much doubted she was one in *his* mind, however. Not that she needed to be.

The only thing she really needed to be in was his bed.

She tried to replace the picture of them sleeping to-gether with the scene outside her window. An early frost covered the ground with a ghostly white sheen. Stars pierced the fabric of the black sky like jeweled needle-points. There had never been this many stars in New York—ever. Not with all the lights and noise and pol-lution. Here, though, everything was quiet and still. The sky, the streets, the houses. Even her heart seemed to slow its frantic pace, her brain seemed to race less.

Unless she was around Burk.

Willa took a sip of wine, her lips curving into a smile around her glass. It was shocking, really, that she'd spoken her ideas about Burk out loud to her friends at the recipe exchange last night. *Ideas* wasn't the right word, though. Neither was *plan* or *agenda*. Those words sounded so calculated, when really, all Willa wanted was Burk.

In bed.

With her.

"You made a great couple in high school, why not again now?" Audrey had asked. Willa didn't have the heart to correct her. She didn't want to be a couple.

She just wanted...Burk. No strings attached. Friends with benefits, she supposed you could call it.

They were consenting adults. She could give him a few wild nights; he could give her a few in return. It wouldn't have to be anything exclusive or complicated. Just great sex. And then they'd have something between them besides the past.

She giggled involuntarily, wondering how she was going to approach Burk with all this. Should she sidle up to him in a negligee? Should she ask him, businesslike, over the wet paint of a project? Burk was so regimented. Maybe she should draw up papers and create a contract.

The thought made her laugh out loud. The sound echoed in the empty house, which made Willa laugh harder. She was crazy, cracking herself up in this old space, all alone. The merlot must be going to her head. Willa grinned and decided to pour herself another glass. Why the hell not? She was enjoying herself enormously.

She crossed the battered tile floor to the makeshift

wine rack and was just reaching for the bottle when her cell phone rang. Her mind raced, thinking it might be Burk. What if he was coming over now?

Only she hadn't proposed anything to him yet. The deal was still all in her head. "I'm going crazy," Willa giggled to herself, pulling her phone out of her pocket. But when she saw the caller ID, her smile disappeared.

It was Lance.

And it was his sixth call of the day.

Willa reeled. He'd been calling her constantly since his first text at the Rolling Pin. The calls dredged up a mixture of confusion and compassion—but also apprehension. She might have been slightly sympathetic toward him if his remorse had been genuine, but how real could it be if he was suddenly blowing up her phone, asking for her help?

Maybe it was time to hear what he had to say and be done with it. Emboldened by her plan to seduce Burk—and maybe with merlot as liquid courage—Willa hit *Talk*. "What do you want?" she demanded.

There was a long pause. She could hear Lance breathing—the same high sound the air always made through his long, aquiline nose.

"Hello, Willa," he said after a moment. "It's good to hear your voice."

At the sound of his words, her palms instantly grew damp. "I can't do small talk, Lance. Why are you calling me?"

"Willa, please. I'm not calling to fight."

"I'm not fighting. I'm just telling you to hurry up and spill what you need to spill." She tapped her foot nervously on the battered kitchen floor.

Another pause. "You know I'm sorry. I've said it a thousand times, but I'll say it again. I messed up. I was trying to get us more money, and do it quickly, and I—"

"I know," she said, cutting him off. Her heart pounded. She didn't need to rehash the pain of the past months all over again. She knew all too well what he'd done, and what he'd confessed to. She took a deep breath. "I know," she said more softly this time. "You don't have to tell me again."

She closed her eyes, picturing all the paperwork she'd pawed through when Lance was charged: IRA funds, investment portfolios, savings accounts. She called all the firms and banks, and the story was the same—all the money had vanished.

The only account that still had anything in it at all was the one in the White Pine Bank and Trust. It was a small fund that her dad had set up when she was a little girl. She hadn't touched it—and had never told Lance about it.

The money was still there. All the money she had in the world, in fact.

It was pocket change compared to the fortunes she'd inherited. But once she realized that life as she'd known it in New York was over, she'd counted her assets differently. What had seemed not to matter before suddenly meant everything.

Back in the kitchen, Willa had to lean against the counter as the memories gathered like heavy clouds.

"I love you," Lance said into the silence.

Willa straightened. She and Lance had moved in together, had shared a bed and consolidated their possessions, and she'd assumed the whole time it had been love. They'd said as much, but now she wondered if the words had been true. Deep inside, she wanted love to be more, to mean more, than the scraps of emotions they'd meted out to each other.

"Why are you saying that now?" she asked.

"Because I made such a terrible mistake, Willa. I need you. No one else can get me through this but you."

"That's not true."

"It is. When this is all over, we need to be together."

"This is not going to be over for a very, very long time. And even when it is, you know there's no hope for us."

"There is, Willa. I have to believe you still care for me."

Willa rubbed her forehead with her free hand. "Lance, you've owned up to your mistakes, and that's a good thing. But beyond that, there's nothing for us."

"But—"

"I need you to stop calling me."

"I can't do that."

"Lance, I'm sorry. This conversation is over."

"Wait!" His voice was panicked, urgent. "Remember when we went to Mali and stayed in those huts? Just you and me. I want to go back there with you. I want to start over."

Willa shook her head. She made her voice cold. "Those days are over. You made sure of that when you stole my money and everyone else's."

"I love you. I want to see you. Things here are so hard right now. No one will talk to me. I just need a friend."

"No."

"I could fly into Minneapolis. Rent a car and come see you."

"*No.* Absolutely not. You'll violate the terms of your bond if you do that."

"But I need to ask you something."

"The answer is no."

"But I need you."

Willa ran her tongue over her teeth. This reeked of desperation. "Need me for what?"

"N-Nothing. Just life. Happiness." His voice was beginning to shake.

Willa's mind raced. Her skin prickled with unease. "What are you up to? What's going on?"

"What do you mean?" He laughed uncomfortably. Willa could all but see his pale skin shining with nervous sweat, his narrow shoulders hunched in concentration, his eyes darting back and forth, birdlike.

"Fine. Don't tell me. I don't care."

In the background, Madonna's "Material Girl" started playing, and Willa smiled. It was time to change the station. And get off this call.

"All right," Lance acquiesced, "fine. Here's the deal. I nee—"

But Willa didn't hear the rest. She was thinking about Knots and Bolts, about the painted table, and about coaching the girls at the track.

She was making a go of it in White Pine, and she didn't need Lance messing that up, too.

She clicked *End*, then turned her phone off for the rest of the night.

CHAPTER FIFTEEN

Monday, October 1, 8:22 a.m.

*E*arly Monday morning, Burk brought in a crew to tear out the kitchen. Their efficient swiftness surprised Willa, who watched from a corner of the dining room, sipping coffee out of her mom's old mug. Already there was fresh, bright white plaster drying on many of the house's walls and ceilings, and the new roof tiles sparkled like pennies in the spring sun.

It was satisfying progress to be sure, but Willa was starting to get alarmed at the rapidly dropping numbers in her bank account. She'd forgotten to think about landscaping, which would be a massive expense, and she'd decided that she had to hire a full-time housekeeper. Even if she could keep up with the cooking and the linens, there was no way she'd be able to clean the whole place, too. There was also advertising, because she had to tell people about the B and B; otherwise how would they know to come?

It all meant more money, which was something she didn't have. But she figured it was something she could *get*.

After all, she had her dad's legacy at the White Pine Bank and Trust. She might even still know a few people who worked there, and surely they would give the daughter of Harold Masterson a loan. She'd have no trouble paying it back once the B and B was up and running. She pictured telling the bankers about the food she'd serve in her B and B, about the comfy beds she'd provide, and about the beautiful space she'd create. And just in case things didn't take off right away, she'd make sure to negotiate a loan with a reasonable interest rate. Harold Masterson's daughter could do that, too, thank you very much.

The creak of bending nails caught her attention, and her insides quavered as she stared at Burk, who was tearing out old molding. His wide back muscles flexed underneath his work shirt. His dark hair gleamed in the lights. Next to him, two men were lifting off the top of the old counter, getting ready to haul it to the Dumpster outside. "Next we'll start on the cabinets, okay, boss?" one of them asked. Burk grunted in reply, not looking up from his work. Satisfied with the answer, the men began the slow, careful maneuver of the old countertop through the narrow doorways and outside.

Willa knew she should probably wade into the thick of it—maybe supervise the emptying of her cupboards so they could start ripping out the dated cabinets. Or go over the paint swatches one last time, to make sure the soft yellow she'd picked for the walls was perfect. But here she was, standing off to the side, watching Burk instead.

She swallowed, thinking about the proposition she had

for him. "I think we should spend a few nights together," she imagined saying, running her hands over his chest, playing with the soft hair in the wide fields above his pectorals.

She could imagine lifting her face to his... and then what?

What if he blew her off? Worse, what if he laughed?

Willa clutched her coffee mug. It would be horrible. Beyond mortification. She'd probably have to find a new contractor at that point. Yet he *had* kissed her in the Volvo. And there must be part of him that wanted more, she reasoned. She just had to convince him it was a good idea.

God knows she'd already convinced herself. She watched Burk kick a sharp sliver of molding away from where he was working, and found she was already envying his boots. To be that close to his feet, contoured around them—it almost wasn't fair.

Oh God, she thought, *I'm fantasizing about his feet.*

As if he knew she was watching him, Burk straightened and met her gaze. His blue eyes sparkled like the ocean in summer. Was there laughter there? Blushing furiously, worried that he could read her thoughts, Willa strode away. This wasn't going to work if she was staring at him pathetically all day. What man wanted a woman who would stand around *pining*?

She needed to be more poised than this. More aloof. It was just sex, after all. If it worked, it was going to be a glorious release, and nothing more. She couldn't have him suspecting she was getting all moody about him.

She followed the workmen with the countertop out the front door. While they heaved the giant scrap into the

Dumpster, Willa walked the opposite way—around the house to the detached garage in the rear.

The small structure sported crumbling wood and flaking white paint. Green mold had rotted the roof's tiles, and the whole thing was beginning to list slightly to the left. Still, it was quiet and peaceful—and the perfect workshop, Willa had reasoned. She'd moved a few of her things out here over the weekend. Brushes, the tarp, and a small nightstand that she'd found in the attic. She was going to work on it and use it as a practice piece, until Burk could help her repaint and age the blue coffee table, which was still in the living room.

Willa lifted the old garage door by hand. It rolled upward with a rusty groan. A startled collection of wrens fluttered nearby. They twittered into a maple aflame with scarlet leaves. The tree's splendid color could barely be muted as gray clouds scuttled across the sky. Willa filled her lungs with the fall air, smelling the strong oaks and lean poplars that would soon send their leaves fluttering to the ground.

Inside, the air in the garage was the opposite—dark and musty. She tried not to imagine the mice or raccoons or other creatures that might be in the walls or corners. She flipped the dusty light switch and an old fluorescent light buzzed to life.

The little nightstand sat on the tarp, as if it had been anxiously awaiting her return. It was tall and sturdy, with two planks at the top and two planks that formed a shelf about halfway down its spindled legs. It had a small drawer as well, perfect for a reading light and a book, she thought.

Willa wanted to try a project she'd researched online,

where she painted a color directly on the wood without
the endless primer that Burk had made her use. He was
approaching things as a contractor, and she needed to approach them more as an artist. So she was going to paint
not one but three colors onto the table, then sand them
out, and apply a few other layers of stain as well.

If it worked—if she could make the nightstand come to
life the way it was in her mind—she knew she could finish the coffee table using the same techniques. With one
glaring exception: She would need a palm sander, a machine, because the table would be too big to do by hand.
And she'd need Burk to show her how to use it.

Willa bit her lip, thinking how funny it was that she
was already planning to use power tools, when mere
days before she'd been intimidated about buying paint.
Somehow, working with Burk had given her confidence
she didn't know she possessed. He'd been patient,
interested—and he seemed to appreciate her decorating
ideas. In turn, Willa was able to believe more in herself,
in her entire B and B project, in a way she hadn't been
able to before. She grinned to herself, and reached out to
the table to get started.

She paused, however, when she saw the state of her
hands. Her knuckles were dry from scrubbing off residual
paint, and no amount of lotion had been able to soften
the Sahara of her skin. She'd chipped most every nail, as
well. Not that she minded, but her hands were starting
to look pathetic. If she was going to do this and not ruin
her skin completely, she really needed a pair of gloves already.

Carefully she began pushing aside old boards and
shovels, rooting around the garage for a discarded pair.

Dust swirled and caught in her throat. She coughed and turned away from the debris. As she did, she spotted a shelf above a rusted bike wheel and there—right on top of an old metal can—was a pair of faded leather work gloves.

"Bingo," she said, though the shelf was near the garage's roofline, at least five feet up. Even if she found a chair, she wouldn't even be close to reaching them. With a ladder and a rake, however...

Willa darted toward an old metal rake hanging on the wall, and pulled it free. More dust plumed, and her eyes began to water, but she wiped them and kept looking around. She *knew* she'd seen a ladder. And sure enough, there it was, buried under bundles of old chicken wire. With the handle of the rake, she rolled the sharp wire away, leaving the ladder exposed.

In the humming light, it wasn't hard to tell the wood was rotted. It was soft and moist—but still holding together. The bottom rung was damp and shredded, but everything above that looked okay.

Or if not okay, at least—passable. Sort of. While she wouldn't choose this ladder if she had an alternative, the truth was that she'd be on the rungs for mere moments. Just long enough to knock the gloves off with the rake and climb down. Willa eyed the wood determinedly. Surely it could hold her for a few seconds.

She heaved the ladder to its tottering feet, and spread it into its classic inverted V shape. Chips of old wood rained down, landing in her hair, on her clothes. Ignoring them, Willa placed the ladder under the shelf. She only had to climb three rungs at the most. Not counting the first, which was really just shredded bits.

No problem.

With the rake in hand, Willa placed her foot on the second rung and tested it with a little weight. She felt it give slightly, but then hold. Slowly she added more weight until all that was left to do was grab the sides of the ladder and haul herself up. Taking a deep breath, she did just that, and smiled when she found herself supported. "All right then," she said, placing her foot on the next step.

It held, too. This was going to be a piece of cake. She could already see the gloves, and with just a few more inches, she could swipe them off their tin can perch and be done with it.

Just then, a shadow darkened the mouth of the garage. "What in God's name are you doing?"

The gravelly voice shook the inside of Willa's bones. She paused, trying not to let Burk see how much he affected her. His presence was ten times more dangerous than the ladder, thanks to the way her hands were now shaking. "I just need some gloves. They're up there. I'll be down in a sec."

"Get down now," he said. "That ladder isn't safe. Jesus, it looks like it's *rotting*."

"It's fine," Willa protested as Burk took a step closer. "I need five more sec—"

Just then, the stays on the ladder snapped, separating the sides of the inverted V from each other. With her counterbalance gone, Willa began to pitch backward. The rake clattered to the floor. Horrified and falling, she twisted, trying to land on a leg or shoulder and not her head. She cried out, simultaneously bracing herself for a fall on the hard concrete.

Instead, she landed with a thud against Burk, who

grunted as he caught her. Broken pieces of ladder splintered every which way as his arms wound around her.

Willa was too startled to mind the way he swore angrily. His eyes were aflame—and if she hadn't been so
surprised, she might be alarmed at the fury there. If the
terror of the fall hadn't been so startling, she would have
loved to relish the feel of his chest, the closeness of his
skin against hers, the way the heat from him warmed every part of her.

"Where are you hurt?" he demanded. Willa tried to
breathe normally, to tell him she hadn't been injured, but
her words came out as if she'd just been at track practice
with Audrey.

"I'm...all...right."

And then, as if she weighed nothing more than what
she had in high school, Burk lifted her and threw her over
his shoulder. Her chin was against his back—her ass near
his face. Willa grunted in protest. Whatever he was doing,
she didn't need it.

"Put me...down," she demanded, her breath still
shaky.

"No," he growled.

Willa's blood pounded with every step. "Burk. What
are you *doing*?"

He ignored her, his long strides eating up the ground
from the garage to the house.

Her anger building, she pounded the small of his back
with her fists. "Goddamn it, set me down," she yelled as
best she could with her lungs still recovering from the
fall. "This is not okay. You have no right—"

Whack. Willa's mouth opened in a silent O of fury.
Burk's hand had come down directly on her rear.

He'd spanked her!

So she did the only thing she could think of. She raised her hand and spanked him back, as hard as she could. "Two can play this game!" she cried as he threw open the back door and stepped inside.

The work crew immediately stopped what they were doing to stare at their boss—with the owner of the house slung over his shoulder. Willa's blood pounded. She had never—ever!—been treated this badly by someone she'd *hired*. And here she was, looking like a fool in front of the biggest crew she'd ever written checks for.

She felt Burk's chest expand as he took a breath. "Back to work!" he bellowed to his crew.

Even half upside down, Willa could register how they responded like an army battalion. They returned to their scraping and painting and hauling as if nothing were amiss.

Burk stormed through the kitchen, then rounded the banister and took the stairs two at a time. Willa's muscles tightened as she realized where they were going: her bedroom.

She clenched her fists, wanting to be outraged that he was carrying her upstairs like some maiden in distress. But her fury wouldn't—*couldn't*—overcome the pulse of excitement suddenly beating in her.

Not even the fact that Burk's crew was probably already speculating about the two of them could numb the thrills prickling her skin. She took a breath, but it only resulted in Burk's pine-and-citrus scent filling her head. With her cheek resting against the cotton of his shirt, she could feel the heat from his skin through the fabric. She wondered if he could feel her own heat—the way it spread through her, flaming her desire.

Suddenly Burk was rolling her away from his body, tossing her on her bed. She landed with a jolt on the same full-size mattress that had been there since they'd lost their innocence to each other so many years before.

She blinked. Her indignation returned in a blistering wave. "You have no right!" she cried, trying to sit up. "That was the stupidest, most meat-headed thing—"

"Enough." The single word was spoken in a quiet, dangerous voice. Willa's words stopped in her throat. Burk's face was dark with anger, his muscles strained with emotion.

He leaned over her, his blazing eyes inches from hers. Willa's breath caught.

"You asked for my help," he said, his tone gravelly and low, "and I agreed to assist you. But if you flit around recklessly, getting into things, then I—"

"Flit? Since when do I *flit*?" First of all, it was her house. And second, she didn't need a lecture on top of everything else.

"This home is old," Burk continued, his enraged pulse visible in his neck, "and you can't just put on your explorer hat and race off to any dark corner you like. You could have been seriously hurt."

It was then that Willa saw the fear alongside all the anger in Burk's eyes. It was just a shift—a small change—but it was there. He was scared for her. Her stint on the ladder had *frightened* him.

Because he cares, she thought, her heart pounding.

"I…" She tried to think of something to argue with, something to say, but her mind had gone blank.

"Find me the next time you need something from the garage," he growled, his barrel chest heaving. He pulled back, standing to his full height above her. Willa trembled on the bed, willing her brain to kick into gear. He was going to leave if she didn't stop him.

"What if I need something that's not in the garage?"

He ran a distracted hand through his ebony hair. "Well, then find me for that, too. The point is—"

"What if it's not in the house?"

His head shifted ever so slightly. She lost sight of the freckle underneath his right eye.

"Where else would you need something?"

Willa sat up. Her hands were shaking so much she had to clasp them together.

She needed to proposition him *now*. The only problem was, she was struggling to find the words. She was also having a hard time getting past the fact that there were wood chips in her hair and dust on her skin. And never mind the fact that they were surrounded by the décor of her childhood bedroom. The same butterfly border ran along the top of the lavender-colored walls, now faded and peeling. The same books lined the white case in the corner, now yellowed with age. The same basket with the same pink flowers rested near the window, now dusty and moldy. It had been a beautiful, lavish room for a teenager back in the day. These days, it was just old and tired, and Willa wanted so much to explain to Burk that she was sorry for all of it—for the way she'd left him, for the way she'd left this house, and wounded everyone around her.

Where had all her brazenness gone? Unclasping her hands, she did the only thing she could think of—she reached out and placed her fingers on the bare skin of his arm. The world flickered for a moment, shifting from the charge between them.

Burk's dark blue eyes darted to her fingers, then back at her face. His lips—such a steady line—broke just slightly.

"I might need *you*," Willa said, hating the breathy notes in her voice. She wished she could be more forceful. More demanding.

She flattened her palm on Burk's skin. She could feel the soft hairs of his forearm, and the knots of muscle just beneath the skin.

Burk didn't say anything, but his sharp jawline flexed.

"It doesn't have to be anything complicated," Willa continued, feeling a flush creeping up her neck. "Just us. Here and now. Nothing but the present."

She sucked in a breath as Burk inched closer. "What are you saying?" he asked, his voice impossibly low.

Willa almost smiled. He *would* make her spell it out. His breath was hot on her skin. She feared she would melt into a puddle right there.

"You and me," she replied, her insides shivering. "Let's put something else between us besides the past."

Burk leaned in so far that she was forced to lie back onto the faded bedspread. His hands came to rest on either side of her head. His eyes stormed like a thousand blue waves. He kneed her legs apart, and she gasped as he eased himself lower.

"Like this?" he asked. "Is this what you want between us?" He shifted so she could feel the thick hardness of him. She closed her eyes at the shower of sparks that ignited her flesh.

"Yes," she murmured. "*That*."

She traced the sharp line of his jaw, loving the sensation of his rough stubble under her fingertips. He shifted again, pressing harder this time, and she tilted her head back.

Burk's mouth immediately found the soft skin just above her collarbone. He placed his lips there, working his mouth upward. His stubble rubbed a delicious coarseness along her skin.

By the time he reached her lips, Willa was nearly aching. *Oh God*, she thought, *I'm undone and he hasn't even kissed me yet.*

He paused so long before putting his mouth on hers that Willa finally opened her eyes. He was right there—all fine lips and high cheekbones and dark hair. The rugged handsomeness of him made her chest hurt.

"I'm good at this part," he said, a small smile playing at the corners of his mouth. "But I can't say I'll be good for much else."

Willa tilted her hips up just slightly, pressing against him. "That sounds just about perfect to me."

Burk groaned, and met her thrust with one of his own. Willa shuddered with the hard pleasure of their grinding.

"So you want to bring this thing into the here and now?" he asked, his lips just inches from hers, his hot breath tickling her skin.

"Oh, yes," she replied, her hands flattening on the broad expanse of his back. "Very much."

His smile vanished as he bore his mouth down on hers in a kiss so searing, it left her seeing stars.

CHAPTER SIXTEEN

Monday, October 1, 10:10 a.m.

The roaring passion thundering inside his body was clouding Burk's thoughts. Had Willa seriously just propositioned him in her old bedroom, and had he really just accepted?

The primal drumbeat of his heart pulsed the truth, hammering harder as she emitted hot, breathy whispers underneath him.

Underneath him.

Holy Christ, was this really happening?

The creep of the shadows in her old bedroom was all so dreamlike—he might have believed his imagination was on overdrive, except that the *real* darkness was where his body fit against Willa's. They were perfectly contoured puzzle pieces, blocking out all light. And he might doubt her solidness beneath him, he knew, if he wasn't already flat-palming her ribs, running his hands along her sweet-smelling skin, and lifting her shirt over her head.

Her top free, Burk took in the curves of her flesh, and all remaining doubt about what they were doing vanished. Her lovely breasts molded perfectly to the contours of her plain white bra. It wasn't the searing pink or leopard-print pattern of the women he was used to. It was practical. It was so unlike the Willa he remembered that he grinned.

Willa turned her head away when she saw his reaction, and he realized she must think he was laughing at her. His muscles tensed. He would never make fun of her exquisite shape, her beguiling scent—all the things that were so uniquely *her*. Especially not when he'd told himself he'd forgotten all about them, when in reality he'd just locked them away for twelve years. Now they were out of the cage of his memory, threatening to overtake him.

But instead of saying any of that, he lowered himself and took her mouth, driving himself headlong into the feel and taste of her. She responded eagerly, wrapping her legs around him, plunging her fingers into his hair and pulling him closer still, as if she couldn't bear to have even an atom of space between them.

Reaching behind her, he deftly unhooked the bra and threw it to the side. Her exposed breasts were twin mounds of perfection—pale and rosy-tipped—and he cupped them in his calloused hands. They felt fuller than he remembered—more womanly and sensual somehow. He had never seen a more exquisite pair. Willa breathed a soft "Oh!" as he delicately squeezed each nipple. They hardened underneath him, perfect rosebuds on her skin. He lowered his lips to one sweet peak, then another, sucking gently.

He pulled back briefly, needing suddenly to stare into

the depths of her green eyes. Willa met his gaze fully, but he could see she was blushing.

"What?" he asked, palming one breast.

"I've—I've gained weight. You don't have to pretend I haven't."

The tension in his body returned again—a painful tightness he didn't altogether understand. Why would she think she was anything but beautiful? He wondered angrily if someone in New York had made her self-conscious. If so, it was criminal. Her body was a series of lush curves any man would want to lay his hands on.

But all Burk could do was shake his head. "No," he growled, lowering his head to the rounded flesh of her belly, running his tongue along her skin until she moaned.

Willa's hands dug into the skin at his shoulder blades. "Your shirt," she said huskily, "off."

He left her skin for a moment in order to whip off his shirt and toss it to the ground. Willa pressed her chest against his now bare one. The feel of so much skin on skin had him coiled with desire.

Her fingertips left a wake of fire along his skin as she traced his muscles—from his chest to his shoulders, down his arm and back again. Finally, when he couldn't take it, he crushed her beneath him with another kiss.

Her hands left his skin to fumble with his pants. "I can't—get the—"

Burk lifted his hips so her fingers could slide between them and undo his jeans. She shoved them down, and he kicked them off.

Her hand found the hardened length of him immediately. The spark of her fingers against his sensitive flesh was so intense he nearly recoiled.

"*Mmm.*" Her voice was husky with an emotion he couldn't place. "*Yes.*"

He worked his lips along the underside of her lovely jaw, while she stroked him in long movements that threatened to shatter his composure. He was going to lose himself in her touch alone. It would be like high school all over again when he tried so desperately to control himself but wound up with wetness in his jeans instead.

Grabbing her wrist, he removed her hand from his penis and pinned it behind her head. With his other hand, he unbuttoned her pants and worked them downward. She shimmied and twisted underneath him until her clothes were in a pile at her ankles.

Burk raised himself so he could see the impossible expanse of Willa Masterson. Back in her bed. With him.

The naked length of her brought to mind cream and sugar and sweet fruit. His mouth watered, imagining the taste of her—*everywhere*.

Willa bit her lip, seeming to shrink from his gaze. *Embarrassed*, he realized again. He could feel his brows knotting with confusion and frustration. He wanted desperately to tell her how lovely she was, how much he wanted her, but his throat was closed shut. Burk Olmstead didn't talk that way to women.

Ever.

So instead he took out his fury on her body, parting her legs and finding the center of her quickly. Too quickly. Her eyes went wide as he plunged a finger into her wet depths. "Oh," she breathed, tensing.

Burk's heart constricted. He didn't want to rush this. He wanted to enjoy her, to languidly kiss and press and thrust against her—hearing her moan and cry out and whimper—for the rest of the afternoon. Only he found himself rubbing her center with hurried strokes that left them both wanting. Willa's eyes were dark with confusion. What was he doing? It was too fast, too hard—and they both knew it.

Burk placed his mouth on hers and tried to slow down. He tugged on her lips with his teeth, pulling gently, and she sighed against him. Wrapping her arms around his neck, she whispered his name. "Burk."

Tenderness flooded him. He squeezed his eyes against it, trying to shut it out. This wasn't what he'd signed up for. He hadn't anticipated feeling so goddamn *much* with her. Not meeting her eyes, he spread her legs wider and settled between them. Her neck arched as the tip of his penis pressed against her warm, wet entrance.

Oh, God. He wanted this. He wanted to spend hours here, coaxing out passion in waves that would overtake them both.

Except that her vulnerability, her misplaced bashfulness—it was unraveling him. He didn't like it. *Burk Olmstead did not get unraveled.*

So instead he plunged inside her depths, and she cried out when his thickness filled her up so suddenly. She gasped, her face flushing with equal parts pain and pleasure.

Burk could only grunt at the softness all around him. She was so perfect, and he desperately wanted to savor the moment, the sensation of being inside her, their bodies joined once again after all this time. It was once so sweet and innocent—and this time it could be sweet and sensual, if he'd let it.

Willa placed the palms of her hands against his skin. The gentleness was too much. He wouldn't look at her. He was racing against his own heartbeat, trying to finish what they'd started so he didn't have to think about her anymore. Specifically, how much he found himself caring for her.

He tensed, wishing all this feeling for Willa would go away. That all this raw *emotion* would just vanish. He hadn't signed up for this.

"Burk," Willa breathed. At the sound of her voice, he found himself relaxing, melting into her in spite of all his misgivings. His whole body shuddered at her impossible tightness, the perfect wetness between her legs. It reminded him of their first time together, and he wondered how long it had been since she'd been with someone.

He ground his teeth and closed his eyes, telling himself he didn't care about her past. Who she'd been, who she was. He wanted her right here, right now. And that would be it.

Wouldn't it?

He grasped her buttocks and pulled her toward him, as deep as he could go. She cried out, her voice reverberating through him. Desperate to fill her, to bring her to climax, he pulsed against her flesh. Willa's fingers ground into his skin, and he savored the bite of it. He focused on the pain to keep from spilling himself too early. Better to think about that than the fact that she'd been back for weeks now, and he'd never even asked her what life in New York had been like. He'd never even asked what *happened*.

The brass headboard slammed against the wall with the sound of a repeating gunshot. Underneath him, Willa was a nymph, shifting and coaxing, giving and getting. He wanted to be unmoved, but Burk was undone at the breathtaking sight of her tumbling hair and her flushed skin. She was radiant with pleasure, and he could feel the same sensation wracking his own body. Christ, if being together as teenagers had been good, this was the edge of heaven itself.

And then Willa was crying out his name on her incredible lips once more. The sound of it constricted his heart so much that he put his lips over hers. She pulled him closer still, whimpering as she climaxed. Locked together, the power of her orgasm overtook them both. "Willa," he whispered involuntarily. She clutched him harder as her center massaged and contracted all around him.

He kissed her again, just as a molten-hot burst of pleasure seared his nerves. She writhed underneath him, pulling every ounce of sensation from his body. Bold colors exploded behind his eyelids. For a few moments, he lost himself inside her.

And then he wondered what in the world he was doing.

Pulling back, he took in Willa's flushed face, her sated eyes, her lips twisted into just the tiniest smile.

"My God, I needed that," she purred.

Burk tore his gaze away, fearful she'd glimpse the river of emotion coursing through him. Tenderness. Affection. Compassion.

Except that wouldn't do. Burk wasn't about to let himself feel anything for Willa. At least nothing beyond the acknowledgment that she'd given him a good lay.

Rolling off her, he tried to convince himself everything was fine. They'd had sex. They'd put something between them besides the past—and that was what Willa had wanted. He'd accepted her offer and that was that.

"Thanks," he said, working to keep his voice flat and even.

The bed shifted as he sat up and began pulling his clothes on wordlessly. The late-morning shadows deepened, darkening both the room and his mood further.

"What, you're leaving? Right now?"

Burk could hear the subtext of the query: *Don't you want to stay and do that again?*

The temptation was nearly unbearable. Burk stood. He couldn't look at Willa. He knew if he did, his heart would be shredded by the vulnerability and beauty he'd see there. He cleared his throat, telling himself it was time to go. Their bargain was fulfilled. She'd wanted it. And she got it.

He should be patting himself on the back, really.

"See you," he grunted, striding toward the door.

There was only silence as he pulled it shut with a click.

* * *

Willa sat on the cold bedspread, half dressed and trembling with hurt and anger. Burk had taken her with every ounce of passion she'd hoped for, giving her the most glorious release she'd had in years—and then he'd sprinted away.

Not to put too fine a point on it: He'd fucked her and left.

Willa smoothed her tousled hair, too shocked even to throw a fit. Part of her understood that was the deal: She and Burk would have sex without strings attached. Fine.

But she'd never anticipated that being with him again would be so...abrupt. Glorious and spine tingling to be sure. But did he have to race out the door like he couldn't wait to get away from her?

Cripes. What a dick.

Willa shook her head. What a dick *indeed*. His penis had been thick and hard and so much bigger than she'd ever remembered. It was exquisite, and had filled her up so completely. She'd felt fused to him when he was inside her, if that was possible. For a moment, she'd found herself thinking that this was more than just a physical release, that they were genuinely connecting to each other. But apparently she'd been deluded to think he was doing much except getting laid and walking away.

She groaned in frustration, rolling off the bed. She pulled on the rest of her clothes and then sat back down for a moment. Her skin still felt tingly and her muscles were relaxed in a way they hadn't been for months. Maybe *years*, if she was being honest with herself.

At least she had an afterglow, even if Burk hadn't stuck around to enjoy it with her.

She took a deep breath, letting herself savor the moment. But savor wasn't what happened. Instead, her body reheated with something like hurt. It clawed at her insides and turned her face red. Over and over she asked herself why Burk hadn't stayed. Was it the weight gain? Had she done something wrong? Worst of all, what if she'd enjoyed it but *he* hadn't?

His corded muscles and the way he'd whispered her name—well, it spoke to enjoyment. But what did she know? It wasn't like her recent experiences with Lance were a good playbook to work from.

It all led to one infuriating conclusion: She had wanted
Burk to stay, she had wanted him to want more, and when
he didn't—well, it stung.

The sharp hurt had her reeling. It shouldn't have mattered really. Willa almost couldn't understand it. They
both got what they wanted. They were both satisfied,
at least physically. But somewhere, deep down, she'd
clearly wanted *more*.

Willa squeezed her eyes shut, knowing there was nothing she could do about it. So instead, she allowed herself
a few more minutes wallowing on the edge of the bed,
then told herself it was time for whatever was next.

Even if she wasn't sure what that was.

Burk would probably just go back to work, no doubt accepting the jeers and high-fives of his crew, who had surely
heard the headboard slamming against the wall. While
Willa... what? Waited up here until they went home?

No, she thought, sitting up straighter, *that wouldn't do*.
Why should Burk get to go back down to his crew like a
hero, while she waited in her room like some seventeenth-
century maiden?

Screw that. She stood and tugged on the faded bedspread, ignoring the faint smell of Burk that lingered
there. She didn't even have the chance to get his scent on
her sheets, she realized. There'd been no time to dive under the covers and revel in each other.

Disappointment wanted to rear its head again, but
Willa pushed it aside. Instead she made her way to the
bathroom to shower and think about her next steps. Underneath the spray of lukewarm water, she decided she'd
head to the Rolling Pin and grab a cruller. Then she'd
swing by the bank, get her loan, and meet Audrey down

at the track in time for practice. Coaching the girls today, she could work off any residual frustration. It was wrong, she knew, to want Burk for more than he'd given her. Oh, but she felt like she could go eight—ten! a hundred!—more rounds with him and still not be satisfied. She watched the water drip down her body, wondering if she'd opened the door to a deluge of desire she had no idea how to control.

* * *

The bank had the same smell Willa could remember as a child: a mix of leather, paper, and polished wood. It was a scent that would cling to her dad's clothing when he came home at night. Willa's heart ached with missing him as she sat in one of the wing-backed chairs near the entrance, waiting to see a loan officer.

Beyond the velvet ropes, a woman with long coppery hair talked with the teller on duty. A few employees walked here and there, their heels muted on the plush carpets covering the hardwood floors. The sleepy space was a far cry from the marble and high ceilings of Willa's New York bank, which always seemed to be crowded with people. Their voices, cell phone ringtones, and loud transactions were forever echoing off the cold, stony floor, reverberating in sharp notes. Her bank had been one of the few things about New York that Willa had disliked. She much preferred the homey, comfortable feeling of the White Pine Bank and Trust.

"Willa Masterson?" a woman with stylish horn-rimmed glasses and bright red lips asked her. Willa nodded and stood.

"Right this way," the woman said, leading her down a short hallway to an office with a huge oak desk and a south-facing window. She gestured for Willa to have a seat, then placed herself at the computer behind her steamship of a desk.

"My dad's office was at the far end of this hallway," Willa said, straightening the pearls around her neck. "Harold Masterson? He was president here for a long time."

The woman smiled. "Of course. There's a lovely oil painting of him in the conference room." She pulled out a business card and passed it to Willa.

"I'm Chelsea Aldermann. I was hired long after your dad's tenure here ended, but I have been in this business for over fifteen years. I'll be glad to help you if I can."

"Thank you," Willa said, accepting the card. She wondered if she should ask after some of the employees she once knew here—Lois Maylock, who used to give her peppermints, or Cal Hoopstra, who was the security guard for a time. Then again, Willa didn't want to seem like she was desperate for Chelsea to realize exactly who she was. How important her dad had been.

"So what can I help you with?" Chelsea asked, peering over the tops of her glasses.

"I need a small loan for a bed-and-breakfast I'm starting on Oak Street. It used to be my family home, but it's just me in it now. I've got the renovations under way, but I need twenty thousand more to finish a few projects up, do some advertising, and to make one hire. A cleaning person."

Chelsea nodded. "I see. And when do you anticipate you'll be open?"

"As soon as possible. Midwinter at the latest."

"Good. And do you have a proposal for the space?"

"A proposal?"

"A document with, say, your room rates and your P and L?"

Willa blinked. "P and L?"

"Profit and loss. A statement that outlines all your costs—your employees, your advertising, your utilities, your food—as well as how many people have to stay in the hotel each week for you to make money."

Willa pulled at the cuffs of her navy suit. She decidedly did *not* have a P and L statement. She didn't have anything except a half-finished house and a table she'd painted blue. She sat up straighter in her chair. "I can, of course, draw all that up for you, but I'm confident this B and B will be profitable quickly. And if not, then I'll just work extra hard to make it so. There's no need to worry about me as a financial risk."

Chelsea folded her hands on top of the desk's smooth wood. "Tell me, how much did you think you'd charge each night for your rooms?"

On the East Coast, she wouldn't hesitate paying three hundred dollars or more to stay at a nice B and B. That was per night. White Pine might not have exactly the same clientele, but Willa knew that she'd need to charge a premium for her establishment, same as the other B and B's.

"I was thinking two hundred dollars," she replied. "That would be the average."

Chelsea studied Willa over the tops of her glasses. "There are certainly wealthy people in White Pine as well as tourists, but do you think the market as a whole can sustain that?"

Willa nodded. "I certainly think it's in the range."

"All right, let's say that's ballpark," Chelsea said after a moment. "I'm willing to entertain it, but you need to show me evidence."

"Excuse me?" Willa asked, wondering if she should remind Chelsea that this was a bank, not a courtroom.

"Willa, I know from the bit of paperwork you filled out here that you haven't lived in White Pine for some time. So you may not realize that this is largely a working-class community. The majority of people—not all, but a majority—might not have two hundred dollars to spend on a hotel room for a night. If tourists or other clientele will supplement the hotel's profitability, then show me that."

"It's not a hotel. It's a bed-and-br—"

"Here me out," Chelsea said, holding up a hand. "My point is that a bed-and-breakfast here could work, but you still need to assess the market. Do some research. What do people want? What would they pay for? Show me in data, don't just make a guess. I have stayed at the Great Lakes Inn, I have put relatives up there when they've come to town, and God knows I would love an alternative to that dump. But at two hundred per night? You'd better show me why and how that price point is going to work."

Willa felt the blood drain from her face. "So are you saying you need this information before you'll give me money?"

"I'm afraid so."

"So I won't be getting a loan today?"

Chelsea shook her head. "I'm sorry. Not now. Not with your current business model. Or lack thereof."

"But I'm telling you, this is going to work."

"You can't tell me. You need to *show* me. On paper."

Willa's anger kindled. "My dad—he *owned* this bank for years. He practically built it. You wouldn't even have a job if it weren't for him."

"Is he cosigning on your loan?"

"No, he's dead."

"Then I'm sorry, but it's not relevant."

Willa sat back in her chair, the air gone from her lungs. They were turning her down for a loan. They were saying no. She didn't know whether to cry or throw a fit, or both.

Across the desk, Chelsea offered her a compassionate look. "I'm sorry. I know this isn't what you wanted to hear. But there's more. I'm being extra picky about all this because you technically *are* a risk. On paper anyway. You have no savings. You have no job. The only asset you have is the house, which is currently in a half-finished state of remodeling. I'm sorry, but this just doesn't look very good."

Willa swallowed the knot of emotions in her throat. *I had money*, she wanted to say, *but it was stolen from me. And I had assets, but I had to sell them.* She wanted to argue for days, but what good would it do? Unless she changed her B and B plans drastically—and figured out how to write a P and L statement—she wasn't going to get a dime from this bank.

She stood, and reached out a hand. "Thank you for your time."

Chelsea gave her a firm shake. "I'll reconsider this situation if you bring me a viable proposal. Until then, I'm sorry we couldn't do business."

Willa lifted her chin. Her proposal was just fine. She wasn't going to alter it just because some number cruncher behind a fancy desk told her to. "Have a good day," she said, and strode out the door with as confident a swagger as she could muster.

It wasn't until she got to her car that she let her face fall. She put her forehead against the steering wheel and let the tears plunk onto her navy skirt. They'd turned her down. Never in a million years did she think that would have been possible. Harold Masterson's daughter denied a loan at the White Pine Bank and Trust.

"Oh God," she groaned, her emotions raw from all the disappointment of the day. First Burk's hasty departure; now this.

She wasn't going to change the past. And she wasn't going to carve out a future. Which left her with exactly nowhere to go from here.

"Except track practice," she grumbled, starting the engine. Not even a grueling workout could make this day any worse.

* * *

Willa and Audrey turned their backs to the biting autumn wind that whipped over the Birch River and onto the field where the track team was practicing.

"Man, it got cold!" Audrey said, jogging in place a little. "That's Minnesota for you. One minute it's sixty and sunny, the next minute it's snowing."

For her part, Willa was plenty warm, thanks to the mile she'd jogged with the track team, and the back-and-forth coaching she'd done. Plus, frustration at how her day had gone—from Burk to the bank—had her insides flaming with irritation.

"Earth to Willa," Audrey said, tugging gently on her sleeve. She started.

"Sorry, what?"

"Where did you go? You've been spacy all practice." Audrey's brown eyes flickered across her face, trying to read her.

"I just—it was a tough day," Willa admitted as another gust of wind tore through the trees on the edge of the field. Around her, the girls were finishing up their practice, long legs flashing as they carried the hurdles and starting blocks and shot puts back to the gym. Willa watched them feeling a pang of envy. Track practice, then homework. She'd give anything to have an agenda as simple as that.

Audrey reached out and linked her arm with Willa's. "The girls are out of earshot. You want to talk about it?"

Willa stared into the gray edges of the darkening sky. The weather had changed right along with her mood. "It's Burk," she said, feeling her skin prickle involuntarily. "We had sex."

Audrey's brown eyes went wide. "Really?"

"Really."

"You're frowning like it was bad. Was it?"

"No, it was amazing. I mean, mind-blowing. It's just that he took off right after. Like he regretted it or something."

"You're kidding."

"I wish I was."

Audrey shivered a little—whether from the cold or from the idea of Burk bailing after sex, Willa wasn't sure.

"Was it that way when you guys were in high school?" she asked. "Is it a...pattern?"

"No! I mean, we were kids, we barely knew what we were doing. But still, he always stuck around after. He was patient. So sweet about everything. And just the right amount of..."

She trailed off, unable to finish. Talking this way about Burk was starting to get her riled up again. It was the feeling that had started all this—the one that had led her to proposition him in the first place.

Audrey squeezed her arm. "I'm sorry. That's so frustrating."

"It's not the only thing," Willa said. "I went to the bank and tried to get a loan to finish the B and B, but they turned me down. They were asking me for things like market research and P and L statements, and I didn't have anything to show them. This woman about laughed at me for what I wanted to charge per night per room."

"What *do* you want to charge?"

"Two hundred."

Audrey's brown eyes widened. "Two hundred dollars?"

Willa rolled her eyes. "Not you, too!"

Audrey shook her head, her glossy ponytail swinging. "Sorry. It's just—a lot for locals. But maybe that's not who you had in mind to stay there. Is it?"

"I don't—I'm not sure."

"Maybe you could talk to Betty about it? She's kept Knots and Bolts in the black for years now. Plus she's got that whole Halloween business on the side. She might be able to help you formulate a plan."

"Right. Because she totally wants to help the girl who bullied her in high school."

Audrey shrugged. "The past is the past. We said so the

other night. You might be surprised at people's willing-ness to move on."

Willa stared at the leaf-littered ground. It was the same thing Burk had told her. Just because you stayed in a lo-cation didn't mean you stayed the same person.

"Have you ever had anything like this happen?" Willa asked.

"No, I've never tried to start my own business before. The only loan I've ever gotten was for my car."

"No, I mean, the other stuff," Willa said, "the Burk stuff." She didn't mean to sound hopeful, but she was dy-ing for someone to be able to relate.

Audrey shook her head. "Well, it's not like White Pine is brimming with bachelors. And even if it was, I'm not sure they'd go for me."

Willa took in Audrey's lean shape, her lovely eyes and thick hair, and doubted very much that was the case. "But you've had boyfriends, right?"

"Sure. In fairness, my most recent one bolted after-wards, too. After two weeks, I thought I was in love. Then he was gone."

"So quickly?"

"Without even a good-bye," Audrey said, her eyes dis-tant.

Willa sighed, leaning into her friend. She couldn't help thinking about how she'd left Burk the same way all those years ago. She wondered if it was the destiny of humans to always be hurting one another. "Love sucks some-times."

"Is that what this is? Love?"

"No," Willa said quickly, "today was about sex. It was burn-the-house-down-it's-so-hot sex. Which I'd like to have *again* if I could. Only I'm not sure if that's possible."

Audrey smiled. "Well, one thing that I *do* know is that we are going to freeze to death if we don't get inside soon. Let's head over to Knots and Bolts and see if any of the girls are there."

"All right," Willa agreed as they started walking briskly toward the gym to round up the girls and send them home. "We'll get you warm, but we can't talk about this anymore at Knots and Bolts."

"Why?"

"If Anna's there, I don't want to discuss it in front of her. It's one thing for her to hear some of this stuff secondhand from Betty or whatever. But I'm not going to sit there and spill the beans about Burk and me doing it."

"Doing it well."

"Very well."

Willa sighed. It was such a shame Burk had to take off, but there was more to it than just disappointment. The part she didn't want to admit to herself—or to anyone else— was that he'd hurt her. She didn't know how to describe the crumpled piece of her heart that she couldn't seem to smooth out since Burk had closed the bedroom door on her. She'd felt so close to him, so connected. But it had clearly been one-sided. He'd fled as if he'd been full of regret.

"I won't say a word," Audrey promised. "Silent as the grave, right here." She paused. "We can still eat Anna's pie, though, right?"

Willa nodded. "I think that's allowed."

"Good." Audrey grinned. "Because if you'd said no, I would have told Anna *everything*."

CHAPTER SEVENTEEN

Monday, October 1, 5:18 p.m.

Half an hour later, Willa was already feeling better, thanks to a slice of apple pie with a thick hunk of cheddar cheese on top. Anna, who was at Knots and Bolts when they arrived, was dishing it out. "I would have blabbed for this, too," Willa whispered to Audrey. "No secret is worth giving this up for."

Audrey was about to reply, when Stephanie barged in the back door. A blast of cold air followed right behind. She didn't even take off her coat before she collapsed at the wide table where Anna, Audrey, Willa, and Betty were already seated. Clearly the whole group needed a Knots and Bolts fix tonight.

"Someone please get me a drink," Stephanie pleaded. Her red hair gleamed under the back room's soft lights, but her freckled skin looked paler than usual. There was dried food smeared across a swath of her jacket. No doubt from one of the four-year-old twins.

"Tough day, Momma?" Anna asked, pouring straight vodka into a mug for her.

"The worst," Stephanie replied, taking a sip and grimacing. "Adam got out a tub of peanut butter and made a sandwich—out of the carpet. Because the floor was brown, he said, just like the bread." She took another drink. "And then Molly cut her own hair. It looks like she was run over by a lawnmower."

Willa bit back a smile.

"That's why I never had kids," Betty offered, her blond hair swishing as she shook her head. "Kids are always tearing things up and ruining everything."

"You also don't have a husband," Anna offered.

Betty's eyes blazed. "In this day and age, you do not have to be married to have a baby."

Anna held up her hands. "That's true, but I don't know what I'd do without Sam. Having a partner makes the whole child-raising experience a lot easier."

"Pfft," Betty replied. "It never gets easy with kids. Did you see *Cujo*? That's what I think being a parent is like. Everything is fine and then, *bam*, next thing you know, you're trapped in a car, drinking your own pee, because you can't ever escape them."

Stephanie paused, mid-drink. "Did you just compare my kids to a rabid dog?"

Betty shrugged. "Would *The Exorcist* have been better?"

Stephanie threw back her head and laughed. "Touché," she said, and took another sip of vodka.

"You know, you're only thirty," Anna said to Betty after a moment. "You might change your mind about kids. Or a man."

Betty stopped folding the candy corn tablecloth she

was getting ready to ship to a customer in Virginia. "When I could have peace and quiet? Hell no."

Stephanie groaned. "I don't need that much peace and quiet. I just wish I could get out a little more. Do something productive. I feel like I'm going crazy."

Betty's face softened. "You're always welcome here. Day or night."

"Thanks," she replied. "I know that. I just wish I had something to do besides be a mom"—she lifted her glass—"and drink."

"Some days, the two things go hand in hand," Anna empathized. She walked to the kitchenette and returned with a slice of apple pie for Stephanie as well.

"Willa's helping out at track practice," Audrey said after a moment. "You could come, too. It's fun. The girls are really sweet, and they work so hard. It's a great sport."

"I appreciate that," Stephanie replied. "I was never an athlete, though, and it just doesn't seem like a fit. I want to do something that I'd really enjoy, you know?"

"You could help Willa, then," Audrey said. "She needs some guidance on her business."

Willa gave Audrey a sharp look, but it was too late.

"Guidance how?" Betty asked.

"Turns out the bank doesn't think my B and B is going to fly," Willa admitted.

"Why not?"

"I might be charging too much, so they say. And I don't have a P and L statement, whatever that is."

Betty shrugged. "Those are good reasons. You open a business, you need to know what a P and L statement is. For the record, how much *are* you charging?"

"Two hundred per night."

The group of women fell silent. "That *is* a lot," Anna said a few beats later. "But I suppose it depends on who your customer is. Do you know?"

"No." Willa set her jaw, tired of hearing the same refrain. "But it's going to be a first-class establishment! Isn't it enough to know that much? How am I supposed to charge less if I'm giving people the best wine, the best food, having them sleep on the best sheets—the whole nine yards?"

Betty arched a brow. "You sure that's what folks around here want? Or are you just giving them what *you* want?"

Willa opened her mouth, then closed it. She'd never thought about it that way. This whole time she just assumed that *of course* folks in Minnesota would want a taste of the East Coast right here in their own backyards. But maybe that was the wrong way to look at it. Maybe it wasn't about giving them an escape from White Pine, which was what *she'd* wanted so badly all those years, but rather an *extension* of White Pine. People who loved it, whether they lived here or were visiting, and would just want more of the same.

"Cripes," Willa muttered, staring at her pie and feeling like an idiot. She suddenly wasn't hungry.

"At least in the meantime, you've got Burk helping you with... other stuff, isn't that right?"

Betty's teasing tone made Willa nervous, especially with Anna right there. "The house is coming along, yes."

"You sure that's the only thing that's coming?"

"Betty!" Audrey scolded. "*Stop.*"

"Oh, I'm just trying to find out how Willa's plan to seduce Burk is going. That's all."

Willa found she couldn't breathe very well. So much

for keeping things from Anna. She felt her face redden, mortified that her plan had come to light so publicly.

"Willa might not want to talk about all this in front of Burk's sister," Audrey said pointedly.

"Oh, poo." Betty waved her off. "Anna's a grown woman. She can handle a little gossip about her brother. Can't you?"

Years ago, it was easy to deflect Anna's questions about how kissing felt and what second base was by telling Anna that she and Burk didn't do any of those things. "It's for married couples," Willa had lied, "and Burk and I aren't married."

Now she struggled with how much to share and how much to hold back. Anna was an adult with a baby, but she was still Burk's little sister. Not to mention Willa's friend—or at least Willa wanted to think so. The confusing intersection of roles had Willa's brain reeling.

Willa could feel Anna staring at her, and she knew she had to look up. When she did, she found Anna's dark blue eyes disconcerting, especially considering she'd been so close to their matching pair earlier today.

To her great credit, Anna did her best to smile.

"Willa deserves some privacy," Anna said. She pushed a stray piece of her raven black hair away from her face. Like Burk's, only longer. "Burk likes fixing stuff, and Burk likes ladies. If both of those things intersect over at Willa's house, that's none of anyone's business. Willa's not obligated to share it."

Willa exhaled, grateful that Anna was giving her privacy some traction. Certainly she wasn't a little kid anymore, asking for any in-depth relationship details she could get. At this point, Anna would probably rather stick her fingers in her ears and hum than listen to tales of her brother's sex life.

Betty huffed. "We don't keep stuff from each other at Knots and Bolts. That's the rule here. You want to be private? Go somewhere else."

"Rules can change," Anna said.

Willa cringed, hating the fact that things were becoming awkward and she was the cause of it. She was nearly ready to confess her mortifying afternoon and get it over with, when Anna stood. "I think the solution here is that Willa should feel free to share whatever she likes with the group, but not be forced to do it when I'm around." She reached for her jacket. "So I'm going to head out. I have to pick up Juniper anyway."

"Is she at the sitter's?" Audrey asked.

"Nope. She spent the last couple hours at her uncle's." Anna grinned. "And don't think for a moment that I won't get all the dirt from *him*."

Winking at Willa, she headed out into the bitter evening.

Betty banged the table and hooted. "That's my girl."

Willa sighed, and ate another bite of pie to keep from having to say anything else.

* * *

Juniper curled her small, sticky fingers into Burk's enormous ones. "Again!" she said, looking at the book he'd just finished reading her. Burk's heart filled as he took in her enormous sea blue eyes, her doughy, round cheeks, and her sweet smile. He leaned down and kissed the top of her button nose.

"You got it, kiddo," he said, knowing she could ask for the moon and he'd work his whole life trying to find a way to get it for her. He grinned, so glad he'd kept his word to watch her for Anna. After being nearly undone in Willa's bed, he'd almost reneged. But now Juniper was a welcome distraction from the coldness that had sunk into his chest after that morning's misguided tumble.

He turned to the first page of the book—a story about a cow that only wanted to eat vowels—and began again.

"Callie Cow wanted an A. Not her hay on this fine day, but only an A. Frog carried an I as he hopped right on by. Callie could munch on that I, if Frog would trade it for flies.

Burk let out an enormous moo that filled up his whole apartment. Juniper giggled. "More!" she cried, kicking her legs a little.

He was just getting ready to moo once more when there was a knock at his door. He glanced at his phone and was surprised to see it was after six o'clock. Anna was here already.

Scooping Juniper into his arms, he galloped to the entrance, Juniper shrieking with delight. When he opened it, Anna was already smiling. "I can hear you guys having fun from out here," she said, wrapping her daughter in her arms.

"Come on in," Burk said, trying not to think about how empty he already felt knowing Juniper would be leaving soon. The apartment was already dimmer, the silence more pressing. He always watched her every chance he could get—when his sister went to Knots and Bolts, or when she and Sam needed a date or had someplace they both needed to be—but no matter how often Burk had Juniper around, it never felt like enough.

For the next few minutes, Juniper played tour guide, showing her mom everything they'd done that afternoon. Story time on the plaid couch, *Ticklesaurus rex* in the hallway, and dress-up in the bedroom, which mostly consisted of Juniper shuffling around in Burk's old tennis shoes.

"Sounds like you guys had a great time," Anna said, smiling.

"She's a great kid," Burk replied, his full heart aching. He looked away, suddenly embarrassed to be so emotional. It was excessive, really, and he couldn't help wondering if that morning with Willa had made him oversensitive. He was having a hard time compartmentalizing what she was churning up in him, and it was beginning to spill over into every part of his life.

He needed to make it stop.

"So how about dinner Friday night with us?" Anna asked from the kitchen table, where she was packing up Juniper's bag with toys, diapers, and wet naps. "I was thinking of making a chicken potpie from scratch. All I can keep thinking is that it's fall, and I need to get comfort food back on the table."

"Sure," Burk answered distractedly. He picked up the few remaining board books from the couch while Juniper tossed CD cases from the top of his stereo onto the floor.

"Want The Who!" she demanded, discarding case after case in her search. They clattered to the floor, bouncing and spilling open.

"Oh, honey, *no*," Anna said. "Burk, tell her to stop. Junie, you need to respect Uncle Burk's things. Don't touch unless he tells you that you can."

"No big deal," Burk replied, wondering if he'd ever

be up for the challenge of parenting. He was such a pushover. Love made people so weak. He'd probably just wind up giving his kid everything they ever asked for, and raising a monster.

Anna raced into the living room, pulling Juniper away from the CDs. "Honey, no," she said firmly. "Those are Uncle Burk's things."

"Sowwy," Juniper replied, and Burk's insides melted.

"It's okay, sweetheart," he said, walking over to give her a quick hug. She grinned up at him, and in his mind's eye he could suddenly envision towheaded toddlers with bright green eyes—miniature versions of Willa Masterson running around with their sweet skin and sticky hands, filling him with joy and happiness.

He pulled away, alarmed. He used to think about having kids with Willa when they were together as teens. They'd wait, of course, until they were older, but he could always picture them raising a family together. Since then, he'd told himself he'd want kids with the right girl when she came along. Until she did, being an uncle had always been enough. Until now. It had been years since he'd pined for a family. But here he was, back to having those same thoughts about children swirling in his mind. He shook his head, trying to regain his bearings.

"You get everything?" he asked his sister, distracting himself by looking around for anything Juniper may have left behind. During one visit, she'd forgotten her blanket, and he'd had to drive it over at ten thirty at night, Anna pleading with him to hurry, as a distraught Juniper howled in the background.

"I think so," Anna replied, her eyes flashing concern and—something else he couldn't make out. Burk wondered suddenly how much she already knew about that morning. Certainly she could see the emotion flickering across his features—subtle changes only she could read. Maybe Willa had already spilled any details of that morning to the Knots and Bolts crew. Well, so be it. *His* crew had certainly heard the banging upstairs at Willa's house, the headboard slamming into the wall, but his scowl had no doubt kept them from saying anything about it. At least to his face.

"All right," Anna said, crossing her arms. "Spill it. Tell me what's going on, because you look downright *lost*."

Burk paused. Was *lost* the word for it?

Jackass was more like it. That was what you called someone who'd shut down like he had this morning, especially to someone as beautiful and irresistible as Willa.

He tried for a moment to tell himself it was better this way—keeping her at a distance would make her imminent departure from White Pine so much easier—but it felt disingenuous. He was beginning to lose sight of how he'd even get her to sell him the house at this rate.

"All right," he admitted finally, "I'm just not sure the project over at Willa's is going as smoothly as I'd hoped. It's frustrating."

"The project is frustrating, or she's frustrating?"

"Both," he replied. "She just darts around, painting furniture as if she's an expert, and putting herself in harm's way. Not to mention she took up a big chunk of my time, asking for help redoing that coffee table. Plus, she's making these collages that I just don't even know what to do with. And I can't even—"

He stopped when he realized Anna was smiling at him. "What?"

"Nothing. Keep going."

"No. Why are you grinning like that?"

"Because it's nice to see you have some emotion about a woman for once. You never talked this much about what's-her-name from the Paul Bunyan Diner."

"Brittany."

"Right. Her. I just like seeing you take an interest in someone. It's nice."

"I took an interest in Brittany. We dated for a year."

"You banged her for a year. That's different."

Burk opened his mouth to argue, then found he couldn't. He also found he didn't like the way his sister kept grinning at him, as if she were up to something. Sure enough, she broke their stare-off to look around the apartment.

"You know, you've lived here for five years now, and it strikes me that you've never once hung up a piece of art."

"I don't have any art."

"Exactly. Or any throws for the couch, or any candles for the bathroom, or a kitchen table that isn't from a garage sale."

"It was a bargain at twenty bucks," Burk replied, irritated that his sister was suddenly critiquing his décor. "How's my decorating your business again?"

"Because from what I hear, Willa seems to have a knack for it. Or at least making old things look good again. I bet she could do wonders with your space."

"My space is fine."

"She probably has a list of tips she could give you. Five easy things you could do to make this place less college dorm-y."

"I like it this way."

"I should probably invite her over to dinner one of these Fridays, you know. Give you guys a chance to talk about it."

Burk's frustration surged. "I don't need her help. In fact, just the opposite. She needs mine." He thought about her lying on her bed, inviting him to join her, to experience something new together. "And she needs to stop complicating things already. She's making things harder than they need to be."

Anna raised an eyebrow. "Complicating things how?"

Burk shook his head, wishing he hadn't let his thoughts come out of his mouth. "Nothing. Never mind."

Anna unwrapped Juniper from Burk's leg. He hadn't even noticed she was there. "Well, either way, I think she'll be a great addition to a Friday dinner. Maybe a week from this Friday? I'll let you pass the invitation along to Willa."

Burk didn't bother answering. She wasn't really asking him if it was okay. She was telling him what she was doing, and daring him not to be all right with it. He kissed Juniper's cheek as they headed out the door. She waggled her chubby fingers at him, and he knew the answer. He'd be at Anna's house on Friday, on time and with a bottle of wine to share. Any excuse to spend time with Juniper was a good excuse in his book.

But there was another part of him that prickled with something like excitement at the idea of seeing Willa, too. Both of them outside the house. In clothes not spattered with paint. A date, kind of.

Except not a date, he told himself firmly. Just a chance to talk. Away from their projects.

Even if all they were going to do was talk, he was going to have to smooth things out with her beforehand. Maybe even apologize for the way he'd stormed out of her bedroom after sex.

He tried to ignore the small thrill pulsing deep inside. He'd shoulder the burden. He'd find a way to get back in Willa's good graces and—

He didn't let himself think about the possibility of them sleeping together again.

No. First things first. Patch it up.

Once it was all worked out, *then* he could fantasize about Willa. *Then* he could imagine her laid out on the bed, wet with desire and anticipation. He could think about the ways he would kiss her, stroke her, enter her, and make her feel special, feel beautiful, feel worshipped. He could—

The uncomfortable press of his erection against the seam of his jeans stopped him in mid-thought. He shook his head.

He was going to have to figure out how to crack the door on his emotions about Willa without being overwhelmed by them.

If there was a pinch of doubt in his gut, he ignored it. This was going to work.

Burk puttered around, wiping the remnants of Juniper's grape juice and cookie snack off the kitchen table and tidying up. Then he paused, wondering what the sound was that was suddenly filling the apartment.

He blinked when he realized it was himself.

He'd been humming.

CHAPTER EIGHTEEN

Sunday, October 7, 9:54 a.m.

Willa hesitated before crossing the threshold into the White Pine Lutheran Church. With all the sinful thoughts about Burk Olmstead she'd had rolling around in her brain—and other parts of her body—these past few weeks, she worried she might burst into flames if she stepped foot in this holy place.

But Audrey had insisted she come because people needed to see her out and about, as a member of the community. "Even if you get your B and B up and running, local people won't stay there unless they *know* you," Audrey had argued. And Willa admitted she had a point. It was time to show her face in places besides Knots and Bolts and track practice, and to let people know she was serious about sticking around.

Thankfully, nothing ignited as she stepped into the high-ceilinged space. Her heels were muted on the center aisle's red carpet as she hunted for a seat in the pews.

Morning light filtered through the windows, where all the apostles were posing with Picasso-esque features, thanks to the blocks of color on the stained glass. A great organ piped a languid hymn into the air, while Pastor Sondheim sat on a bench just to the right of the pulpit, frowning over his Bible, not looking at the congregation as everyone settled in.

"Willa, over here!" She turned to see Stephanie waving at her. The twins, Adam and Molly, squirmed at Stephanie's side. Willa slid into the pew, grateful for a familiar face.

"I didn't know you were Lutheran," Stephanie said, shoving a pack of fruit snacks at Adam, whose lower lip had started to quiver.

"Only technically," Willa replied. "I haven't been to church in more than a decade."

Next to her, Molly gave a little whine. "I have to use the bathroom," she said. Stephanie exhaled, and Willa couldn't help taking in the dark circles around her friend's eyes, and the tired lines around her mouth.

"Sweetheart, we just got our seats, and the service is about to start. Can't you hold it?"

"Noooo," Molly replied, squeezing her legs together.

"Normally Alan's here to tag-team the service," Stephanie said, brushing crumbs off her skirt, "but he got called into work today. He works for the utility company, and a transformer blew somewhere."

"Here, let me take Molly," Willa offered, standing before Steph could. She didn't wait for a reply, but scooped the four-year-old into her arms. "You sit. We'll be back in a jiffy."

Stephanie nodded gratefully, and Willa walked back down the carpeted aisle with the girl in her arms.

"I don't know you, and Mommy says I shouldn't go with strangers," Molly said, staring at Willa.

"I'm your mom's friend, and we're just going to the bathroom. If I don't take you immediately there and back, you have my permission to scream."

Molly's eyes grew large. She and her twin brother had Stephanie's red hair and freckles, but their builds were stockier, their faces rounder, which must have been their dad's genes. "I can scream in church?"

"If I don't take you straight to the bathroom and back, yes."

Molly grinned, and Willa stopped by the sanctuary entrance, searching for a sign pointing the way to the restrooms. Down a set of steps was the church's main entrance, where the doors had been thrown open to welcome visitors on the crisp, sunny morning. She blinked into the light just as Burk approached. Behind him were Anna and another man, whom Willa presumed was Anna's husband, Sam. There was also a doughy, adorable toddler, who she could only guess was Juniper.

"Shit," she muttered, and Molly giggled.

"You said a swear in church!"

She set Molly down. "I did. And it's going to happen again if we don't get out of here."

She saw Burk grab Juniper and lift her into the air. The sight of Burk with a child made her heart ache suddenly. Not that she was about to stick around long enough to think about why.

She grabbed Molly's hand. "Let's go this way," Willa said, pulling her toward the nursery. But Molly dug in her heels and wouldn't budge.

"It's not that way," she said, her eyes shining.

"What's not?"

"The bathroom." And with that, Molly opened up her mouth and began screaming at the top of her lungs.

* * *

By the time Willa and Molly were settled back into the pew, Pastor Sondheim had already started the service. The entire congregation had stared as they'd noisily taken their seats toward the front. Willa flushed, realizing that she'd wanted people in the town to know she was back—and now they did, probably thinking that she'd abused a four-year-old girl in the short time she'd been around. The screaming, after all, had been *epic*.

Thankfully, Anna had raced over and had been able to calm Molly down, and Burk had even offered to go into the sanctuary and explain to Stephanie what was going on. The result of all of it was that the group of them were now seated together, taking up an entire pew. And, of course, she and Burk were stuck on the end, next to each other.

As Pastor Sondheim read the announcements, Willa tried not to notice the way her shoulder brushed against Burk's in the cramped space, or how the edge of her thigh pressed against his. When it came time to sing, they both reached for the hymnal, their fingers brushing.

Willa ignored the sparks on her skin and forced herself to glare at him. If he thought he could fuck her and then leave and pretend like everything was fine, singing songs like a pious Christian, he had another thing coming.

Of course, it didn't help one bit that Pastor Sondheim's stupid sermon was all about forgiveness. Willa wanted to ignore the hunched preacher at the pulpit, but for all his boorishness, he really was a great orator. He talked passionately about Peter betraying Jesus and getting a second chance. He painted the picture of Mary Magdalene's past not being held against her. "Even Judas would have been forgiven, I believe," Sondheim said, his booming voice carrying out across the sanctuary, "if he'd just *asked* Jesus for another chance."

By the end of the sermon, Willa's heart felt like someone had taken a meat tenderizer to it. She didn't know what to think about anything, and she filed along, dazed, with the entire congregation to the basement, where they were serving coffee, donuts, and hot dish.

In the cramped space, with kids' drawings of lambs and shepherds all around them, Willa helped herself to a donut, as well as coffee so weak it was tea-colored. She tried not to think about her favorite café on the Upper West Side, and the rich espresso it had served.

"That was sure something." Willa turned to see Betty standing next to her, a paper plate piled with hot dish in her hand.

Willa could only shrug. "I *told* Molly she could scream. It's my fault, I suppose. I just got turned around trying to find the bathrooms."

Betty arched a brow. "I meant the sermon."

"Oh," Willa replied. "Well, yes, I suppose it was."

"Got me thinking," Betty said, shoveling some of the casserole into her mouth. She chewed thoughtfully for a moment. "I could look at whatever business plan you drafted for that B and B. Maybe help you out with that a little. You know, point you in the right direction."

Willa nearly dropped her coffee cup. *Betty was offer-*

ing to help her. "Th-Thank you. That would be amazing."

"Don't thank me, thank Sondheim. It was a good sermon."

There was a throat clearing behind them, and they both turned to see the good pastor, clad all in black, gazing at them. "I'm glad you enjoyed it."

He looked uncomfortable in the crowd, his brow shining with sweat, and Willa wanted to say something to put him at ease, but she wasn't sure what.

"You ever have someone in your life you couldn't forgive?" Betty asked him. Willa was surprised at the direct question, but the pastor seemed to actually relax at the inquiry.

"No. But that's not to say it's easy. Forgiveness is one of the hardest things there is."

Betty grunted. "You can say that again." Willa shifted uncomfortably.

"I appreciate you coming," Sondheim said to Betty after a moment, and Willa watched as his mouth almost twitched into a smile. Almost.

"Every Sunday. Like clockwork."

This close up, Willa was astonished to observe how much younger the pastor was than she'd originally suspected. He was barely forty from the looks of it. If her dad were here, he'd call Sondheim an old soul. Before today, Willa might have opted for calling him a curmudgeon.

"Next week's sermon is on courage and boldness," the pastor said, looking right at Betty as if Willa had ceased to exist. "I hope to be able to inspire everyone in the congregation, but most especially . . . myself."

Betty was just opening her mouth to reply when a pair of similarly dressed older women waved from a few feet away. "Pastor!" the shorter of them said. "We've been looking for you. We need you to settle a disagreement for us."

The pastor's expression strained visibly as he took in the women with their matching flowered dresses. "Be right there," he said before turning back to Betty.

"It appears that Rae and Mae need me to settle another one of their bets," he confided in a low voice. "The last one was about whether Chippewa Indians were descended from the ten lost tribes of Israel." The pastor smiled wryly. "At this point, I just make up answers and hope they don't find out."

Next to her, Betty emitted a high-pitched sound. It took a moment for Willa to realize it was a giggle. Sondheim's entire countenance brightened. He looked at Betty for a long moment before heading off to see the sisters. When he was gone, Willa faced her Knots and Bolts counterpart.

"What was *that* all about?"

Betty gave her a blank stare. "What do you mean?"

"Come on. You and the pastor? There's totally a spark there!"

Betty frowned, her smooth skin wrinkling. "I think you're imagining things. The pastor and I are friends. Besides, I have no use for sparks unless it's in my fireplace."

Willa was just about to argue when she spotted Burk elbowing his way through the congregation. He looked as if he was going to approach them.

"Excuse me," Willa said to Betty. "All this talk of sparks and I realized I left my iron plugged in at home." It was an awful lie, and she was sure Betty saw right through her. Nevertheless, she tossed her Styrofoam coffee cup into the trash and raced up the stairs and out the main doors. She prayed Burk wouldn't follow her.

She had nothing to say to him, after all. No matter how you looked at it, she'd invited him into her bed, not the other way around, and if he chose to race away afterward—well, that was something a thousand prayers for a thousand years couldn't fix. What was done was done.

The irony of the whole situation wasn't lost on her, either. She'd left him twelve years ago without so much as a backward glance, and now he'd done the same to her, in a manner of speaking.

They were both too good at leaving.

"Lord have mercy," Willa muttered, speeding toward her car and squinting against the bright Sunday sun.

CHAPTER NINETEEN

Thursday, October 11, 7:35 a.m.

Willa was up and dressed, ready to get her day going before the work crews descended at eight o'clock. She had checked out a couple business books from the White Pine Library, and she was determined to read up before she met Betty later that afternoon. She also had her cell phone in hand, ready to make some calls to figure out how much the Great Lakes Inn charged per night, as well as hotels in some of the surrounding communities. Betty had called it market research, although Willa figured it was more like summoning the courage to talk to the people who might take your customers.

Beyond that, she had groceries to get, track practice, and the recipe exchange. She was determined that wine wouldn't be her contribution to this week's gathering. Audrey had promised to teach her how to cook a hot dish, and if the two of them could get to the Knots and Bolts kitchenette tonight right after track practice, she could ensure that each of the ladies left with a Tupperware container full of her very own casserole.

"And the great thing about a hot dish is that you can make it for any meal," Audrey had told her. "There's breakfast hot dish, dinner hot dish—so if you open your B and B knowing how to cook a couple of these, you'll be able to feed your guests pretty well. And cheaply, too."

Willa couldn't wait for her hot dish lesson, but even bigger than all that was the palm sander.

Today was the day she was going to go get a power tool of her very own, and finish that blasted blue table in the living room once and for all. She was tired of waiting around for Burk's help, which, after the sex debacle, seemed like it would never come.

Who needs him? she thought as she hurried along the threadbare hallway runner. Sunday's sermon had only steeled her resolve to make things work in White Pine—on her own.

In spite of all her rushing, Willa paused as she caught a glimpse of herself in the full-length mirror by the stairs. She'd seen herself in this same glass a thousand times growing up and since moving back, but something about her now was different. She stared, and struggled to place her finger on it.

Her hair was a little longer and maybe needed a trim, but that wasn't it. Her skin was glowing without the aid of makeup, but that was nothing new, either. It was all the Minnesota fresh air, she was convinced. As she placed her hands on her hips, trying to determine what had changed, it suddenly dawned on her.

Muscles.

All the sanding and painting and track practices and

moving furniture had given her a solid strength she wasn't used to feeling. This wasn't the aerobic leanness she'd tried—and failed—to achieve in New York, but rather a firmness she could feel underneath the band of her jeans. She ran her hands up the length of her own arms, loving the newfound shape of them. They were harder, some-how, but not bulky. Just sturdy. *Unshakable*, she thought, and smiled.

"I'm becoming a hardy Midwesterner," she said to her-self, and laughed. The thought delighted her, instead of leaving a bad taste in her mouth as it once had. Maybe, Willa thought, if she was becoming a little more like the people around her, she could open up a B and B that was the same way. Something that belonged in White Pine, in-stead of being forced on White Pine.

The idea tickled her, until she remembered how her curves—sturdy or no—had been bared to Burk during their brief encounter, and how he'd grinned when she'd taken off her bra. She'd confessed she'd gained weight and in reply he'd said...nothing.

Willa swallowed back a pang of hurt, wondering if her shape was what had driven him away so quickly. Sure, she'd gained weight recently, but she didn't think she was *odious*.

Surely that couldn't be it. Could it?

She shook her head, knowing that she was making his post-sex departure worse by overthinking it—by not be-ing able to just shove it into the past, where it belonged—but she couldn't help it.

She was still struggling to piece together what, exactly, had happened between them. The sex had been mind-blowing—as hot as she'd hoped, with the added bonus of actually feeling connected to Burk—so why had he acted like it was horrible? Sunday's encounter didn't make it any easier, either, with heat burning between them as they sat there in church, pressed next to each other in the pew. She simply couldn't grasp why he was sprinting away when there was clearly so much magnetism between them.

Unless she was imagining it.

The question was made even more pointed by the fact that they hadn't really even *talked* to each other since Willa's bedroom. Except for when Burk had blurted out that Anna wanted her to come to dinner this Friday night. Before she could open her mouth to refuse—because she couldn't think of anything more awkward than a dinner with Burk *and* Anna—he'd already strode away. After the odd invite, there were times when she'd catch him looking at her, and she'd think, *Now. Now we will get over this horrible hurdle and get back into bed.* But then he'd just shake his head and go back to barking orders at his crew.

Willa brushed back a piece of dark blond hair that had fallen on her forehead. No matter, she thought, straightening and enjoying the sight of her strong shoulders, her firm waist. If Burk didn't want the goods, someone else would.

Certainly *Lance* was wishing he could get back in her good graces.

Lance.

The name stuck in her head as she descended the stairs and headed toward the kitchen. Or what was left of the kitchen, since the old appliances had been taken away the previous afternoon, the flooring ripped out, and the cabinets removed.

Willa thought of the same text she'd gotten, over and over, since Lance's call the other night.

I'm sorry. Please help me. I love you.

Over and over. Eight words that shook her hard enough to make her vision blur every time she read them.

Not because she believed them. Just the opposite, in fact. They reeked of something so desperate, something so sad, that she pitied how low he had to be to send them over and over. She was sure he was desperate for someone, anyone, to cling to as he faced the charges against him. But even still. She couldn't be the one to help him. Whatever kind of support he needed, he'd made sure she'd never be the one to give it when he'd taken all her money.

The thoughts rattled around in her brain as she hunted for her coffeemaker. Yesterday she'd run an extension cord from an outlet in the kitchen to the dining room table, where she'd been able to brew her Folgers. It was one of the last pieces of furniture on the lower level, and one of the last safe places for any of her things. Now the dining room table was gone—no doubt hauled out to her workshop in the garage or down into the basement—and her coffeemaker was nowhere in sight.

She swore softly. *To the Rolling Pin, then*, she thought. But as she turned to grab her coat from the downstairs closet, there was Burk, standing near the front door with two cups of coffee in his hands.

She cried out, startled. No matter how many weeks it had been, she still wasn't used to him just coming into her house like he owned it.

"Sorry I'm so early," he said, shaking his head and sending fat, wet snowflakes falling from his damp hair to the floor. "I had some measurements to make and some plans to draw up before the crew gets here. I brought you this, in case you were up, too."

He extended a hand, offering her one of the coffees he was holding. Willa found her steps unsteady as she went to take it. The man was a sight in his gray peacoat. His perfectly fitted jeans hit his thighs and calves just right.

"Snow this early," Willa said by way of conversation. "How about that." She forced herself not to stare at the way the tiny beads of cold moisture clung to his glistening hair.

"It can start early here," he replied evenly, not taking his eyes from hers. "This storm's supposed to dump a lot. And it's heavy stuff. I saw a couple tree limbs down already."

Willa looked past Burk to the wavy glass on the front door, wondering if the old oak out front was going to come crashing down on them at any second.

"I'll shovel for you, if you want. You got one in the garage?"

"One what?"

"Shovel."

"Oh," she said, pausing to think. "I think I saw one out there when I was working."

"Do you remember, was it flat on the bottom or pointed?"

"Uh, pointed, I think."

"And probably rusted."

"Well, a little bit maybe, but I'm sure it will do the job." Willa had to work to keep the defensiveness out of her voice. If Burk wanted to stand there and play gentleman, he didn't get to be choosy about which shovel he used. That wasn't how it worked.

Burk smiled widely, revealing straight, even teeth that almost took her breath away. "I think what you have in there is a rusted garden shovel, so we'd better get you something else. Don't suppose you have any salt, either?"

Willa felt her ire rising. "What, so you need to cook now, too?"

Burk laughed so deeply, the whole house seemed to shake with its rumble. "No, it's for the front walk. Salt, to melt the snow?"

"Oh," Willa said, staring at the lid of her coffee cup and feeling foolish. "No, I don't have any of that."

She could feel heat in her cheeks, and she didn't like it. Here she'd been, ready to run out and buy a palm sander, and Burk was busting her chops about a shovel and some salt. *Basics*. If she didn't even have those around the house, how could she expect to run an entire B and B?

Willa set her jaw. It didn't matter. She'd figure it out. And she didn't need Burk's help to do it.

"You know, that's okay, I'll take care of the shoveling. I have to head down to the hardware store anyway when they're open, so I'll just get everything at once."

"What else are you getting?" Burk asked. Like it was any of his business.

"A palm sander. I'm finishing that blue table. Today."

"You don't say."

Willa didn't like the way he was staring at her, his blue eyes blazing with something she couldn't read. Was he doubting her?

Some nerve he had, bailing right after sex and then laughing at her about *this*. Friday night dinner at Anna's was going to be awful if he kept this up. She might just need to skip the whole thing—either that, or she was in danger of walking out in the middle of it if he kept acting like a jackass.

"Thanks for the coffee," Willa said, wrapping her hands more tightly around the cup. "I'll see you later."

"Wait," he said, reaching out and placing his hand on her forearm. Willa felt a flutter deep inside. Before she could tamp it down, Burk took a step closer, and the flutter became a vibration.

"What coarseness are you going to get?"

"Excuse me?"

He leaned closer, as if there were a million hammers pounding and a million saws whirring, and she couldn't hear him over the cacophony.

"Sandpaper coarseness. What do you think, for a table like that?"

Willa wanted to close her eyes and relish the feeling of his breath so close to her skin. She wanted to inhale deeply, filling her lungs with his smell—alive and fresh and all around her. Instead, she straightened and forced herself to ignore it.

"I'm sure I'll figure it out at the hardware store."

"I could help you," he said, his eyes searching her face.

"No, I don't need any—"

"Then stick around for a minute and let's go over some things. I have some project questions."

"I have a full day," she hedged, wary of his sudden interest in talking with her. After their frigid week, why was he suddenly bringing her beverages, offering to shovel, and needing to talk about the house?

"It would be helpful if we could get your final say on everything," he said, finally removing his hand from her forearm. She hated the chill on her skin the moment his fingers were gone. "Floors, wall colors, appliances, cabinets. There are only a few more things to knock out before we can start putting everything back together. So we need your final say sooner rather than later."

Willa swallowed. It did make sense to talk about that. Only she wasn't sure if she could *pay* for any of it. Not unless the loan from the bank came through. Her stomach twisted with unease. She supposed she *could* pay Burk, but it would drain the little bit of money she had left. And then what would she do for food? For gas? Never mind the B and B—she'd be struggling just to live. She wasn't about to admit that in front of Burk, though. "All right. Just let me get my samples."

Willa set her coffee down and went back upstairs to her piles of paint swatches, flooring tiles, and collages. She could barely carry it all as she came back down the stairs.

"Here," Burk said, "let me help you." Willa noted his coat was off, and he was wearing a collared pullover that showed off his broad shoulders spectacularly. As he grabbed half of her pile, their fingers grazed, and both of them stopped moving.

She wanted to hate the fact that he was here, standing in her house. She wanted to loathe him for leaving after sex and avoiding her this week. She wanted to flip him the bird and walk away, but she just couldn't drum up the animosity. The truth was, he was being kinder than he had been for days. And on top of all that, she was thrilled to be able to show someone all the ideas she'd pulled together for the B and B. Especially now that she'd had time to figure out how to bring the flavor of White Pine into the space a little more. Even if it might never come to pass—if she might not get the money from the bank to finish it—she was delighted to be able to show someone her plans.

"I guess we could use the blue table, as long as it's still there," Willa said. "To spread everything out on, I mean. There's a lot to go through."

Did she imagine it, or did Burk's eyes darken at the mention of spreading things out on the table?

"I guess we'll kneel," he said, "since there are no chairs."

"We'll bow at the altar of my design, you mean."

His eyes flashed. "Will you require a human sacrifice?"

"Today I only require a caffeine sacrifice. Which you've made, so you're in luck."

Burk took his notebook out and Willa tried to ignore it. She hated that damn thing. "Start with the kitchen, then?" Burk asked. "I have your paint swatch for the walls. But we'll need to get the flooring ordered. And the cabinet specs are set, but you need to choose the color."

Willa pulled out the flooring sample she'd found, as well as a kitchen collage she'd put together the previous weekend. "I want the cabinets white, like this. I know Gary down at the hardware store can order them; we talked about it last week. And look, see this sample? The flooring is cork, so it's more sustainable than hardwood. And there's something about the texture that feels a little more homey, don't you think?" She knew she was talking quickly—nearly blathering—but she didn't care. "And the wall color you already know, and the appliances are all here, in this folder." She handed him a manila file, on the side of which was neatly printed *Kitchen*. "They all fit the specs you gave me."

When Burk reached for the folder, Willa wondered briefly if his hands were shaking. *Too much caffeine*, she thought, and barreled ahead.

"I've got the dining room color picked out here, along with trim color, which is the same as the ceiling. Floors in all the rooms should be restained in this tone…" She rummaged through some samples until she found the one she wanted. It was also labeled. "It's not too dark, but it does have a hint of red in it, which I like. It reminded me of the trees around here."

She smiled at him, but he just blinked. *Okay, maybe not* enough *caffeine*, she thought, and kept going.

On she went, handing him folders full of orders, samples, and pictures to meet all the specs he'd given her. When she was finally done, the crew had already filed in for the day, and were starting their work. But Burk barely seemed to register their presence.

"So what do you think?" Willa asked above the noise around them. "It's a lot, I know, but it's—"

"Perfect," Burk replied, his Adam's apple bobbing in a way Willa had never seen before. "I never imagined it could look like this. I never knew…"

He trailed off. Willa's heart raced as he leaned closer. "It's almost too much," he said, low enough so Willa had to strain to hear him above the crew noise. "It's almost too unbelievable to see it come to life this way."

Willa struggled to keep pace. "What do you mean? To see it come to life in what way?"

Burk smiled and shook his head. "Nothing. I just— Willa, I can't think of a more beautiful home. I really can't. Did you learn to do all this in New York?"

New York. Why was he asking about her past now?

She wanted to answer carefully, but before she could stop them, the words were tumbling out. "There was an art gallery I liked, the Bishop. I gave them some money and they let me futz with the exhibits. I liked to think about how the space and the art worked together. I suppose it's a little like decorating. Now I'm just learning to work with used tables instead of priceless Manets."

In spite of the joke, Burk's face remained still. Too still, Willa realized, as if he were fighting a great battle inside, and was determined not to let any of it show.

"In all that time you were in New York, did you ever get married?"

"No," Willa answered. "I did live with a man, though. Lance."

The green flecks in Burk's eyes darkened, like the sea before a storm. "Were you happy?"

Willa swallowed, suddenly nervous to be sharing all this. "For a while I thought I was. But now that I look back—no. I don't think I was."

"Why?"

The back of Willa's neck prickled. The magnetic pull toward Burk threatened to overtake her now that he was asking about her. Taking a genuine interest in her, it seemed. It made her desire surge: made her want to hook her arms around his neck and bury her fingers in his thick hair and kiss the straight, strong line of his jaw over and over. She wanted to invite him back to her bed *now*, and spend the afternoon there—never mind track practice or the recipe exchange or any of it.

The problem was, sex hadn't worked. Sex hadn't changed anything between them last week, and it wouldn't change anything this week, either. She wanted it to—the ache in her muscles and the heat between her legs told her how very, very much she wanted it to. Only it was a lost cause.

Sex was not going to fix what was broken between them.

But maybe an apology could.

No matter how Burk acted, no matter how he treated her now, she owed him an "I'm sorry" for the past. She owed their relationship that much. If they were going to move forward, *that* was what it would take.

He'd asked her why she hadn't been happy, but it wasn't because of Lance. It was because she had never faced up to who she was.

The time to tell him was now or never. She took a steadying breath. "Burk, when I left White Pine all those years ago, I was already so broken. My dad had died, my mom was spending all her time with Max, and you were the only one I had in my life. You held me when I cried, and you took my crazy two o'clock in the morning phone calls, and then I just—I left you. It was horrible. And unfair."

Burk's body went still. She'd never seen him so immobile. She pressed forward.

"I left because I was afraid that you'd abandon me first. That you'd stop loving me and take off, too. So I ran away before you could. I was dumb and blind, and I thought I'd just... start over or something.

"You were such a good boyfriend, and I was such a terrible girlfriend. You deserved better. I'm sorry I broke your heart and abandoned you. And I'm sorry it took coming back here for me to realize that. And to apologize."

She held her breath, ready for him to chastise her for taking so long to admit how wrong she was, but when his eyes locked with hers again, there was a smoldering fire there. She almost inched backward from it. His desire was so openly apparent, she automatically looked around to see if any of his crew were watching them.

"As long as we're apologizing," Burk said, leaning closer, "then let me add one to the pile." His heat was all around her, searing her skin even though they weren't touching. "The other day, you had a great idea and I— frankly, I ruined it."

Willa's heart lurched. "You thought it was a great idea?"

Burk arched a brow. "A very, *very* great idea. I'm sorry I left so abruptly. I probably gave you the idea that I wasn't—that is, that I didn't enjoy it. But that's far from the truth."

Someone started hammering in the kitchen, scrambling Willa's thoughts. She couldn't think straight.

Burk leaned in farther. His stubbled cheek brushed against hers, his warm breath tickled her ear. She could no longer distinguish the pounding in the kitchen from the pounding in her head. "Let's go to dinner tomorrow," he said, "at Anna's. And afterward, maybe we can try this again."

Every bone in Willa's body turned liquid. She was going to disintegrate into a puddle right there on the floor, and the crew was going to have to clean her up and put her in the Dumpster in the driveway. "All right," she said faintly.

He pulled back and ran a finger down the skin of her jaw, leaving a wake of fire behind. She trembled as he grasped her chin and tilted it up.

"I'll stick around this time," he said, brushing his lips

across hers gently. Sparks flew along her skin, along every nerve in her body. He nibbled her bottom lip, nearly unraveling her right there on the floor.

"But before we do anything," he murmured, his mouth curling into a smile, "I'm going to help you with that palm sander."

CHAPTER TWENTY

Thursday, October 11, 10:34 a.m.

Downtown White Pine was sagging under piles of wet, sticky snow. It didn't flutter from the sky so much as rain down in thick, heavy flakes that coated everything. Great clumps of the stuff slid off trees and plopped onto Main Street as Willa and Burk pulled up to the hardware store. In front of the Paul Bunyan Diner, a man in a white apron was hard at work trying to shovel the stuff off the sidewalk. His cheeks were pink and his forehead shiny with the effort.

Burk killed the engine and looked at his watch. "I don't think we should be here too long. I need to get back and dismiss the crew so they can get home before the roads are impassable."

"Of course," Willa agreed. She smiled at him, liking his concern for his employees. "I just need the sander."

"And a shovel."

"Right. And a shovel."

"And salt."

"Yes, salt. Not the cooking kind."

Burk glanced at her feet. "And maybe some boots?"

Willa stared at her leather shoes. Technically, they *were* boots. The only boots she had, in fact, sporting a heel and a lovely zipper up the side. Only they didn't exactly keep the cold out. She could already feel the wet slush seeping into her socks.

"Maybe," she hedged, "if they have a cute pair or something."

Burk shook his head. "I guarantee you, White Pine Hardware will *not* have a cute pair. They're going to be green or brown. Rubber and leather. And they're going to be ugly as sin."

The lines at the corners of his eyes deepened with amusement. Willa felt a smile starting on her own face.

"You want me to wear ugly boots?"

"I want your feet to be warm. I don't much care how they look."

"Next you'll want me to buy a John Deere hat."

"They have those here, too. Also in green or brown."

Willa laughed. "Overalls?"

"That can be arranged."

"Suspenders?"

"To hold up your waders? Yes."

Willa giggled helplessly. Burk smiled back, and Willa experienced a lightness she hadn't known in a long, long time. *Happiness.*

"I don't care what you wear, Willa Masterson," Burk said, leaning over to give her a light kiss that had her muscles aching with pleasure. "You don't need to worry about how you look."

Willa pulled back, surprised.

"You—you didn't think so the other day."

"How do you mean?"

"When we were in bed. You laughed at me."

Burk's brows crowded together. "No, I did not. I would *never*—"

"You pulled my shirt off and you were grinning. Like it was hilarious or something."

Burk's eyes widened. "Only because you looked so different from what I remember. But not bad, different. I never meant for you to think that I was making *fun* of you. Good God, you're..." He ran a hand along the back of his neck, as if struggling for the words. "You're just fine is what you are."

"Fine?"

"No, no. More than fine. You're great."

"Great?" Willa crossed her arms. "Next you're probably going to tell me I'm *swell*."

Burk glanced up at the sky, as if he could find the right words in the fat snowflakes. "Listen, I've blown a lot of hot air at women in my day. But I'm not doing it now. So will you just trust me that I wasn't laughing at you? I wouldn't do that. I *wasn't* doing that."

His blue eyes were boring into hers, alarming in their intensity.

"I can prove it," he offered.

"How?"

He leaned over and placed his warm, perfect lips on hers. His hand grasped the back of her head, pulling her toward him. With a firm tenderness he parted her, claiming her mouth entirely with his own. The kiss was all about Willa—slow and deep and giving. He offered pleasure with every stroke of his tongue, matching his lips to hers and keeping them in perfect unison. The kiss ignited every part of her body, leaving her breathless. He nipped gently along her lower lip, causing her to nearly collapse like the damp snow around them.

"You believe me?" he murmured as he finally pulled away after what seemed like hours.

Willa nodded, unable to speak. She had no doubt that he wanted her now. *All* of her.

Her spine still tingling, they exited the truck. They both turned at the sound of another shovel scraping, only to see Betty laboring to remove snow from the sidewalk in front of Knots and Bolts. The plow had already come by and piled up damp mounds of white along the street, and Betty was working to carve what looked like a small mountain pass in front of the shop.

"Oh, we have to help her," Willa said, starting down the sidewalk. Burk chased after.

"Betty!" Willa called. "We're coming!"

Betty leaned on her shovel, her chest rising and falling underneath her tan parka. Behind her, the awning of Hair We Go creaked under the weight of all the snow, threatening to rip at any moment. "Well, that's a relief," Betty said at their approach. "I was wondering when a New Yorker might come save me in a snowstorm."

Willa might have been irritated, if it weren't for the fact that Betty was going to be helping her draw up a business plan later that afternoon.

"All right, muscles," Betty said, handing the shovel to Burk, "let's see what you can do."

With a pointed glance at Willa, Burk began to shovel. The scrape of the metal on concrete made her shiver.

"It's like God's dandruff," Betty said after a moment. "And the Good Lord just keeps itching his scalp."

Willa grinned. Behind them, geese honked on the banks of the Birch River, riding out the storm in feathered clusters. *Bad timing*, Willa thought. If they had any sense, they'd be in Florida by now.

"I thought I'd be here all afternoon," Betty said, watching Burk. "This is downright Sisyphean."

"Sisa what?" Willa asked.

"Sisyphus. Greek guy. Rolled a rock up a hill every day, and just when he was at the top, it rolled back down and he'd have to start all over again. Every day. For eternity."

Willa tried to catch a snowflake on her tongue. "Thounds awfthl."

"Zeus did it," Burk said, hurling a pile of snow onto the bank the plow had created. "Sisyphus thought he was smarter than Zeus, so Zeus punished him."

Willa stopped catching snowflakes. "Since when do you know Greek history?"

"Greek *mythology*," Burk said, sending another heavy pile of snow flying. "And I make it a point to memorize stories about people who get too big for their britches. Cautionary tales, you can call them."

Before she could respond, there was a flap of black among the flakes, and Randall Sondheim was standing next to her. "It's always valuable finding lessons in texts other than the Bible," the pastor said by way of greeting.

"Hello to you, too," Willa said, taking in the man's grumpy, rounded posture, made worse by the elements.

Betty looked the pastor up and down. Snowflakes coated her eyelashes. "Only preaching I want to hear today is in relation to this snow."

The pastor met Betty's fierce gaze. "Do you have a Bible verse you think is applicable?"

"*Jesus wept.*"

Willa snorted laughter, then quickly covered her mouth.

Betty crossed her arms. "Pastor Indecisive came in a week ago for fabric to recover his favorite chair, wasted two hours of my time trying to pick one out, and then left without buying anything."

"I was coming back today to make my choice," he said evenly, though Willa thought she detected a flash of frustration in his eyes. Betty could flap the unflappable, Willa thought.

"We're closed today," Betty replied. "See this snow? That means no business lesson or recipe exchange tonight, either, Willa."

Willa nodded, repressing a wave of disappointment. She'd been looking forward to talking with Betty, not to mention learning how to make hot dish.

"Perhaps I could implore you to reconsider," Pastor Sondheim said, his black coat standing in sharp contrast to the white all around him. "I could run up to the bakery and bring you a donut. Make it worth your while."

Willa realized suddenly that today wasn't Wednesday. *That* was the pastor's donut day, but here the regimented man was, offering to buy donuts on *Thursday*. He must really want to spend time with Betty if he was willing to switch up his pastry purchases.

Suddenly Willa wondered if Randall Sondheim hadn't stalled in Knots and Bolts because he couldn't make up his mind about fabric. Maybe there was a different reason altogether.

She glanced at Betty. She couldn't be sure, but she thought she saw a softness in her face. It was very possible Betty had deeper feelings for the pastor than she was letting on.

"Burk," Willa said, grabbing his arm, "maybe the pastor here could finish up, so you and I can get our things and get back to the house."

"Be happy to," Randall replied, stepping over to take the shovel.

Burk was about to protest, but Willa elbowed him sharply. "Bye, Betty!" she called, practically dragging Burk up the street. Betty just stared at them with raised eyebrows as the pastor continued moving the heavy powder.

"What was that all about?" Burk asked, brushing damp snow off his coat when they were safely inside the hardware store.

Willa grinned. "I'm positive Randall Sondheim likes Betty!"

"Because he wants to buy fabric from her?"

"And also because he's going to buy a donut on *Thursday*."

Burk considered it. "I did wonder why he'd changed his donut-buying day."

"Also I saw some sparks flying between the two of them after Sunday's sermon."

"What do you mean you saw sparks? Were they making out or something?"

Willa laughed. "No. They were talking in the church basement."

"Oh," Burk said dryly, "of course, the perfect place for romance to bloom."

"I'm serious. I think there's something between them."

"Something like?"

"You know. Starts with L. Ends with OVE."

"L'Ove? Is that French?"

"*Love.*"

Burk laughed. "Come on," he said, "let's go get you some boots and a sander."

"And salt and a shovel."

"Yes. And those, too."

If Burk had said they were going to buy diamonds, Willa wasn't sure she'd have been any more pleased.

* * *

Later that afternoon, Audrey called Willa to tell her track practice was canceled—schools were closed and kids were sent home. Outside, the snow kept piling up in thick mounds that snapped branches off trees and weighted down power lines and blanketed the fall colors that had been at their peak of brilliance.

Willa watched the white flakes with increasing anxiety. She wasn't sure what she'd do if the power went out, or if she couldn't get her car out of the driveway. Burk had sent the last of his crew home, and was packing up his toolbox now. When he left, it would just be Willa against the elements.

"I'll be fine," she muttered to herself, going into the kitchen to make some tea. But then she realized she had no stove since it had been carted away the day before. Her kettle was packed away. And who even knew what box the tea was in?

Not a problem, she thought to herself. Burk had encouraged her to stop by the grocery store for a few bags of food, and she could always make a peanut butter sandwich and drink water out of the bathroom faucet if she had to. As long as her pipes didn't freeze.

She paced the torn-up floor, suddenly worried. What if the power gave out, and she was without heat? What if the food ran out and she was trapped here?

"All right," Burk said, striding into the kitchen, "everyone's out for the day, so I'm going to head—" He took one look at her face and stopped short. "Are you okay? What's wrong?"

Willa forced herself to smile. She was not a baby. A little snow was not going to take her down, for crying out loud. "Nothing," she lied, "I'm just trying to figure out how to use that palm sander if the power goes out."

"Well, you've got a generator, right?"

Willa shook her head. "No."

Burk looked suddenly concerned. "Propane?"

"Like the gas?"

"Yes, like the gas."

"No."

Burk sighed. "Are you telling me we were at the hardware store earlier today and you didn't think to pick up *any* of this stuff?"

Willa clenched her hands. "How was I supposed to know I needed it? In New York, if there's a blizzard, you just go find a Chinese place that's open, and then watch movies."

Burk arched a dark brow. "Well, you're not *in* New York anymore. You're in Minnesota. You came back here in September, and you didn't think you might want to plan for some snow?"

Willa's insides sank. Her cheeks burned with embarrassment. She was such a fool. Just when she thought she was getting the hang of White Pine again, Mother Nature showed her how little she knew. She thought of the army green boots she'd purchased today and shuddered. If it weren't for Burk, she wouldn't even have the right *footwear*.

"I didn't know," she said, studying her cuticles. "I haven't seen snow like this in a long time, okay?"

Burk sighed. "All right, look. This is only going to get worse. You're going to have to go somewhere."

Willa raised her eyes. "Like where?"

He took a step closer. Their gazes locked. "We'll have to think about this."

His voice was an octave lower. The way he'd emphasized the word *think* made Willa tremble. She wanted to reach out, to run her finger along the sharp line of his jaw. The sudden dark desire in his eyes was like a gravitational pull. "I'm sure someone will take me in," she said slowly.

"Pastor Sondheim, probably." Burk stepped closer, his lips turning into a small smile. He blocked out what little light was left between their bodies.

She was close enough to feel the heat from his massive torso. "He'll feed me donuts and we'll watch wholesome television," she murmured.

Burk placed a warm hand on her neck, letting his palm slide across her skin, down to her clavicle. "It will be very chaste, I'm sure," he said, his hand slipping lower, lower. Willa sucked in a breath when he found her breast, his broad thumb tracing the outline of her nipple through her shirt.

"You want me to go then?" he asked wickedly.

"I would hate to keep you," Willa gasped. Her head tilted back. Burk brought his mouth to her exposed skin, his teeth nipping gently at her throat, up to her jaw, and then to the edge of her earlobe. Her knees weakened; her breath came in rasps. She wrapped her arms around his neck for support, fearing she'd crumple to the floor if she didn't simply hang on. She sank her hands into his thick hair, pulling her body more tightly against his.

Burk uttered a noise that seemed more animal than man. In one swift movement, he picked her up, carrying her like a bride across a threshold.

"This isn't the way to the pastor's house," she teased, her heart hammering with excitement.

Burk's mouth hardened. Emotion stormed behind his eyes. "You're goddamn right it's not," he said.

She could feel every muscle in his body tighten as he carried her up the stairs to her bedroom. The second time in a week she'd been spirited away to her bedroom by her teenage lover.

"We're riding out the storm here," he growled, shoving her door open with his foot. Outside her curtained window, the world was quiet and white. Heavy flakes fell in infinite number, blanketing everything.

Willa's whole body trembled. "Then I hope it's an avalanche," she whispered thickly as Burk placed her on the bed.

CHAPTER TWENTY-ONE

Thursday, October 11, 1:10 p.m.

*I*t took every ounce of willpower Burk had not to rush things with Willa. Suddenly, he was seventeen again, and it was his first time and they were both trembling, their hearts hammering amid their breathless whispers. She'd cried out that night they'd first lost themselves to each other—part pain at the sudden expanse of him inside her, and part pleasure at the overwhelming joining of their bodies.

Burk closed his eyes against the aching tenderness of the memory. You never forget your first time, it was true. And if he was honest, he'd never forgotten *anything* about Willa Masterson. Buried it, yes, under piles of detachment as deep as the snow outside. But her warm body underneath him now was melting all that away, sending rivulets of tender affection into every part of him.

As he pressed his lips against her temple, murmuring her name as he inhaled the scent of her skin and hair, part of him wondered if his heart hadn't been in hibernation all this time. He'd been a player, bringing women near, but never letting them get *close*. Maybe he'd just been asleep, he reasoned, waiting for Willa to come back so he could feel alive again. *So he could love again.*

Burk squeezed his eyes shut, tamping down the tide of emotion rushing through him. *Easy*, he warned himself. Love was a dangerous thought. Love had gotten him into trouble years before, crushing him when the woman he'd wanted to marry had gone east without a good-bye.

Love didn't mean cracking the door open to his heart and letting a little trickle of feeling in, as he'd planned. No, love was an earthquake of emotion, generating a tsunami of affection that threatened to wash him away entirely.

Underneath him, Willa slid her fingers along his arms. Her hands cupped his shoulders and trailed down his back. He answered her touch with a kiss so deep her whole body trembled.

Desperate to have her naked form spread before him, Burk lifted her shirt and unclasped her bra. Beneath him, she twisted and pulled off her pants. He raised himself to a sitting position to take her in, and his heart constricted.

The only sound in the room was his raspy breathing. He tried in vain to control the air in and out of his chest at the sight of her smooth, perfect skin; her breasts, round and tipped; and the sweet, wet space between her thighs. The length of him hardened to a tortured fullness.

"Willa," he said, unable to keep her name off his lips. She responded by sitting up and lifting off his shirt, pressing her soft, delectable chest into his flat, muscled one. The skin-on-skin contact had him hissing with pleasure.

He crushed her to him, needing her as close as possible. His lips found hers once again, and he claimed them, worried for a moment she'd pull away from the force of his kiss. Instead, she gave in to his hunger again and again, matching it with a need of her own that had his muscles burning.

"My king," she murmured, her hands flattening along his abdomen, then unbuttoning his pants. Burk's throat tightened at the name she used to call him, after they were crowned king and queen at prom senior year.

The memory had his brain buzzing, his heart hammering, his manhood aching.

Only a little feeling, he reminded himself, cupping her rounded breasts in his workman's hands. He lowered himself to a nipple, sucking gently on the blushing tip. Willa writhed underneath him. Her thighs clung to his naked legs; her hands plundered his hair as he let his tongue wander languidly from one breast to the other. She mewled with pleasure, and he smiled at the sound.

She caught the movement of his mouth. "You're grinning," she said, and he noted the worried tone of her words.

She still thought he was laughing at her.

"You are beautiful," he growled. He ran his hands along the outside of her shapely thighs, up to her soft belly, and finally to her face, which he cupped gently. "Never doubt that. Ever. Please. You're too stunning to even put into words. I hate the idea that you would think—"

Burk stopped, suddenly embarrassed at how verbose he was being. He shook his head. "You're beautiful. That's all."

Willa's green eyes glittered. "Thank you," she whispered, her fingers brushing the hair of his chest, lowering to the downy trail on his abdomen and to—

He tensed as she grasped his penis in her soft hands. His whole body shuddered as she began stroking him gently.

Good God, he was going to spill himself all over her bedspread if she didn't stop.

And that wouldn't do at all, because he wasn't even close to being done with Willa Masterson.

He grasped her hand and pulled it away, then pressed himself along the naked length of her. She moaned as skin met skin. Her damp, aching center pressed against his hot, pulsing need.

He lowered a hand to the inside of a thigh, and moved slowly upward.

"Your body is beautiful," he murmured, surprising himself with still more words. His lips hovered above hers, their breath mingling, as his hand inched upward. "Your shape belongs in a museum. Sculpted into marbled perfection alongside Venus."

She arched against him, aching with need, but he forced his hand to stay the course. Steady, steady.

"You would be chiseled enchantment," he whispered, his fingers gently rising until finally he could trace the outline of her sex.

She sighed at his touch. "Chiseled enchantment?" she murmured from inside her fog of pleasure. "Where is Burk Olmstead, and what have you done with him?"

Burk smiled, and placed a kiss on the hollow of her throat. "I'm right here," he replied, loving the way she tilted her head back to give him more access. So eager, so willing. "And I won't have you doubting for a minute what your body can do."

His hand was at the hot center of her, and the sweetness was too beguiling to resist. He parted her folds and slid a finger inside her, losing himself in the delicious softness of her core.

She strained against him, pressing him deeper. How had he been so foolish to sprint away from this the other day? He wanted to smack himself in the head with a two-by-four for squandering the chance to savor every inch of her.

Leaving her elongated throat, Burk let his lips wander down, down her flesh—all while his fingers churned waves of pleasure inside her body. Finally, his lips were just above where his fingers were working, and his tongue found the center of her, swollen with desire. He placed his lips on the soft bud, kissing gently as she cried out.

Her fingers tangled in his hair; her pelvis arched to meet his mouth. He grasped her rounded buttocks in his free hand and squeezed, letting his mouth possess her sex fully. In deep, wet kisses he tasted her, savoring the center of her, while his hand gave her pleasure within.

"Burk!" she cried, and his body tensed with a sharp thrill at the sound of his name on her lips.

"Say it again," he demanded, sliding another finger inside her.

"Burk," she gasped, her green eyes opening to find his own. "*My king.*"

The words fueled him like adrenaline. His body was charged, sparking the room with sexual energy. Willa arched her back as he pressed himself deeper into her, as his mouth hungered to taste every inch of her. He was overwhelmed by her softness. She never pulled back, never hampered his efforts. Her beautiful vulnerability had his heart racing.

He would give her everything he had, dammit. He would spend himself to make her happy. He would be Sisyphus, rolling the rock up the hill every day if he knew she'd be there at the top, and he could glimpse her emerald eyes lighting with happiness at the sight of him.

All at once, her pleasure broke like a dam, spilling over them both. She cried out, pulsing against him, her hands clutching him in desperate need. The whole house rang with her cries of ecstasy—free and pure in the quiet afternoon.

She rocked against him, shattering in his arms. The ribbon of her orgasm wound through her body and then his own, binding them both. Burk could feel the sensation of it in his bones. He clenched his jaw and fought not to spill himself.

Finally, after the long waves subsided, Willa's body relaxed against his. When her breathing had steadied, he withdrew his hand from her still-pulsing core. He lifted his head and kissed her flesh from navel to neck. Finally, he found her contented lips with his own. "Mmm," she murmured against him, her breath warm and tickling. He pressed his thick hardness against her and she smiled lazily.

"I should let you deal with that on your own for the way you raced out of my bed last week," she said.

Burk grinned, pushing a lock of her dark blond hair away from her forehead. "And I wouldn't blame you," he said, kissing her clavicle, her neck, her forehead. She sighed.

"But that's not how this is going to end," he said, and placed himself between her warm thighs. She tensed and he could feel the hunger building in her again.

He took her mouth in his and kissed her until they were both breathless. Placing the tip of his penis against her slick entrance, he paused to study Willa's face. She was glowing with both pleasure and desire. Her emerald eyes were bright and alive, her mouth quirked with a kind of playfulness.

Gently this time, he eased himself inside. Her fingers clutched the muscles of his back, but not painfully so. He closed his eyes as he lost himself in her soft flesh.

Words collected in his throat—so many at once he didn't know what to do with them.

This feels so right.

I won't leave this time.

He moved against her, burying his face in the place where her shoulder met her neck. He busied his lips against her flesh so they wouldn't form words that scared and thrilled him at once.

Eagerly, she rocked with him, grasping him so he filled her up completely. Her lashes quivered as her eyes squeezed close. A groan escaped him, deep and unbridled. Affection surged—a sudden desire to always be with her, to keep her safe, to let her know how beautiful she was and how hard he would work to cherish her always.

Pulling her body closer, Burk thrust himself inside, demanding every inch of her and getting it all—and more—in return. She opened herself up, stretched herself to fit all of him, panted and writhed for everything he had.

Dear God. Her hands worked up his sides, to the flat

planes of his back as he plunged deeper and deeper. He was losing himself, getting swept away with Willa and this moment and the impossible rightness of it all.

Her head tilted back and another cry escaped her long, lovely throat. She called his name as her core contracted around his shaft, sending him into a spiral of his own. Dark waves pulled him down, down into a rabbit hole of enraptured ecstasy from which he wasn't sure he could ever escape. He clutched her harder, deep animalistic noises emitting from within him: primordial sounds that proclaimed a need for her so deep, words could never translate them.

They tumbled over the edge of pleasure together, falling into each other's arms when they were spent, gasping like they'd just run a marathon.

When he could move again, he eased off her relaxed body, pulling her spent frame closer to his. As she sighed against him, the words collected again—a jumble of emotions and phrases mashing in his brain and in his throat.

I need you.

I think I've always needed you.

All he could do was pull her closer, whispering her name over and over in her hair, along her skin.

"Willa."

Just before they drifted off together in a spent slumber, she smiled at him, as if somewhere, somehow, part of her understood what he was trying to say.

CHAPTER TWENTY-TWO

Thursday, October 11, 3:22 p.m.

Willa awoke and stretched like a contented cat. Next to her, Burk's body radiated enough warmth to melt the piles of snow that had fallen outside. She stared at his still-sleeping form and wondered at what had occurred between them. Not only had the sex been mind-blowing—again—but Burk had stuck around this time. Plus he'd shown enough affection and tenderness to make her contemplate whether what they'd just done had crossed from casual sex into...something more.

Willa smoothed back her tousled hair and took a steadying breath. This didn't have to get complicated if neither of them wanted it to. She stole another glance at the rise and fall of Burk's strong chest, at the peaceful line of his mouth, and told herself this was enough. If it never went beyond having this much, right here, she'd be happy.

Burk stirred and opened his dark blue eyes. Willa

smiled at him, brushing back a mass of his thick, dark hair. "Hey, sleepy," she murmured, kissing his lips gently.

He sat up. "What time is it?"

"Not late. Just after three. We napped a little, I think."

Burk grinned and flopped back on the pillows. "We wore ourselves out." Willa snuggled into the cavern between his chest and bicep.

"I think we did," she agreed.

Outside, the snow had stopped, but the blanketed world was still. No cars puttered down Oak Street; no kids shouted to each other from front lawns. Everyone was holed up, and Willa was delighted that the world had seemed to pause so that she and Burk could enjoy each other. She felt a thrill upon realizing that it wasn't really even dark yet. She and Burk had *hours* left in the day. If they wanted them.

Burk pulled her closer, letting his hand slide down her bare chest to her nipple, which he traced in lazy circles. It hardened at his touch, and Willa shifted as desire stirred inside her all over again.

"You know," he said lazily, moving his hand to the other breast. "The work my crew and I have left to do here is pretty invasive. Floors, walls, installations. You might want to consider leaving the house for a few days while it all gets done."

Willa's flesh trembled as his hands continued their march on her breasts. "Where would I go?" she asked breathlessly, heat stirring in her innermost parts.

Burk grinned. "I suppose I could make room for you at my place. It would be a shame to see you off in a motel somewhere."

"The Great Lakes Inn gets such good reviews, though."

"I can think of a few things the Great Lakes Inn can't provide," he said, placing his mouth on her taut nipple and running his tongue over it in slow circles. Willa gasped and pulled his head tighter against her chest. He paused only to move his mouth to the other nipple, to give it equal attention.

Willa's brain was unfocused and pleasure-heavy, but in one corner of it was the nagging reality that she wasn't going to be able to pay Burk for any of this work. Or if she did, then she wouldn't have anything to live on. She was going to have to talk with him about it. Maybe now that they'd been able to finally…*connect*, he'd understand her situation a little better.

She struggled to gather her thoughts. "Burk, I need to tell you something."

Burk nuzzled her neck with his lips. "What's that?"

"The house repairs. I'm not sure I can *oh*—"

Burk had slid a finger inside her. Willa's muscles liquefied at the unexpected jolt of pleasure.

"The costs may be too high," she gasped as he began to stroke her.

"We'll work something out," Burk murmured, nibbling her earlobe. "We can talk about it later."

Willa wanted to relax, to give in to the ways he was bringing her closer and closer to an edge she so desperately wanted to experience again, but she couldn't let herself. She needed to tell Burk the truth.

"Wait," she insisted, stilling his hand. His eyes darkened with confusion.

"What?"

"I need to tell you about the house. About the repairs, I mean. I'm not sure I can let you continue with everything."

Willa shifted and he withdrew his hand. She tried to ignore the cold ache left in his absence. "I'm running out of money. I went to the White Pine Bank and Trust for a loan," she continued, "but they weren't so keen on my B and B idea. At least, not as it stands. Betty's going to help with a business plan, and I think I can get there. But I don't think I can—I don't think I should let you continue if I can't afford it."

Burk eyes darkened. "I don't understand. You're stopping this project? Now?"

Willa nodded. "I'm sorry. I'm sure the bank loan will come through eventually. But I can't let you continue if I can't pay you."

Burk sat up. Willa followed suit. "I would have been looking for other work if I'd known this was going to end so suddenly. The crew—they'll need another project." His brow was suddenly lined, and Willa hated the stress she saw on his face.

"I'll pay you every cent I owe you for what you've done," she said. "I'm good for what's been completed so far. I just—I can't guarantee anything more."

Burk pulled away from her, and the motion had Willa's chest feeling hollow. For a long moment he didn't say anything.

"I could still buy it," he offered finally. "To help you, I mean. I could even finish the remodel, and you could subtract it from the final price of the house."

Willa started. She thought they'd be able to talk about this as . . . friends. That she'd be able to trust him with the reality of the situation. She never expected he'd try to negotiate in the midst of her confession.

"So I pay you to finish a house I won't live in?" she asked.

"Please. Listen to reason. You won't sell it any other way. A half-remodeled home will sit on the market for months. What I'm offering—it makes sense for *both* of us."

She shook her head. "But my B and B—"

"If you can get the loan, you can set up shop anywhere. The idea's not dead, but if you can't finish what you started in this house, then let me help." Burk's voice was warm, and yet there was something about his words that still seemed too...insistent.

"Look," he said, reaching out and placing his hand over hers, "maybe it's best this way. We could even work out a deal where I could pay you to help with the interior decorating. It'll still have your stamp on it. And it's not like you won't ever see the place again. But if you let me, I can finish this. I can give this house what it deserves."

Willa's blood heated, in spite of what sounded like Burk's good intentions. "What this house deserves?" she asked pointedly. "What is that, exactly?"

Burk didn't flinch. "Someone who can take care of it. Someone who knows what's best for the structure."

"And that would be you, obviously."

Burk nodded. "I want the house, Willa. I won't deny it. I've wanted this place since it was abandoned. I've been taking care of it for years, and I even started purchase negotiations with your mom about it before she died. When the title passed to you, I thought for sure you'd just put it on the market. When you didn't and you came back to White Pine, I thought..."

He trailed off.

"You thought what, exactly?"

"I thought you would just leave again. Like last time."

The words stung. "But I haven't left. I'm not *going* to.

And I'm not sure how you can sit there and talk about taking the house back like you don't care what I'm trying to do here."

Burk scowled. "Because I *don't* care. Not about the B and B anyway. It's your dream, not mine. And as for you, I had no idea we could be close again. When you first turned up, I thought you were the same person who left and broke my heart. I didn't want you to take my house, too."

"Your house?" Willa stood and snatched her clothes from the bedroom floor. "This is my house, Burk Olmstead. Let's both be goddamned clear about *that*."

Burk exhaled slowly. "That came out wrong. I'm not trying to—"

"Was this part of it?" Willa asked, yanking on her jeans and shirt. "Was getting me into bed part of a plan to get the house back? Because who's going to be easier to fuck over than someone you've *literally* fucked, right?"

"Willa, no. This was your idea—"

"Oh, sure. My idea, which you conveniently agreed to because maybe it will get you the house faster."

Mortified that tears were suddenly coursing down her face, Willa turned away. Her chest stung with the same hurt she'd felt when she'd discovered Lance had been stealing from her.

"Get out," she said, marching to the doorway. "Get out of my house."

"Willa, please, I can't leave like this. It's a misundersta—"

"You can and you will," she said, her whole body shaking. "And you'll take your stupid crew and never come back. Do you understand me?"

Burk's brows drew together. His jaw hardened. "Twelve years I've been looking after this place while you've been living in New York. I've cut weeds and mowed the lawn and replaced boards on just about every surface. This place meant something to me before it *ever* meant something to you. So don't sit here and lecture me like you have loved this house the same as I have."

"Loved it enough to hurt someone over it, apparently," Willa retorted, walking back into the room so she could scoop up his pants and shirt from the ground.

"Hey, give me those."

Willa turned her back to him and stomped down the hallway. She heard him grumbling and swearing behind her.

She dashed down the stairs and headed for the front door. "You will never come back here," she cried, opening the front door. "You will never touch me again!" She flung his clothes into the piles of snow outside.

"Jesus!" he cried, pushing past her and wading into the mounds of powder wearing just his boxer shorts. "You are crazy, you know that?"

"I'd rather be crazy than care about a bunch of wood and nails more than a person!" she yelled as he worked to retrieve his jeans and shirt.

Willa was ready to slam the door—never mind Burk's coat and car keys and boots—when both of them realized there was a figure at the end of the walkway. He was hunched and shaking, silently watching the fight.

"You got a problem, nosy neighbor?" Willa shouted into the deepening twilight. Her voice echoed along the quiet street.

The stranger raised a single hand. "Hello, W-Willa."

Her stomach churned. She wondered if she might be sick.

Lance had decided to pay her a visit after all.

* * *

Burk pulled on his clothes right there on the front porch, his eyes darting from Willa back to Lance. His feet were bare, and he must have been freezing, but he never let on that he was cold.

"Can I help you?" he asked Lance. Willa elbowed him out of the way.

"Oh, for crying out loud. Don't try and play hero now." She motioned for Lance to come up to the house.

"You picked a hell of an afternoon for a visit," she told him as he waded through calf-high snow to get to her.

When Lance reached the porch, she realized he was dangerously pale. His lips sported a bluish tint, and his brown hair, normally curled and styled to perfection, was hanging limply around his face.

"My c-car stalled out about a m-mile away," he said, his perfect teeth chattering. "I c-couldn't get any r-r-reception on my phone a-and I had to w-walk."

Willa glanced at his feet and grimaced when she saw he was wearing loafers.

"Cripes," she swore. "Get inside."

She didn't even argue when Burk followed them both in. "Take off your shoes and socks," she told Lance. "Go upstairs and get in the shower right now. Bathroom's the second door on the right. The shower only gets lukewarm, but it's probably going to feel scalding to you. I'll get you a towel and something else to wear."

Lance nodded and headed up the stairs—too tired and dazed even to question her logic. Burk turned to Willa the moment he was out of sight.

"Who is that?"

"None of your business. Now *go*."

Burk straightened, towering above her. "I will not leave you here with a strange man."

Willa folded her arms. "He's not a stranger. He's my ex. Now will you please *get out*?"

For a brief moment, Willa almost regretted the ferocity in her tone. Burk's eyes flashed hurt and something else. Regret perhaps. He shook his head.

"I was trying to help," he said. "I can't apologize for trying to save a place I've already saved for years." He looked like he was going to say something more, but stopped in mid-thought. Instead, he grabbed his coat and boots and truck keys, and walked silently away. Willa bolted the door shut behind him and tried to ignore the dull ache in her heart.

* * *

Willa scrounged around while Lance was in the shower, and managed to find two mugs. The microwave had been tossed into the basement, so she could at least plug it in and heat some water. Never mind that she couldn't find the tea. Hot water was better than nothing at all.

She busied herself around the house so she didn't have to answer the nagging voices at the back of her head.

Were she and Burk over?

Were they ever not *over?*

What was Lance doing here?

Did he expect to spend the night?

When she finally heard the water in the bathroom stop, she grabbed the biggest pair of sweatpants she had and a sweatshirt, and left them just outside the door, along with a fresh towel.

"Everything you need is outside the door," she called to Lance. "I'll be downstairs when you're ready."

"All right," came the muffled reply.

There was nowhere to sit downstairs, really, so Willa lowered herself next to the blue table in the living room. Beside her were extra blankets she'd pilfered from the hallway closet, figuring Lance might still need them to warm up. As she listened to her ex puttering around upstairs, she took a deep, calming breath. *Everything is going to be fine*, she told herself, even though her heart was shredded into a million frayed pieces after what had occurred with Burk.

White Pine is not New York, she thought determinedly. *It's all going to work out.*

Except that she'd just been hurt by someone she'd unexpectedly come to care for all over again. If she was honest with herself, then she had to admit there was a part of her that had hoped she and Burk might get close again—maybe even truly be together instead of just screwing around.

She placed her face in her hands. What a fool she'd been. She'd told Burk the truth and he'd tried to take the house from her. If he had to pick, he'd pick the *structure* over her.

The reality made her breathless with hurt.

"Are you all right?"

Willa looked up to see Lance at the foot of the stairs

wearing her gray yoga pants and an oversized white sweatshirt with a heart on the chest.

"I should be asking that of you," she replied, stifling an unexpected grin at his attire. "How are you feeling?"

"Warmer," he said simply, walking toward her. His long, lean legs ate up the space between them in a few steps. He folded himself next to the table, grabbing one of the extra blankets and draping it across them both. Willa scooted away a few inches. She still wasn't sure what Lance was doing there, besides violating the terms of his bond, and she wasn't convinced she was going to let him stay very long.

"That's your water," she said, motioning to the steaming mug on the blue table. He wrapped his hands around it.

"Hot water?"

"It's all I had."

"In that case, thank you."

A moment passed, during which Lance sipped from his mug and took in the roughed floors, the bare light-bulbs, and the bright white plaster. *It must be taking all his willpower not to tell me what a dump I'm living in*, Willa thought. Of course, it was better than a jail cell, which was where he might be headed, so he was in no place to judge.

She studied Lance's aquiline nose, his light brown hair, his lean frame and small chin. It was the same as she'd remembered, and yet so much about Lance was strange to her. She hadn't left him that long ago, but he still seemed like someone she barely even knew anymore.

"You shouldn't be here," she said finally. "If the judge finds out you've left New York, you're going to be in huge trouble."

Lance smiled at her, but there was little warmth in it. "I came to talk. In person."

"About what?" Willa knew she sounded rude, but she didn't feel like sugarcoating anything. It had already been a long day.

"About our situation. About how sorry I am."

"Right. You made that clear."

"I need you," Lance said. "If I get through this, I want you to know, I'll spend my life making this whole mess up to you."

She studied his eyes, a dark so brown they were almost black. Flinty, she used to call them. "Lance, this has to stop. I appreciate it, but you need to go back to New York. I've had enough of guys I can't trust for a while."

Lance's eyes glinted with cold amusement. "Lovers' quarrel earlier, I take it?"

"That's none of your business."

"No, of course not," Lance agreed. But she could still detect the humor in his tone.

He set down his mug and turned to face her fully. "I have insulted you enough, Willa," he said, folding his long, lean fingers together. "You deserve the truth, so I'm not going to beat around the bush here."

She almost sighed with relief. Finally, someone was going to be forthright.

Lance cleared his throat. "I need cash, and I need you to give it to me."

Her mouth nearly fell open. "Excuse me?"

"I'm broke, and I need cash. I will pay you back, even though I realize trusting me on that front will be exquisitely difficult."

Willa could only stare at him.

He continued. "I am going to prison, Willa. It's foolish to think that I won't. I know the outcome of this trial before it's started. We all do. And while I admit that what I did was very, very wrong, I'm not sure I want to be ass-raped for the rest of my life as a result. I admitted my wrongs, and I'm sorry. Truly. But I need to make a new start somewhere. Except I have nothing left with which to do that. So I need your help."

"You want me to give you cash so you can flee the country?"

"In a manner of speaking, yes."

Willa could feel her eyes widen. This guy was unbelievable. "I'm suing you, for crying out loud. I'm listed on the lawsuit. Do you not get that?"

"But I need money. Badly."

"So do I, as it happens. You wiped me out."

"I was trying to help us. I was trying to make more. I was stupid, but not malicious."

"You still lost it."

Lance looked around. "But you still have some funds *somewhere*. I saw a Volvo in the driveway, and you're doing repairs on this house. You must have a honey hole stashed away somewhere. Please, just give me a few grand. That's all I'm asking for."

"No!"

Lance smiled sadly. "You sound so sure."

"You can beg until you're blue," Willa said icily, "but you're not getting a dime from me. In fact, I think you should go before I call the judge and tell him where you are."

Lance's face crumpled in desperation. "If you help me, Willa, I will never forget it. When I'm back on my feet, I'll return the favor. With interest."

"How about you return to me the millions that you *already* stole, and then we'll talk?"

Lance shook his head. "I'm so sorry, and I wish that I could. But I can't. Not now anyway. This is a last-ditch effort to save my skin, and I'm appealing to the love you certainly must still feel for me. I need help. I don't want to die in prison."

Willa set down her mug angrily. "You should have thought about that before you *stole everyone's money*."

Lance stared at her. "I know you must be furious. We had a good life in New York, you and I. Before I fucked it all up. And I am so sorry. For hurting you. If you don't hear anything else I say tonight, at least hear me on that front. I hurt you, and I'm very sorry."

Willa studied his bottomless eyes and grudgingly allowed herself to admit that perhaps he wasn't lying about that. Lance was smooth, but he wasn't prone to sentimental bullshit. Still, Willa skated past it, more interested in getting him out of her house already.

"I need you to go," she said, standing. "I need you to leave and go back to New York before I tell everyone where you are."

Lance stood, too. He stared at her. "Come with me."

"What?"

"When I go, you should come." He waved his hand at the sparse room. "This isn't you. This small town? You're better than this. Fly away with me. Tomorrow, we'll find my rental car and return to the airport. We'll go somewhere warm and remote and beautiful, and you can leave this Podunk holler behind forever."

Willa swallowed. Much as she hated to admit it, there was some honey in Lance's words. The idea of fleeing this impossible situation—with Burk, with the house, with the bank—had its appeal.

But that appeal had nothing to do with Lance. She could never trust him again. And if Willa had learned one thing from her time here, it was that she was *part* of this "Podunk holler" now, and it wasn't so bad. It was time to stop running from her roots, and start embracing them.

"You can sleep on the floor tonight," Willa said finally. "In the morning, I'll take you back to your car. That's all I'm going to do."

Lance grasped her hand with his. His fingers were still icily cold.

"I understand. I appreciate you hearing me out. It's more than I would have done for someone who had hurt me as much as I hurt you."

Willa pulled her hand away. At least she'd gotten a face-to-face apology from his unexpected visit. But now she was ready for the snow to stop so he could be on his way.

"I still love you, Willa. I always will."

She rolled her eyes. "Get some sleep. In the morning you can leave and try to find someone else who cares about your crap."

CHAPTER TWENTY-THREE

Friday, October 12, 7:31 a.m.

Willa spent a restless night, tossing and turning, worrying that the heater would give out, that the pipes would freeze, or that all the fallen snow would collapse the garage in the back of the house, or even the front porch. There was also the gnawing anxiety that Lance would leave his pile of blankets in the living room floor and try to enter her bedroom. She'd latched her door, but she worried that he'd start murmuring more dark words, lacing them with enough sweetness to convince her to do something foolish.

She would never, ever give him money or help him flee the country. But she just didn't trust herself beyond that. She had been so stupid, after all. Naïve in thinking she could start an East Coast B and B in her hometown; ridiculous to think she could ignore her past; ludicrous to think she could rekindle things with Burk.

Willa squeezed her eyes closed.

Something deep inside her ached at the memory of Burk's leaving, his hastily pulled-on clothes rumpled and askew. His truck had rumbled to life with enough noise to jar her heartbeat.

She'd closed the door on him, hating that he was leaving.

But she hated that he would put the house before her even more.

She clutched her pillow, still able to smell Burk's piney scent on the sheets. This time, he'd stayed long enough in bed for his smell to rub off on the fabric, on her skin, on her *heart* if she was honest.

Wrapped in bed with Burk, she'd been stupid enough to believe that he liked her. Cared about her, even.

It was a ridiculous thought. She should have let their relationship end after the first fuck.

Willa wiped away a tear that had found its way down her cheek. She sniffed and sat up. Crying wouldn't do at all. It was time to figure out what was next. And to move forward. Whatever that meant.

"It means I should get dressed," she muttered, pulling on a pair of athletic pants and a sweatshirt. Her whole body ached as if she'd had back-to-back track practices.

When she went downstairs, she found Lance wasn't faring much better. There were dark circles under his eyes, and he moved stiffly. Sleeping on the floor must have left him sore all over. His now dry designer clothes were back on his person, but they were water stained and rumpled from yesterday's adventures in the snow.

"Morning," he said, folding the last of his blankets and stacking them next to the blue table. He tried to smile, but it ended up looking more like a grimace. "You don't happen to have any coffee, do you?"

Willa shook her head. "No. The coffeemaker is all packed away. If we can get the car out, though, we could head down and see if the Rolling Pin is open."

Lance arched a brow. "The Rolling Pin?"

"The coffee is good. So are the donuts."

"I'm sure," he said, in a way that made it clear he wasn't.

Ignoring him, Willa walked to a front window and looked out the wavy glass. The sun was just up, and twinkling on all the fallen snow. She could hear the pluck, pluck of melting snow dripping off the roof. The day was warming already, and with any luck the snow would start to disintegrate in earnest.

She pulled on her new boots, then shrugged on her jacket. "I'm going to see if I can't shovel us out a bit."

Lance placed his hands on his lean hips. His eyes lingered on her functional boots. "You? Are going to shovel? Isn't there someone you can...*hire* to do that?"

Willa nearly laughed out loud. "I'd make your privileged ass do it, but you don't have the right attire. You'll freeze all over again."

Lance poked a cheek with his tongue. "You're seriously going outside?"

"Either I do this, or we're stuck here. Without coffee."

She turned toward the door, but he grabbed her upper arm, stopping her short. She glanced at his long fingers sinking into the fabric of her coat, and felt a prickle of unease.

"Willa," he said smoothly, "please, just stop a minute to look at yourself. Look at what you're *wearing*. Look at what you're doing. It's as if you've been taken hostage by someone else. A stranger."

Willa yanked her arm away. "I have not."

"Those boots? Manual labor? Look, I'm not saying this is a bad life for some people, but this isn't your life." He leaned in, and brushed her cheek with the back of his hand. "Willa, please. *Leave with me.* I'll call the tow truck and get the rental car out. I'll book us tickets. We'll leave today."

She shook her head, wishing Burk could want her half as much as Lance seemed to right now. "Excuse me," she muttered, twisting away from Lance's hand and walking out the front door. She waded into the mounds of snow in her practical boots, and started heaving piles of the stuff away from her car.

When her chest rose and fell with the effort, when her skin burned and her face was streaked with sweat, she was glad. She was grateful to feel anything besides the cold hollow of hurt inside herself.

* * *

The day was heating up into the forties, and the Rolling Pin welcomed customers as the snow puddled into drains, washing down to the Birch River. The coffee was warm and fresh, and they even offered a "snowpocalypse" special: two powdered donuts for the price of one.

Willa ordered the special, eating both donuts in quick succession as she and Lance sat at a small enamel-topped table near the counter. He barely picked at his, but Willa hardly cared if he had an appetite. Let him starve for all it mattered.

Lance called the tow truck as they finished up their coffees, and got the rental delivered back to Willa's house.

"It'll be there soon. We can drive it to the airport together. You and me. And we can leave together."

Willa shook her head. "No. I can't."

"Why's that? Give me one good reason that this town should keep you."

Her overwrought brain worked to formulate an answer. Because of Knots and Bolts and the recipe exchange. Because of the track team. Because of Burk. Because in spite of everything, she was *finding* herself here.

"I belong in White Pine now. I'm not leaving."

Lance frowned. "Is it that man who was in your house last night? Is he keeping you here?"

"No."

"Oh, you never were a good liar, Willa. Tell me, is he a mechanic perhaps? No, wait, a *farmer*?"

"He's my contractor. And my high school boyfriend."

Lance snorted. "Oh God," he said, "you cannot make this stuff *up*. It's too good to be true. And yet you stand here like there isn't more for you in the world. Like there isn't more for us."

"Because there isn't," Willa said, standing. "I'm done listening to you."

Lance followed Willa out and stood by the Volvo as she unlocked the driver's side. When she didn't unlock the passenger side, he tapped on the window. "Hello?"

Willa started the car and cracked the passenger window. "You know what, Lance? I grew up here. This place means something to me, even if it's just a big joke to you. Maybe you can think about that while you walk back to my house and wait for the tow truck. And then think about it some more when you go back to New York and face the consequences of ripping people off. Oh, and I recommend getting some boots from the hardware store before you set out. The walk's likely to be slushy. They open at ten."

Lance's face darkened. "Willa, stop. You can't be seri—"

She pulled away from the curb, leaving him standing there, mouth half open, in a state of shock that had her smiling into the rearview mirror.

* * *

It had felt so good to leave Lance behind that Willa almost didn't notice Pastor Sondheim as she drove past Knots and Bolts. He was peeking in the windows, presumably trying to see if Betty was around.

She pulled the Volvo over and climbed out. "Pastor Sondheim, can I help you?"

He squinted at her in the morning sun, scrunching up his face as if all the light were distasteful and he preferred the snow and cold.

"Is Betty here?" he asked, taking off his knit cap like a gentleman caller.

"Not from the looks of it," Willa said, "but you're more than welcome to come in and wait for her if you want."

Willa knew it was a ballsy move, inviting the pastor into Knots and Bolts like that, but she wanted to think maybe Randall and Betty might be able to kindle the flame flickering between them. Besides, it was much more fun to think about the two of them, versus her own problems with Burk and the house.

"I—I don't know," the pastor stalled.

"Come on," Willa insisted, leading him to the back.

Grabbing the key from the potted plant, she let them both in. Her eyes took a moment to adjust to the dim interior—a stark contrast to the brightening day outside.

"Betty?" she called, not entirely surprised when she didn't get an answer. Most likely Betty was running errands, probably shipping some vintage Halloween gear at the post office. It wasn't as if the morning after a huge snowstorm was a big time for fabric purchases, after all. That is, unless you were Randall Sondheim.

She flicked on some lights and peeled off her coat. In the kitchenette, she started water for tea. "Hope herbal is okay; it's all we have," she said.

The pastor stood there, his thick brown eyebrows drawing together like fuzzy caterpillars, his rounded shoulders hunching even more. He hadn't even taken off his coat.

Willa thought he was probably wondering about the propriety of the situation. If Betty were here, no one would question them being alone together because it was her place of business. Willa, on the other hand, was an unknown.

He studied her with his piercing gray eyes. "You're friends with Betty, then?"

"I'd like to think so."

"You know her pretty well?"

"We went to high school together," she said, "but there was a long period when we didn't see each other. You could say we're getting reacquainted."

"But you could—you know her, ah, preferences?"

It dawned on Willa that the good pastor was after intel on her friend. "You'd better come in if you want to *really* talk about this, Pastor Sondheim."

With barely a nod, he replied, "Call me Randall," and shrugged off his coat.

He relaxed just slightly as Willa poured the tea. "The table is red," he observed, and she fought the urge to giggle. How did this man think he was going to keep up with *Betty*? Then again, she thought, gesturing for him to take a seat, maybe it was about putting together two complementary personalities instead of those that were exactly alike. The pastor would certainly provide a quieter balance to Betty's outspoken ways, which might not be a bad thing. Maybe Randall could even exert some influence on her.

She caught him opening up a cupboard filled with booze, then closing it quickly.

Once their mugs were filled, Willa took a seat across from him. "So you're interested in Betty?"

He shifted, his thin lips pressing together so much they almost disappeared. His manners were octogenarian-like, making him seem ancient. Yet with a full head of hair and high cheekbones, Randall wasn't unattractive. In fact, if it weren't for his slumped posture and his dowdy disposition, he might actually be okay looking.

"I was, uh, hoping Betty and I could get to know each other, um, better, yes," he stumbled.

"Does she know you're into her?"

He took a nervous sip of tea. "I don't—I haven't declared my intentions, no."

Willa smiled. "Well, it's not the 1800s. You don't have to court her formally and fill out her dance card. But if she thinks you keep coming into her store for fabric for your chair, you might want to tell her that it's not exactly a bolt of cloth you're after."

The pastor's face reddened. He concentrated on dunking his tea bag into his water, over and over. "It's certainly difficult," he said, not looking at Willa. "I'm not sure I'm her type."

"Betty's a pistol, it's true, but hopefully that's what you like about her. She's certainly straight to the point."

At this, the pastor's gray eyes found hers. "It's remarkable," he said, "her forthrightness. I've never met anyone with such a gift for being frank. It's terribly admirable. It's forced me to—well, as you can imagine, I'm not much of a suitor. But I am compelled to pursue her. I just lack the, ah, refinement for the process."

Willa felt a surge of sympathy for the poor pastor. He was attracted to Betty for the things that made her Betty, and she couldn't fault him for that.

"All right," she said, "it's show time. Are you ready?"

The pastor blinked. "You think I should take her to a show? Perhaps a play of some sort?"

Willa laughed. "No, no. It's just an expression. Show time? Like, the curtain is—oh, never mind. Look, I think the fastest way to Betty's heart is by being as honest with her as she is with everyone else. I think she respects that. So the next time you see her, you can't beat around the bush. You have to be straightforward. Practice it if you have to, but say something like, 'Betty Lindholm, I like you and I want to take you out on a date. I think next Friday night is perfect. What do you say?' And then go from there."

Randall didn't look so sure. "Maybe this is all a terrible idea. Perhaps I'm just not meant to date anyone."

Willa folded her arms. "Are you required to be celibate?"

"No, of course not. I'm Lutheran, not Catholic."

"Then stop putting up roadblocks. She might say no, it's true, but you should try. You seem like a decent guy. And Betty's watching way too much *Law & Order* these days. You could get her out of the house."

For a moment, there was the hint of a smile at the corners of the pastor's mouth, then it vanished. "Well, you know what the Bible says."

"Go forth and multiply?"

"I was thinking more along the lines of, 'You have not because you ask not.'"

"Oh. Right."

Randall pushed his chair back from the table. "You've been very helpful. I appreciate it. It's not always easy for me to talk with people, but you've made this very enjoyable." He drank the last of his tea, then stood.

Willa walked him to the door. "It's a funny profession to be in," she said after he'd pulled his coat back on, "being a pastor, I mean. Especially when talking to people isn't your thing."

He nodded. "It's true. I often don't feel qualified to do what I'm doing, but I can't seem to escape my calling. I'm better at the pulpit than in person, I think. And no matter what, I have it easier than Moses."

"Why, what was his deal?"

The pastor surprised her by smiling fully. She caught a glimpse of his teeth, of all things.

"Moses was a stutterer," he said. "I'm grateful not to have a speech impediment on top of all my other deficiencies." With a last nod, he pulled on his cap, and stepped back into the bright afternoon.

Willa closed the door behind him, laughing to herself.

If the pastor did ask Betty out, she had no doubt the Knots and Bolts crew would hear about it at length. Betty would tell them all in her no-nonsense way, and probably have them wheezing with laughter within minutes.

She was already looking forward to it.

CHAPTER TWENTY-FOUR

Friday, October 12, 6:02 p.m.

Anna opened the door, took one look at Burk's face, and dropped the towel she was holding.

"What's *wrong*?" she asked, pulling him through the doorway. Inside her home, it smelled like fresh bread, chocolate, and warm spices. No doubt Anna was getting the meal pulled together for tonight, without the faintest idea of what had transpired with Willa the day before.

"I have to talk to you," he said as she led him to the kitchen. Juniper was at the table, coloring, until she caught sight of her uncle.

"Burby!" she cried, opening her chubby arms for a hug. Even in his wretched state, Burk still smiled at her nickname for him. His heart stirred at the sight of his niece's round cheeks and her delighted smile. He gave her a squeeze, pausing to take in the scent of her hair and skin. It was a precious smell, sweet enough to give his aching insides a brief respite.

He set her down, but she pounded on his outer thigh. "Horsey!" she demanded.

Burk looked at his sister. "Um, I think we'd better get Sam in here. And maybe let Juniper watch a princess movie or something."

At the word *princess*, Juniper's ears perked up. "Ariel!" she cried, for *The Little Mermaid*.

Anna nodded. "Come on, babe," she said, taking Juniper's tiny hand. "We're going to break all the rules and let you watch a movie before dinner. How do you like that?"

Juniper giggled, and Anna got her set up in the next room, calling for Sam as she did so. Her husband came into the kitchen, and grasped Burk's strong hand with his own.

"Heya, Burk," he said, grinning his lopsided smile. The men had been friends ever since Anna had introduced Sam to the family, and Burk had always liked his brother-in-law. He appreciated Sam's passion for classic rock, liked that he held a steady job as an IT professional over at the hospital, and was flattered that he seemed to look up to Burk like a big brother.

But most of all, he knew how deeply Sam loved Anna. And for that, Sam could be a garbage man with halitosis and Burk wouldn't care, so long as Anna was happy.

"What's going on?" Sam asked, pushing his floppy brown hair away from his forehead.

"I'd better wait to tell you and Anna together."

"Sounds serious. Is it beer serious?"

"This might be whiskey serious."

"Uh-oh," Sam replied. "Beer and a bump, then." He got a bottle of whiskey down from the cupboard above the fridge, poured them each a shot, and opened two beers. They'd just downed the shot at the counter, grimaces still on their faces, when Anna returned to the kitchen.

"It's *whiskey* serious?" she asked, studying them both. "Good Lord. Pour me one, then."

She did her shot, grabbed her own beer, and then the three of them settled themselves at the kitchen table.

"All right, Burk," Anna said, her cheeks already pink from the warmth of the whiskey, "you have forty minutes before Willa arrives for dinner. So spill it."

"Well, that's the thing," Burk said, taking a deep breath. "I'm not sure she's coming. We had a falling-out and I don't know what to do."

Sam reached over and covered his wife's hand absently. It was a small thing, a tiny gesture, but it started a dull press behind Burk's sternum. For the first time, he longed for something like what Anna and Sam had. Something steady, something real—not the series of one-night stands he'd cultivated for the past twelve years.

He'd been so close to it with Willa. He'd tasted it, sensed it was within his grasp. And then he'd thrown it away.

"Falling-out?" Anna asked. "What do you mean? Like, a fight?"

"A big fight," Burk replied, taking another swig of his beer.

Anna searched his face. "Is this about the house? Did you do something stupid?"

Leave it to his sister to cut to the chase. He nodded, staring at the polished wood of their kitchen table. "She told me she'd hit a financial bump with the house, and I offered to buy it from her. Again."

"Well, that's not so bad," Sam offered. "It's a big project."

"It's just—I don't think she was telling me so I'd take it off her hands. I think she was…confiding in me. That is, she told me when we were together."

"When you were *together* together?" Anna asked, eyebrows raised.

"Yes," Burk said, suddenly overcome with the memory of Willa's skin against his, the soft brush of her hair against his shoulder, the way her nipples had hardened as he traced a line from her throat to the plunge between her breasts.

"She was explaining how she had to put everything on hold until she could get more cash together," Burk said, pushing away the vivid images. "And I told her maybe the B and B wasn't such a good idea right now, and she should probably sell the house."

Anna groaned. "You said this while you were in bed? Jesus, Burk. I mean, there's stupid, and then there's that."

"Okay, okay, hold on," Sam insisted. "It's not *that* bad. Even if Burk picked the wrong time to offer to buy the place, he was still trying to help. Right?"

Anna's mouth hardened. "Maybe, but think about it from Willa's perspective. She lets Burk in on the reality of her situation, and Burk tries to turn it around to his benefit." She faced her brother fully. "What's more, you belittled her dream. You *have* to realize she is considering the possibility that you only slept with her to try and change her mind about the house, right? I'm trusting that it wasn't your motivation, even though at this point I'm not—"

"It wasn't," Burk interrupted. "I swear, it wasn't."

Acid churned inside him as he realized the full weight of what a fool he'd been. He'd had Willa *right there* in his arms, but even still his lust had been for the house. He'd wanted it for so long that when the possibility of having it was in front of him, he couldn't help trying to get it. He'd put wanting a structure above wanting her.

And he regretted it with everything he had.

"I need to tell her I don't want the house," Burk said. "I need to tell her things have changed."

Anna and Sam shared a glance.

"Changed how?" Anna asked.

"Well, you know. How things can change. With people."

"If you want our help, Burk, we can't beat around the bush here. Changed *how*?"

Burk searched for the right words. How could he explain to them that his mind burned every day with the collages that Willa had made? How could he tell them that she'd taken a bricks-and-mortar project he'd been obsessed with and turned it into something more? She'd added charm and warmth to all his plans—a thousand touches that he could never have known he wanted—and made his house a *home*. Even if she agreed to sell it, the weight of the truth had hit him this afternoon: He wouldn't want to be there without her.

Yesterday, when he'd finally allowed himself to crack the door to his emotions toward Willa, his feelings had completely overtaken him. The door had flown open, had torn off its hinges, and was lying somewhere at the bottom of his heart, splintered and broken. And there was simply no way to close it again.

"Wait, do you *love* her?" Anna asked, her eyes impossibly wide.

Love. He'd felt it once for Willa. Was it so impossible for him to feel it again?

The house only worked if he was in it with her. That wasn't love, was it?

No, that was living together. And living together didn't mean marriage or a family, though suddenly his chest hurt all over again with the thought of little girls like Juniper running around, only with Willa's sparkling green eyes.

He shook his head. "I don't know. I can't think about that right now."

Anna's face softened. "How can we help?"

"Tell me what to do," Burk replied, his eyes locking on to his sister's. "Tell me how to fix this."

Sam sat back in his chair. "I'm no expert, but have you tried apologizing?"

Burk opened his mouth, then closed it. He tried to think back to yesterday afternoon—to shouting and putting his clothes on in the snow and the fury he felt when her ex had shown up. There was no apologizing in all that tumult.

"I didn't," he answered finally.

"Well, it's a good start," Anna said. "It also wouldn't hurt to tell her how you feel. Even if you say it's not love, you must feel *something* for her, or you wouldn't be here, drinking and looking like a lost basset hound."

Anna gave him a small, amused smile, as if part of her was tickled by this whole thing. He brushed past it. She could laugh at him all she wanted, if she helped get him back in Willa's good graces.

A timer on the stove dinged, and Anna stood up to pull her chicken potpie out of the oven. The golden, flaky crust steamed with the rich contents underneath.

"Such a shame," Anna said, placing her hot pads on the counter. "All this food and not enough people to eat it."

Burk glanced at the clock. It was five minutes past seven. Willa wasn't coming.

Not that he was surprised. Why would she? Burk had screwed up, her ex was back, and she'd told him never to set foot in her house again.

"Maybe I should let you two munch on this," Anna said thoughtfully, "while I call an emergency meeting of the Knots and Bolts crew."

"An emergency meeting?" Burk asked. "What are you, a league of superheroes?"

Anna squared her shoulders. "We're a league of women who care for one another," she said crisply, "and I imagine Willa's feeling pretty low right now. She might need some *support*."

"Oh," Burk said, feeling foolish. "That makes sense."

"It does," Anna said, "and if you were using your brain, you'd realize that I could put in a good word for you if I saw her tonight."

Burk sighed. No one could ever accuse him of being... intuitive.

"You guys hold down the fort," Anna said, pulling out her cell. "I'm off to Knots and Bolts. I'll see you later."

Burk watched his sister go, feeling a mix of hopefulness and helplessness he couldn't quite reconcile.

CHAPTER TWENTY-FIVE

Friday, October 12, 10:04 p.m.

*W*illa checked her phone as she climbed into her car, getting ready to head down to Knots and Bolts. She had three missed calls and six missed texts from Lance.

Have rental again.

Getting ready to leave. You can still come with me.

I need you.

Why can't you help me?

You're being a bitch.

Goddamn it.

Willa closed her eyes, wondering if she should contact the New York authorities. Lance needed to leave, and having him around was starting to unnerve her. She took a deep breath, resolving to turn him in if he tried to contact her again. In the meantime, she sent him one final message:

It's over. Go home.

Throwing her car into Drive, she pulled out into the dark night.

* * *

Anna's cell beeped as she hunted around for the key in the pot outside Knots and Bolts.

"Here," she said, handing the device to Willa, "can you see who it is?"

Willa took the phone, marveling at how putting *EKB* (Emergency Knots and Bolts) in front of a text to these women meant everyone dropped what they were doing and came downtown.

"Steph's on her way," Willa said, drawing her coat more closely around her. Though the day had been warm and most of the snow had melted away, a fall chill had returned, cutting through all of Willa's layers.

"Got it!" Anna said triumphantly, opening the back door and flicking on the lights. Willa was instantly warmed by the homey furniture, the friendly rugs, and the lingering smells from past recipe exchanges. No matter that she was still a little muddled about why she was here in the first place. She thought Anna might be irritated she'd missed the dinner, but not only was Anna *not* irritated, she suddenly wanted to hang out.

Anna's phone beeped again, and Willa handed it back to her. "Audrey and Betty are on their way," Anna said, her cheeks still pink from outside. Not even the miserable cold could keep these ladies away, Willa realized.

Willa sat in a painted purple chair, suddenly bone tired. "I don't know why we're doing this," she said, rubbing her neck. "It's nice to want to get everyone together, but it seems a little odd."

"It's never odd to get friends together," Anna said, finding a bottle of Chianti and uncorking it. She got two glasses from the kitchenette and set one down in front of Willa. "Besides, Burk told me about what happened between you two. I figured you could use some cheering up."

Willa gazed at the table, wondering exactly how much Burk had confessed to his sister. She pictured his strong chest, the tangle of their limbs in bed, and blushed involuntarily. She hoped he hadn't told Anna *that*.

Anna raised her glass, the Chianti swirling in deep maroons and violets, and toasted Willa. "To you, for not slugging Burk when he pissed all over your B and B idea. I don't know if I could have restrained myself."

Willa smiled slightly, clinking glasses. Whatever Burk had said, it had certainly backfired with his sister.

"He may have a point, though," Willa said after taking a sip. "About the house, I mean. Maybe I did bite off more than I could chew with this B and B idea, you know? Maybe I should just sell."

"Oh, no, you're not out of the game yet," Anna said. "The bank will help you if you get your ducks in a row. And if you have a strong business plan, you can be profitable. You just have to be smart about it."

Willa shook her head, her heart renewing its ache. "But in the end, maybe Burk really should have the house. He has cared for it all this time. What if I'm just being stubborn and keeping a good man from what should be his?"

Anna placed a warm hand over Willa's. "Maybe he hasn't wanted the house as much as he thinks. Maybe he just wants the *feelings* that are connected to the place. I mean, think about it, Willa. Of all the houses in White Pine, he fixates on that one? It was always a question lingering in the back of my mind—why Willa's house?—but once you came back, it was answered for certain. He still cares about you."

Willa waved the words away. "No. He made it clear today that he only cares about the house. He'd rather have the structure than me. And maybe I should just *let* him have it."

Anna shook her head. "Don't give up yet. You deserve your dream B and B and a man who cares about you. And you can have both."

Willa lowered her eyes, embarrassed at the tears pooling. She wanted so much to believe that was true. But the idea of having it all seemed so far away—so impossibly remote.

Anna squeezed her hand just as the back door flew open. Audrey and Betty stomped in, their eyes bright with worry.

"Somebody better be dying," Betty said, "because I was in the middle of a *Law & Order* marathon."

"Your television can wait," Anna replied dryly. "This is more important."

"I'll be the judge of that," Betty said, shrugging off her coat and grabbing more glasses from the kitchenette. She squinted at the Chianti bottle before pouring for Audrey and herself. "At least somebody brought the good stuff."

"Leftover from the ex's collection, I think," Anna said.

Willa nodded. "Definitely. This was a varietal we picked up in a vineyard on the Tyrrhenian Sea."

"Where's that?"

"Tuscany."

"Fancy," Betty said, taking a large swallow.

Audrey didn't touch her glass. "What's going on?" she

asked, her brown eyes darting from Willa to Anna. "Is everything okay?"

"It's fine," Anna said. "My brother's just being an ass, and we need to help our friend. Once Stephanie gets here, I'll explain everything."

As if on cue, the back door opened one last time, and Stephanie scurried in. "Sorry I'm late," she said breathlessly. "The twins didn't want to go down without a fight. Not that that's anything new."

"Pour yourself a glass of the good stuff and take a load off," Betty said. "We just got here ourselves."

"I hope everything's okay," Stephanie said, peeling off her layers and joining them at the table. Her red hair was a disarrayed halo around her porcelain face. "I can't remember the last time we had an emergency recipe exchange meeting."

"Oh, I can," Betty said. "It was when Audrey here got her heart broken by that bike rider. What was his name?"

"Kieran Callaghan," Audrey muttered, her eyes fixed solidly on her wineglass. Willa had never seen her look so glum. It must be the man Audrey mentioned the other day—the one who left her after two weeks.

"The Irish asshat," Betty said.

"What happened?" Willa asked, wondering at the hurt that sagged Audrey's normally bright features.

"I was a fool," Audrey said, her high cheekbones coloring. "I believed Kieran loved me. But he was just messing around."

Betty scoffed. "He had us all fooled. And it's hard to pull one over on me."

"He was very handsome," Stephanie said. "That's probably what distracted us."

Betty pushed an errant blond curl away from her face. "It didn't help that he rode around on that Harley like some kind of Celtic god."

Willa giggled at the image.

"He was superhot," Anna said. "Audrey liked to go on and on about what a handsome stud he was."

"I did not," Audrey protested, but a scarlet flush along her neck betrayed the truth.

"She loved to tell us how she'd kiss the Blarney Stone," Anna continued. "Only I think Audrey called it the Blarney *Bone*, after they did it."

Willa snorted, and Stephanie stared into her wineglass, trying not to lose it. Audrey frowned at all of them, but her eyes sparkled with laughter.

"His good luck charm was his four-leaf boner," Betty grinned.

Willa let out a full-blown laugh at this. She tried to cover it up, but the others had already joined her.

"There was a pot of gold at the end of his rain*bone*," Anna chimed in.

At this, the whole group collapsed into helpless peals. Willa laughed until her sides hurt, until she couldn't see or breathe. When she could finally sit up straight, she felt as if an enormous weight had been lifted from her shoulders.

Eventually, she was able to collect herself enough to speak. "I needed that," she said, raising her glass to toast the group. "Here's to Audrey's awful choices in men."

"Hear, hear," Stephanie agreed, taking a swallow.

"What the hell," Audrey said, grinning. She joined them in the toast. But when they'd all had a drink, Audrey's face turned serious once again.

"As much as I *love* reliving the old days of Kieran Callaghan, can someone tell me why we're here? Is everything okay?"

"It's fine," Anna said, sitting up a little straighter. "At least it's going to be once we're done here. As it turns out, my older brother has been a jackass, and now Willa's doubting whether she should keep the house and turn it into a B and B. I thought we could all help her out."

Betty's forehead wrinkled. "I'm sorry, but I have no idea how to finish a remodel. This may be out of our league."

"Not like that," Anna said. "In *other* ways. Like baking her a pie and reminding her that she's got what it takes to succeed."

"Oh," Betty replied, drumming her fingers on the table. "Well, we *were* going to go over some business plans before the snowstorm got in our way. We could do that tonight, Willa, if you want."

"And I can still teach you how to make hot dish," Audrey offered.

"I can do my impression of my twins accidentally eating lemon slices," Stephanie said. "It's guaranteed to cheer you up."

Willa shook her head, unsure how to explain that it wasn't just her dream of starting the B and B that seemed so suddenly tenuous. It was her dream of rekindling things with Burk. She wanted so much to escape this feeling of helplessness. Of not being in control.

Of being in love.

"Aw, shit," Betty said, studying her. "You're not just busted up about the B and B; you're busted up about Burk. You went and fell for him."

Willa tried to argue, but found she couldn't. She wouldn't lie to her friends.

"Really?" Anna asked after a moment. "You love him?"

Willa couldn't be sure anymore. She was so tired, and she didn't know if she could trust anything she was feeling. "If I do, I shouldn't," was all she could bring herself to say.

"But this is *not* the end of the road," Anna protested. "Trust me, I know my brother. Ladies, has Burk Olmstead ever loved a single woman since Willa?"

"No," they chorused, clinking their glasses.

"And haven't you all thought it was odd that he kept up the house where she used to live?"

"Yes," they chorused again.

Anna was really getting whipped up now. "So don't throw your dreams away yet. This isn't over."

Willa was so overwhelmed with the outpouring of support, she found she could hardly speak. When her throat was finally working again, she could only utter a simple "Thank you."

"Don't say thank you," Betty said. "Say that Stephanie has to do that impression of her twins eating lemons, and crack up before we get to work here."

Next thing they knew, Stephanie was stuffing apple slices in her face to mimic her twins' lemon debacle, and the Knots and Bolts crew was laughing so hard, they were holding their sides. Betty's mascara ran down her face in black tracks and Audrey laugh-snorted so much, Willa thought she might never recover.

And amid the giggles and guffaws, Willa felt something else, too. It took her a while to place exactly what it was, but then, suddenly, she knew.

It was hope.

* * *

It was after two o'clock in the morning when Willa finally made it home. She struggled out of her Volvo, not only because she was weary, but because she was carrying a heavy glass dish filled with warm casserole and a manila file folder with the draft of a business plan inside.

While the business plan had been all numbers and columns—with Betty using Knots and Bolts as the blueprint for how to do things—the hot dish had been a much more creative endeavor. As a group, they'd filed into the kitchen to see what odds and ends they could throw together. "This is the best kind of hot dish," Audrey said. "You don't necessarily have a recipe. You just see what's there, and try to be creative. It'll totally work for the B and B because you'll figure out a way to feed your guests no matter what you have on hand."

"Sometimes more successfully than other times," Stephanie said, smiling. "I made a chicken, Brussels sprouts, and curry hot dish that my husband still talks about. And not because it was good."

They'd chopped up an onion, with Anna teaching her to sauté it on the stove in a bit of butter until it caramelized. Then, they'd mixed it with some wild rice they'd found. "I'm not sure how old that is," Betty had admitted when they'd boiled it up. They added some frozen broccoli—brushing off the frostbite—and pulled it all together with heaps of cheddar cheese.

"That's pretty much the secret," Betty said, watching Willa grate until her arm was sore. "Cheese. Tons of it."

While the hot dish had baked, the women had opened another bottle of wine—this time a cabernet from France—

and talked until the timer dinged. Willa thought they'd all get out forks and taste it, but Betty had insisted Willa take it home intact.

"You're going to need it more than we will," she said, bundling back into her coat.

Now, Willa realized she had no refrigerator in which she could put the casserole. She supposed she could always pack it in some of the remaining snow on the back deck, and pray the raccoons didn't get it.

As she climbed up the steps to her dark, empty house, she fought a pang of longing. She'd so badly wanted to see the whole thing completed and renovated. She'd wanted to serve margaritas on the porch in the summer and plant flowers along the front walk. She'd wanted to have bonfires in the backyard, handing out s'mores to guests. With Burk's help, she'd wanted to transform the whole place. She still could, but she'd have to finish her business plan first, and then find a new contractor if things didn't work out with Burk.

It's all doable, she told herself. She lifted her chin and thought about her friends, the way they'd helped her tonight. With this much support behind her, there was no way she'd fail.

Willa was fumbling for her keys, trying to balance the hot dish, when a sudden throat clearing startled her. She jerked to attention, and the hot dish tilted out of her arms. It shattered on the porch's frozen boards, sending steaming casserole and broken glass everywhere. Willa gave a startled cry.

"I'm sorry to alarm you," Lance murmured, stepping forward out of the shadows on the porch's edge. "But I couldn't leave without seeing you again."

Instinctively, she took a step back. "What are you doing here?" she asked, her heart hammering at Lance's steady advance. She could perceive a glint in his eyes, even in the deep night.

"I'm here to get you to change your mind about helping me," he said, reaching into his pocket. Was there some kind of weapon in there? Willa wondered. She felt her whole body begin to tremble.

"Please, open your door, and we'll go inside and talk."

Willa stopped cold. Her mind raced. There was a look on Lance's face she'd never seen before. *Desperation*, she realized. If she went in that house with him, no good would come out of it. But what else could she do?

There was only one alternative.

She reached a foot out, as if stepping forward, then turned at the last minute and bolted down the front steps. "Help!" she screamed into the night as she raced toward her car. Her hands shook violently as she tried to press the panic button on her keys.

She'd almost reached the car when her heeled shoes hit a patch of ice and flew out from under her. The air whooshed from her lungs as she landed hard on the concrete. Bright light exploded in front of her eyes.

And then everything went black.

CHAPTER TWENTY-SIX

Saturday, October 13, 3:36 a.m.

*B*urk twisted in his sheets, hoping to find a comfortable position but knowing it was useless. Sleep was never going to come. Not until he talked to Willa anyway.

He sat up and raked a hand through his hair. The red lights on his bedside alarm clock told him it was too late—or too early—to go over to her house. But he suddenly didn't feel like he could wait. He had to talk to her.

He'd lain in bed with her and made a house more important than her. More important than her dreams and her feelings, even. What an ass he was.

He got out of bed and pulled on his shirt and jeans. In the early-morning darkness, his brain was as tangled as his sheets.

She'd told him the reality of her situation, and he'd tried to use it to his advantage. Really, he should have taken her face in his hands and kissed her senseless. He should have told her the house didn't matter to him—not without her in it. Why he hadn't was beyond his own logic.

If he could do it over again, he'd tell her to forget about paying him. He'd tell her that he'd finish the project for free if it meant she'd realize how much he cared about her. He'd take her lips in his mouth, suck on them, and run his tongue over their dewy sweetness. And that was only the beginning.

Instead, he'd acted like a jerk. He'd prioritized a structure over her heart.

Because the alternative was...what?

His heart hammered recklessly.

The alternative was feeling more for Willa Masterson than he had for any woman. The alternative was letting every emotion he had for her course through him, unabated, until he was consumed. Overtaken. Swept under with feelings that had never really gone away since high school. And now he had the chance to feel them anew—and even more deeply.

The prospect was terrifying. If he let himself love her, Willa Masterson could wreck him all over again.

But the alternative was worse.

If he didn't let himself love her, he'd wreck himself.

Burk strode to the front door, pulling on his workman's boots. He had to tell Willa how he felt. And he had to apologize. He didn't care what time it was.

He didn't care if he had to pound on her door for hours, or climb up the back trellis, or wait on the front steps until the first pale streaks of dawn lit the sky. It didn't matter anymore. Willa had left White Pine once, taking his heart with her.

He'd be damned if he was going to give her any reason to leave again.

In fact, he was going to give her a reason to stay.

* * *

Willa awoke to a pounding head and burning arms. She tried to move and immediately discovered the reason for the pain in her extremities: Her hands had been bound to a chair.

Panic surged through her as she recalled Lance and the confrontation on the porch. A release of adrenaline helped clear away her fog of unconsciousness. Her mind sharpened; her thoughts crystallized in spite of the pain at the back of her head. She held perfectly still, trying to see around her. Trying to put together what had happened.

She'd fled. Slipped. Lance must have carried her somewhere. But where?

Willa squinted in the darkness, trying to see. She saw a tiny orange light close to the floor, and tried to make sense of it. She wasn't cold, so she couldn't be outside. She had to be indoors and—

The water heater! It dawned on her suddenly that she was staring at the base of the tank. The orange glow was the flame from the pilot light. She was in her own basement.

Her ears strained for the sound of footsteps, but everything was silent all around her. She wiggled slightly, testing the bonds at her hands, but they held fast. She closed her eyes, trying to picture the basement. Was there a tool anywhere she could grasp and use to free herself? Could she scoot her chair to any part of the room and—

"I can hear you thinking." Willa's head snapped up at the sound of Lance's voice. He was in the room with her, but she couldn't see him.

"Your breathing always gets deeper when you're trying to puzzle something out." He clicked on a flashlight from a few feet away. Willa shuddered at how near he'd been, and she hadn't even realized it. The flashlight beam illuminated his face in an eerie play of light and shadow. His eyes looked hollow. His face seemed gaunt.

"I'm sorry I had to tie you up," Lance said, taking a step toward her. "I truly am. This hasn't gone at all like I'd hoped. It's rather—barbaric. I'm hoping we can do away with the drama and just talk. You and me."

Willa locked her lips together and nodded, even as cold dread seeped into every muscle. The same look of desperation she'd seen on the front porch was beginning to creep back into his face.

"Lance," she whispered, "what is happening? What's so bad that you have to tie me up in a basement?" She pleaded for a glimmer of her old lover to emerge—the same one who had once rubbed aloe into her back when she'd been badly sunburned in Mexico.

"I told you, Willa," he said, a cold finger reaching out to trace her cheek. She shuddered at his touch. "I am on the cusp of losing everything. Of going to *prison*. So I'm going to need you to help me."

"I will help you. I *will*. But you need to untie me."

Lance nodded. "I know." He knelt in front of her so she was eye to eye with his black pupils, his aquiline nose, "Except not just yet. You see, I tried to give you a rational way to fix this. You give me cash; I leave and start a new life somewhere else. But since you shunned my offer, and then tried to run away from me on the porch, we're moving to Plan B."

He sat back on his heels. As he spoke, Willa tried her hand restraints again, desperately trying to loosen them with subtle movements he wouldn't notice. They were tied tightly, but she could feel them sliding back and forth. He'd tied her too close to the edge of the chair, she realized suddenly. If she worked them a bit more, she might be able to slide them off the end of the armrest completely.

"Are you all right? Do you need some water or anything?"

Water? She shook her head, wondering how Lance could be so polite and so ruthless at the same time. She supposed it was the dichotomy that had allowed him to steal from people and justify it somehow.

"I'm—I'm fine," she said quietly. "Just please think about what you're doing here. You don't want to get into more trouble than you're in already. If you let me go now, I won't say anything. You can head back to New York and we can pretend like this never happened."

"I would love that," Lance said, his face dark with something like remorse, "but it's just not possible."

Willa tested the ropes once more as he turned his back and continued his pacing.

She was almost there.

"I'm not an unreasonable man, Willa, but I need money. And I'm not going to leave until you give it to me."

Willa licked her lips, inching the ropes farther once more. "How much do you want?"

"Sadly, as much as you have. I know it must seem so unfair for me to take what you have left, but it's the only way." Willa's pulse hammered in her neck. "I have a Swiss bank that will accept the transfer you're going to make in my name. Right now."

He turned his back, reaching for a bag. He was getting his laptop, Willa realized. His attention diverted, she moved quickly. She pushed her wrists forward with all the strength she had, willing the rope to stretch and fall off the end of the chair. Twisting and inching, she finally set one hand free, then the other. She dropped them back into place, unmoving, just as Lance turned back around.

"I'll need the name of your banking institution," he said as the laptop powered to life. "The one you so cleverly hid from me. I have to hand it to you, I never once thought you still had any money in this town."

The basement was suddenly illuminated with the computer screen's eerie blue glow. "And of course, I'll need your passwords." He typed a few keystrokes. Then he looked up at her.

Willa froze. She couldn't run away while he was just *staring* at her. And even if she did, there was no guarantee she could get away to safety. If she fled again, would he hurt her?

The desperate look on his face told her anything was possible at this point.

Which meant only one thing. She had to bring him closer.

Dropping her eyes, she mumbled the name of her bank. He scowled, the shadows above his eyes like horns in the light. "What was that?"

She mumbled the name of the bank again, more quietly this time. Shoving the laptop to the side, Lance stood and towered over her. "You need to speak up," he said, his voice hard with frustration.

"I'll whisper it to you," she said quietly.

Lance exhaled, then dropped his head even closer. "All right. What is it?"

She could feel his breath on her skin, he was so close. Quaking with fear, she summoned all her courage and grasped his face in her hands. His eyes widened as he realized she was free. Before he could pull away, she laced her hands in his hair and pulled downward with all her might. His forehead smacked the arm of the chair.

He groaned in shock and pain. Not wasting any time, Willa bolted from the chair. Behind her, Lance lurched and grabbed for her. He caught her lower leg and she went down hard, cracking her jaw on the basement's cement.

White stars crackled briefly in her vision. She shook her head and kicked with all her strength. She connected with something, though she wasn't sure what. Lance howled as she scrambled to her feet, fleeing up the stairs. Her chest was heaving, her adrenaline racing. She ran through the dining room and into the living room. She glanced at the front door, knowing she should *get out of the house now*, but uncertain if she'd make it any farther than she had last time. Her shoes were gone. The neighborhood was quiet. Who would she run to for help, assuming she could make it anywhere in the cold?

No. If she was going to get out of this, it was going to be by her own doing.

Vomit threatened the back of her throat, but she pushed it down. *Think*, she demanded. Glancing around, she picked up the only thing she could find—the blue table. It was heavier than she realized, and awkward. She placed herself at the corner where the living room met the dining room, and waited.

Moments later, Lance was hurtling through the house, swearing and crying. "Why are you doing this? Don't make me hurt you. I just need you to help me." She braced herself as he rounded the corner. This was it.

Just as he came into sight, she mustered all her strength and swung the table as hard as she could. It collided with his face. There was a sickening thud, and splintered wood flew in all directions. Lance stepped back, his nose smashed and bleeding, his dark eyes startled and shocked. And then he crumpled to the floor.

Willa barely had time to process the fact that he was unconscious when she heard a thump upstairs. There was more thundering as someone else raced toward her. Her stomach roiled with the sickening realization. *Lance had company.* He wasn't acting alone.

Panicked, she grabbed thickest piece of wood she could find, and sprinted toward the door. "I'm armed!" she cried as she fumbled with the latch. She was out of options—she had to run. She'd just managed to yank the ancient wooden thing open when someone grabbed her from behind. She wheeled around, eyes wide, arm poised to strike, when a familiar hand stayed her wrist.

"Willa! Stop! It's me."

The sound of Burk Olmstead's voice washed over her. She reared back, disbelieving that he was actually there, in her home. But no—his storming eyes were blazing into hers, his massive chest heaving with confusion.

"I heard shouting. What happened?"

Willa dropped the wood. Her whole body began to

tremble. She jerked her head in the direction of Lance's still body.

"I need you to tie him up."

Burk's face went white. "What in holy hell?" He released her and flipped on a light switch. She blinked in the brightness.

He looked from Willa to the unconscious form of Lance, back to Willa. "Did he try to hurt you? Did he—did he do that to your *face*?"

Lance stirred and Willa strode past Burk to give him a hard kick. Lance didn't move again.

"I'll explain later," Willa said. "Tie him up. *Now*. I need to call the police."

CHAPTER TWENTY-SEVEN

Saturday, October 13, 6:51 a.m.

 $\mathcal{B}$ urk placed a cup of hot coffee in Willa's trembling hands and watched as she drew a deep breath. As she steeled herself to answer still more questions from the Dane County Police, Burk wanted nothing more than to spirit her away to someplace quiet and warm. He wanted to wrap her in his arms and murmur promises in her ear to always keep her safe.

Not that Willa needed a Prince Charming necessarily. She'd proved today that she was a hell of a fighter. Underneath the white bandage on her jaw was an injury that would have felled a lesser woman. Anyone else would have blacked out or panicked at the pain. Instead, Willa had smashed her captor's head on a chair—then with a table—and escaped.

Still, he'd be damned if he wouldn't die trying to protect her for the rest of his life, so that she never had to go through anything like this ever again.

A fierce heat worked its way up his chest as they sat in the well-worn chairs in a conference room at the police station. Willa could have died today. She could have been taken away from him before he had the chance to tell her how he felt. Burk clenched his jaw. There was no chance in hell he was letting it happen again. Ever. Even if the police hadn't insisted on him coming down to the station as a witness, he still would have gone, just to ensure Willa was all right. He'd followed the police cruiser in his truck, wishing he was with her, that his arms were around her, that she knew he'd always be there for her.

Because whatever happened, he *would* be there. She would be his to treasure and keep safe forever—if she would have him, that is.

"And you were witness to this, Mr. Olmstead?" the policeman was asking. Officer Tobino was young and fresh-faced—but didn't ask questions like a rookie.

Burk snapped back to reality. "Sorry, what?"

"You came upon the scene of the crime as it was in progress?"

"I saw some broken glass on the front porch when I got there, and then heard shouting from outside. I was worried. By the time I got inside, Willa had already defended herself. Lance was knocked out."

"Can you tell me how you gained entry into the house?"

Burk shifted. "I climbed the trellis in the back. It provides access to a second-story bedroom, where the window has never latched very well."

Tobino looked suddenly interested. "And you know this how?"

Out of the corner of his eye, Burk saw Willa blush. "Willa and I dated in high school. I got a feel for the house then."

Tobino cracked a smile. "Fair enough. Just a few more questions."

On and on it went until finally the policeman closed his notebook. "I think we got what we needed. You're both free to go."

When she stood, Willa was so wobbly that Burk placed a hand on her elbow to steady her. She smiled at him gratefully, melting his heart like coals over snow. As they filed out the door, Tobino said that Lance would be charged as soon as he was out of the hospital—probably a matter of a few more hours. It would be on top of the charges he'd already pled guilty to, meaning he'd likely go away for a long time.

"And for what it's worth," the policeman said to Willa with a touch of admiration, "you really did a number on him. My buddy down there says he keeps shrieking every time he wakes up and lays eyes on the table in the room."

Burk hoped he'd shriek even more when the prison doors clanged shut. He shook the officer's hand. "Thank you."

As they exited the brick building and walked across the parking lot to Burk's truck, light filtered through the colored trees along the lot's edge. The early snow was gone. The white had been replaced by a last burst of shimmering yellow birch and poplar leaves, and golden witch hazel blooming in spidery clumps.

Willa squinted against the jewel blue sky as she faced Burk on the blacktop.

"Thank you," she said, her voice scratchy with fatigue.

"I couldn't have gotten through this without you. If you hadn't shown up when you did..."

Burk placed a hand on her cheek. Without hesitation, she leaned into his touch. His heart hammered. "You had it under control," he said, relishing the feel of her skin against his palm, "but I'm sorry you had to go through it at all."

"I think I would have fallen apart if you hadn't been there," she said, lowering her eyes. "When Lance was out cold like that, my mind was just on overload. I couldn't think. I was paralyzed—and then there you were."

"Scaring you further," he said, trying to block out the memory of her frightened eyes, the chunk of wood shaking in her hands. "I'm sorry about that."

Willa stared up at him. The bandage on her jaw flashed in the light. "You never said why you were over at my house in the middle of the night, you know. You told the police how you got in, and explained how you tied up Lance, but you never said *why*."

Burk stared at her intelligent green eyes, the endless depths of them pulling at his heart. "I was coming to tell you how sorry I was. For acting like a jackass. And to tell you that I..." He summoned the words, willed himself to say them. "I care about you. So very much."

He pulled in a breath, every muscle in his body suddenly tense. "God knows I haven't figured out how to share my feelings with you. But I was coming over to tell you I wanted to try. To make things right, I mean, between us. The house aside, Willa, I want to...to be with you. To try and make you happy."

Willa's face went slack with surprise.

"I know it's not the time or the place to talk about all

this. But I hope—no, it's not hope. I am *asking* you to give me another chance."

Her beautiful eyes warmed, and a smile pulled at the corners of her mouth. "I will say, that is the second time in the last five hours I've been dead wrong about what I thought the men around me were capable of."

Burk smiled, admiring her resilience—her ability to be clever, even now. He tucked a few strands of dark blond hair behind her ear. Willa sighed and closed her eyes, as if she'd be content just to stand right there on the blacktop and not move again.

There was so much more Burk needed to say—that he wanted to finish the house, for no matter if she could pay or not, he would spend his whole life making up for the jackass he'd been—but he knew Willa needed to rest. "Sweetheart," he said gently, "I have to get you home. I'll take you in my truck, all right?"

At this, her emerald eyes flew open. "You mean back to Oak Street?" The fear on her face tore at his heart.

"Not if you don't want to," he said.

"I can't go back there," she said, trembling. "Not yet. Maybe in a little while but, please, not today."

"Of course," he said, hating the plea in her voice, as if she was worried he'd refuse her. "We'll go somewhere else."

She nodded, opened her mouth as if to say something else, then began suddenly to sob, her composure shattering. She buried her head in her hands, all her strength gone. Her shoulders shook with the force of her breaking.

Burk's throat worked against a tide of emotions. He wanted so badly to take this pain from her. Knowing he couldn't, he crushed her to him, murmuring into her hair, stroking her back, calming her the best he could.

"It's all right," he said over and over, "I'm here. I'm here." He ran his hands across her shoulders, up and down her arms. He kept his body close to hers, praying she'd feel his protective warmth.

By degrees, she began to calm; her ragged breathing returned to normal. Finally, she lifted her head to stare at him with bloodshot eyes and a tearstained face. She took his breath away with her beauty and vulnerability.

"I'm such a mess," she hiccuped.

Burk placed his fingers on her chin, keeping her face tilted toward his. "You are astounding." And then, unable to stop himself, he bent down to kiss her gently, right there in the parking lot.

He could feel the sun warming her skin and hair as he brushed his lips across hers. He meant to stop there, but he found hunger building inside him, even as he knew now wasn't the time or place.

To his surprise, Willa parted for him, and raised her arms so they twined around his neck. He pulled her closer, needing to feel her. He kissed her more urgently, letting his tongue taste her lips, then the whole of her mouth. She met his eagerness with an energy that surprised him, given her tired state. But suddenly she was plunging her hands into his hair, pulling him toward her with surprising strength.

He broke the kiss to trail down her neck, speaking into her sweet skin, his breath hot. "You should come back to my place," he said, not phrasing it as a question.

Her tired eyes blazed with desire. "Yes," came the simple answer. Burk helped her into the truck, then sped toward his apartment as fast as he dared, considering they were peeling out of a police station.

* * *

As much as he wanted to tear off Willa's clothes, throw her onto the bed, and demonstrate *all day* how much she meant to him, first things first. He demanded she take a shower, and when she protested weakly, he simply put a fresh towel and one of his old bathrobes into her hands. "It will help you feel better," he said. "It's literally going to help you wash away this experience."

Willa's brows drew together—she clearly didn't agree—but she finally relented. Burk pulled the bathroom door shut behind her with a gentle click. While he wanted to strip along with her, lather her body with soap, and knead her sore muscles, he gave her privacy instead. She hadn't had any time alone since the attack, and she might need a few quiet moments to collect her thoughts. To come to terms with the wrenching invasion of her house and person. He whistled loudly throughout the apartment, hoping she could hear him over the running water, wanting her to know he was there, and there was no reason to be afraid.

Finally, she emerged, her skin scrubbed and shining, her hair damp and combed. She was wrapped in his old blue robe, and the sight of her in his clothes sent a possessive prickle along the back of his neck. She smiled at him, inclining her head. "You may have been right about the shower."

He smiled back. "I can be correct on occasion, you know."

"Very rarely, but this might be one instance. Should we write it down?" She glanced around, as if hunting for a pad and paper. Burk took her soft, shower-warm hand in his.

"Come on, I want you to eat something."

He led her toward the kitchen, where he'd fixed grilled cheese sandwiches and tomato soup. It was one of the few meals his bachelor-appointed apartment could offer, but it was at least warm, and it would be filling. He pulled out a chair at the garage sale table, and invited her to sit.

"I'm not really hungry," Willa said, eyeing the food. "No offense. I like what you've made, but I just don't feel like eating right now."

Burk sat next to her and handed her a spoon. "Just try a few bites. That's all I ask."

She pointed the spoon at him. "Only because you were right about the shower." A few bites turned into a few more bites, and eventually half the soup was gone, as well as a quarter of the grilled cheese sandwich.

"Twice in one day," she said, her eyes widening in mock surprise. "I stand completely corrected."

Burk smiled at the glow that had invaded her cheeks, at the veil of exhaustion that seemed to lift from her. It would be short-lived, he knew, but he was glad that she at least had a reprieve from the dark weariness that had briefly sapped her strength.

"Will you trust me a third time?" he asked, reaching for her hand. She allowed him to pull her up from the table, and lead her once again down the hallway. This time they didn't stop at the bathroom. They went all the way to the end—to his room.

Burk pulled back the covers on the bed. "It's time to

rest," he said, gesturing to the bleach white sheets. "I'll stay with you until you fall asleep. And I'll be right here when you get up."

Willa eyed the bed from the doorway. "I don't need a bodyguard, Burk. I just didn't want to go back to the house right away. But you don't have to babysit me. You don't have to tell me when it's *nap time*."

She placed her hands on her hips, giving him a glimpse of the raw, red marks on her wrists from where Lance had tied her up. The sight of her wounds had him growling like a grizzly bear. He strode toward her and lifted her into his arms in one swift motion.

"Why do you *insist* on picking me up every time we talk about something?" she said, exasperated. But she didn't struggle.

He placed her gently on the bed, rolled up the robe sleeve, and brought her wounded flesh to his mouth. He blew softly on the tortured skin, cooling it with his breath and lips. Willa sighed, and lay back on the pillows.

"I will never let anyone hurt you again," he found himself murmuring into her skin. "I will always be here for you. I will protect you."

To his surprise, Willa wrapped herself around him, drawing him closer. He left her abrasions to kiss the hollow of her throat, taking in the fresh, clean scent of her. It was his soap, his robe, but still, somehow, the smell was all Willa, filling his lungs and mind.

He knew he should back away, give her space and time to recover, but hunger for her gnawed at him, overtook him. He shifted so she was fully underneath him. Resting his hands on either side of her head, he lowered himself gently to her exquisite lips, capturing them in a possessive kiss. She was his. He would never be apart from her again.

Willa arched and moaned underneath him. The sound sent an electric current along his back. "Burk," she murmured, running her fingers over the flat hardness of his stomach and back, "I want you."

Burk's body tightened with surprise...and desire. The naked want on her face was so compelling. Her brazen desire for him so raw and uninhibited.

She wanted him. Even after all the ways he'd screwed up, she could still trust herself with him.

The revelation unleashed a tide of emotions inside. Possessiveness. Adoration. Kneeing apart her thighs, he settled himself between her soft limbs. "I'll give you what you need," he muttered, nibbling the edges of her ear. She gasped, trembling at his touch. "I promise I'll do right by you."

Freeing the tied robe belt in one movement, he pushed aside the soft fabric and laid her bare in front of him. His heart raced at the sight of her clean skin, her perfectly rounded breasts, and the sweetness between her legs that called to him. He lowered himself to her breasts, nuzzling and licking and caressing them until she threw her head back and cried out. Slipping a hand between her legs, he pushed one finger into her softness, then two. Her hands clutched at his back, pulled his hair, trembled at his touch.

He wanted to pleasure her until she forgot the horrors of earlier in the day. He wanted to bring her to the brink of ecstasy until the only thing she knew was his touch, his caress. He wanted to worship her and fill her and never let her go.

Trailing kisses down her beautiful belly, he kept his

fingers inside her—coaxing and rubbing—until his mouth found her center. He placed his lips on her swollen clitoris, kissing and licking gently. His touch elicited groans from Willa's throat. His name was in her mouth, over and over. The sound of it ignited him, goading him to give her more. He sucked on the divine peak with a rhythm that matched his fingers inside her.

The drumbeat of his touch intensified, pulsing through her body. Her damp hair tumbled back from her head as pleasure overtook her. She shattered in his arms, her muscles quaking with overwhelming sensations. Her core convulsed around his fingers, and she cried out again and again until the spasms subsided.

Slowly, Burk kissed the insides of her thighs, upward to her hips, then her sternum, and finally her lips. She sighed softly against him, her expression satiated and a little dazed.

He settled himself next to her, pulling the robe closed once more, then tugging the covers back around them both. He was still fully clothed.

"Wait, you're done?" she asked thickly, her confused eyes blinking.

He kissed the tip of her nose, then her lips. "I want you to rest. There will be plenty of time for me."

She struggled to sit up, but he urged her back down gently. "Please. I know I'm pushing my luck here, but I might just be looking at four times."

"Four times being right? In *one day*?" she asked, her voice full of mock wonder. "I don't know, that seems awfully extreme."

"It is," he said, stone serious. "It is extreme enough to warrant careful introspection. We should think about this.

You should think about this especially." He kissed her eyelids closed. "You should meditate and reflect on the wonderment that may have transpired today. You should take deep breaths in, exhaling slowly. That's right, good." He pulled her more tightly to him, marveling at the softness of her breath, the steady rise and fall of her incredible chest.

"Inhale in, exhale out," he whispered as her muscles relaxed.

"You're tricking me," she murmured, already half asleep.

"No, Willa," he replied, kissing her brow gently. "No tricks. From now on, you will have my honesty. You will have my devotion. You will have my heart, and all the love I can give you. Because I do love you, Willa. I always have, ever since high school. And I'm only sorry that it took me this long to realize it." He kissed the top of one cheekbone, the corner of her mouth. "Can you forgive me for being the biggest jerk that ever lived, and can you give me another chance?" he whispered in the stillness.

The only reply was the sound of a delicate snore as it left her throat.

CHAPTER TWENTY-EIGHT

Sunday, October 14, 7:08 a.m.

*W*illa emerged from sleep the next morning wondering if she'd dreamed the whole thing. Had Lance really attacked her? And had Burk nearly rescued her, then told her he cared about her?

She rubbed her eyes and sat up. Next to her, the bed was empty, but she could still feel the warmth where Burk's body had been. And she could smell his masculine, outdoorsy scent around her, as if he'd cocooned her in his arms all night.

All *day* and night, she realized, looking at the bedside clock. It was 7:08 a.m.—on Sunday. She'd been out nearly twenty-four hours.

She stretched, wondering why in the world she'd needed to sleep so long. That is, until she caught sight of her injured wrists. The angry marks reminded her acutely of everything that had happened Friday night. She suddenly wondered if she needed to sleep even more.

But no. She wanted to get up, but was unsure suddenly what to *do* once she was standing. Should she go out into the kitchen wearing nothing except Burk's robe? Or should she dress fully and then head back to her own place as if nothing happened?

Her pulse raced as she recalled the way he'd touched her yesterday—so tenderly and affectionately, as if she meant so very much to him. She closed her eyes, suddenly wanting very badly for that affection to be *true*.

Oh, if there could be another chance for them, she'd take it. Not so long ago, she'd believed all hope for them had washed away, like the sandy edges of the Birch River when the snow melted. Yet maybe it hadn't. Maybe there was an island of opportunity left for them. A little place the raging waters of the past hadn't touched, where the ways they'd hurt each other wouldn't override the ways they could love each other in the future.

She stared at her wounded wrists, touched the bandage on her face. She had no doubt that Lance would have hurt her if she hadn't escaped. Her insides quaked with the realization of how close she'd come to harm.

Life was so short, so tenuous. She hugged her knees to her chest, aching with a feeling she couldn't place. It was part fear perhaps. But also part exhilaration. You never knew how much time you had, or how things could change in a split second.

It made her want to live with abandon, full of life and love for the people around her. She was determined to live with her heart and her mind and her soul accessible to those she knew she could trust. Audrey. Betty. Stephanie. Anna. And Burk, too. That is, if he'd meant what he said yesterday. If it hadn't all been a heat-of-the-moment thing.

Willa chewed the inside of her lip. It had been a difficult day. And people were prone to hyperbole when they were stressed.

Perhaps Burk had spoken out of turn. Maybe he was just being effusive out of concern.

Willa took a breath and pushed the covers back.

She supposed it was time to find out.

* * *

Willa padded into the kitchen to find warm coffee waiting, but no Burk. He was gone, but he'd left a note: *Had to run out. Call me when you get up. I am close by. Thinking about you.*

Willa sighed. There was so much to talk about, and yet he wasn't here. Where could he have gone?

She closed her eyes briefly, realizing how much they needed to sort out. How long would she stay here? What would they do about the house?

She wondered if he was letting her stay out of sympathy. Because he felt sorry for what she'd been through. Yet Willa desperately wanted there to be some part of him that was caring for her not out of compassion but out of—affection. Love, even.

She found her cell phone in her purse and dialed his number. He answered on the first ring. "You're up," he said, sounding pleased to hear from her. The tenor of his voice sent chills along her body. She longed for him to be next to her, for his words to be breath in her ear instead of wavelengths over a phone line.

"I got your note," she said. "What's going on?"

"I wondered if you could meet me at the Oak Street house," he said. She could hear the smile on his lips. "I have something to show you."

"Now?"

"As soon as you can. I had one of the crew members drop off your Volvo, and the keys are there on the kitchen table. I know it might be hard to see the place again, but I think what I have for you will help."

Willa shivered, thinking of Lance, of the shattered hot dish on the porch. "I don't suppose you'd ask me if it wasn't important."

"It's important. But good important, not bad important."

A mixture of excitement and dread churned inside her. She was being asked to go back to the place where Lance had attacked her. It was frightening to be sure, but she'd *survived* him. She'd fought him off and won. And now Burk was inside her home, too. Somehow, between her strength and his, it felt like nothing could hurt her.

Willa smiled. "All right. I'll be there in a few."

She hung up the phone, and raced to get ready, wondering at what Burk could have in store for her.

* * *

As Willa pulled up to the house, she noticed right away that it was ablaze with light. It was hard to miss, even in the morning sun, considering how it poured out of every window, reflecting like glitter on the damp streets.

The second thing she noticed was that the light was *warm*. It wasn't the cold, fluorescent beams from the cheap bulbs that she'd thrown into a few of the house's lamps. Instead, these were deep, golden rays from the kinds of lights she had dreamed about in the space. Chandeliers and Tiffany lamps, for example.

She got out of the car, gaping at the golden hues. Walking up the front porch, she could see two of the new lights already, glinting from either side of the front door. They were Arts-and-Crafts-style porch lights—exact replicas of the lights she'd picked out and pasted into one of her collages. But how—

Before she could fully form the question, the front door opened. There stood Burk, paint flecks on his forearms, Spackle in his hair, and dust in every line of his skin. "You made it," he said, his eyes dancing with something that looked like pure joy.

"I made it," she said, staring at the state of his person. She'd never seen him gritty before. For a contractor, he was normally meticulous. That, plus all the new lights, had her mind reeling.

Before she could ask what was going on, he leaned down to brush her lips gently with his own. A steady hum vibrated through her. The delicious tingle of it had her nearly collapsing on the spot. Before she could deepen the kiss, Burk pulled away. The playful light in his eyes was even brighter.

"I have a surprise for you," he said, pulling her inside. "We've been working all day to get it done. Not *everything* is finished, but there's one room ready. I had to show you—"

"Is that my paint color on the walls?" she interrupted, peering around. "And are those the recessed lights we talked about?" She heard her voice shaking but she was unable to keep the tremor at bay.

"That's what I'm trying to tell you. We—"

"The fireplace mantle has been refinished," she said, pushing past him, "and some of these windows are new." She whipped around, disbelieving the transformation. She wanted to pinch herself. "When did this happen?"

Burk reached out to steady her. She was grateful for his hand, since she suddenly felt dizzy.

"The past twenty-four hours, while you've been sleeping, I've been able to get the crews in here to get some of the work done. I wanted you to step foot into your dream. Into what you deserve. I wanted this place transformed so you'd never think about—about the past when you came back here. It's not all done, of course, but it's a start."

"But *why* do all this when you want the house, too?" Willa asked. "Why not wait to see if my loan fails and see if you can just—take it over?"

With a dusty finger, Burk tucked a piece of her hair behind her ear. "I don't want this house," he said quietly, "if you're not in it. In fact, I don't want this *life* if you're not in it."

Willa could only stare at him, speechless. Her heart filled and pressed against her ribs. She felt a poignant ache in every part of her body.

He smiled tenderly. "Come on, come see what we've done."

He pulled her from the living room into the dining room. The wrought iron and crystal light fixture she'd wanted for over the table had been purchased and installed. The trim had been fixed and painted a clean white in contrast to the rich honey color of the walls. The space was still bare—Burk hadn't ordered furniture for any room, of course, not knowing what she'd repurpose or order new—but many of the structural plans they'd worked out together, he'd executed to perfection.

Next to her, he shifted, seeming suddenly nervous, and Willa realized it's because she hadn't really *said* anything yet. Tears sprang into her eyes, and the refinished space around her blurred. She swiped at the wetness with her palms.

"Are you all right?" Burk asked gently. "Is this okay?"

"I don't have words," Willa said, her chest tight. "It's so beautiful. But it only means something if—"

"She's here!" came a cry from behind them. Willa turned to see Audrey, Betty, Stephanie, and Anna filing in from the back door. They were bundled in coats but had workman's boots on, not to mention durable, paint-splattered gloves.

"We were helping Burk!" Stephanie said, her freckled face breaking into a wide grin. "We've been out in the garage all day prepping your furniture. He told us to sand it and get it all ready so you could paint it and redo it in whatever way you wanted."

"This was so much *fun*," Stephanie said, "just the break I needed from my house. Willa, anytime you need help around here, you call me."

"Steph's good with sandpaper," Anna said, smiling. "I'll give her that."

"But we're forgetting the biggest project," Audrey said, her brown eyes squinting with delight. "We have a surprise for you."

"It was Burk's idea," Betty said, "so if you hate it, blame him."

Willa glanced from friend to friend, marveling that they were all here, in her house, helping out. From the sounds of it, they'd been laboring for hours to surprise her. Her eyes filled up all over again, much to her dismay. When in the world had she gotten so lucky to deserve a group like this?

Burk slipped an arm around her, and she leaned into his solidness. "This is too much," she whispered.

"No," he said, his dark blue eyes boring into hers, "it's exactly right."

"You have to turn around while we carry it in," Anna said. "And promise not to peek. Swear?"

Willa nodded, finding it hard to talk. "Promise," she whispered hoarsely.

She turned around while Burk and her friends filed back outside. She heard scuffling and laughing. Then more footsteps as they reentered the house. She couldn't begin to imagine what they were doing.

"Okay," she heard Audrey singsong, "you can look now."

She turned around and her heart dropped immediately into her feet. She could feel it beating in her toes, where it would remain because no way would she ever get over this surprise. *Ever.* Her whole body trembled at the sight before her.

"Do you like it?" Burk asked.

Willa shook her head. She had no words. She tried to speak, but could only omit a tiny gasp.

"Are you upset?" Audrey asked gently. "I can't tell."

Willa shook her head. She was overwhelmed—but with love and affection, not anger or frustration.

"We wanted you to know that Lance can never hurt you again," Burk said as Willa struggled to regain her composure. "We'll never let him near you again. Your friends are here for you. All of us."

Willa took a steadying breath and stared at the blue table in front of her. It was her table—the one she'd started to refinish for her living room—but had cracked into Lance's face the night he attacked her. Only, her friends had meticulously recovered every piece of wood and put the whole thing back together again. She walked forward unsteadily, running her fingers over the refinished surface. There were cracks and lumps where things hadn't fit back together exactly right. She could see the places where they'd had to use wood glue and maybe some wood putty. It was flawed, certainly, but it was the most beautiful table she'd ever seen in her life.

"I love it," she whispered finally. "It's amazing."

"You still have to distress it," Burk said. "All we did was paint it."

"Oh, I think it's plenty distressed already," Betty said. "What are you going to do to it now? Throw it in the Birch River?"

The group chuckled, and Willa thought maybe Betty was on to something. Maybe she'd leave the table just as it was—a reminder of all the imperfections that could exist but still make up something beautiful.

"Thank you," Willa said after a moment. "I don't even know what to say. This is the most meaningful gift I've ever received."

"We love you," Anna said, looking pointedly at Burk. "All of us. We wanted to give you something that would always be a reminder of how strong we are when we stick together. People can try and break us apart, but we'll just get the wood glue and paint out and put ourselves back together again."

"Damn straight," Betty agreed.

Willa was just about to ask if they'd stick around for the rest of the tour, when Audrey looked at her watch. "My goodness, I haven't been home in *hours*."

Anna nodded. "I should really get going. I've left Sam with Juniper for far too long."

"My husband is wrangling the twins and I think he can handle it for a few more hours," Stephanie said, grinning. "I may just go shopping."

After a fresh round of hugs, Willa walked her friends to the front door, still feeling dazed and overwhelmed.

"See you this Thursday at the recipe exchange," Betty said on her way out. It wasn't a question.

When the door closed behind them, Willa was suddenly very aware that it was down to just her and Burk in the refinished space. He leaned against the new built-in bookshelves, his arms folded and a small smile on his face. "You want to see the rest of the house?" he asked.

Willa began to tremble all over again. "There's more?"

Burk closed the distance between them in a few strides. "Just one more thing on the second floor you haven't seen." He leaned in and placed his lips on the top of Willa's head. She found her arms encircling his waist, pulling him closer. The smell of sawdust and paint and plaster was all over him.

"I don't want to get you dirty," he said, pulling back slightly.

"I don't care. I think you could be covered in mud right now, and I'd still want you. This is the most amazing gift, Burk. I don't have words for what you've done."

"I don't care where I live, as long as you're with me," Burk said, his jaw flexing. "Without you, all I have is cement and nails and wood. But with you, the place I live actually means something."

Willa's breath was gone again. She could only nod as happiness coursed through her, warming her body from head to toe. "Then you should move in here," she said. "Maybe we both belong here...together."

Burk brought his mouth to hers, kissing her as the golden light tumbled around them. Sparks ignited behind her closed eyelids. She'd just opened her mouth, inviting his tongue to enter her in pleasure-filled strokes, when suddenly he groaned and pulled away. Lines creased his forehead, and his eyes flashed darkly.

"What?" Willa asked, still breathless from the kiss. "What's wrong?"

He cursed, his face flushed with an emotion she couldn't place.

"It's not enough," he growled.

"What's not enough?"

"Living together." He ran a hand along the back of his neck. "Dammit, Willa, I love you. And I don't want to just *live* with you." He began pacing the floor. "I want to be with you. Forever. I have never loved another woman like I love you—and I never will."

Willa gasped as he returned to the space in front of her, and got down on one knee. "I don't have a ring to give you. Not yet anyway. But I have my heart to give. And it's yours, if you'll take it."

His throat worked as she stared at him. "Willa Masterson, will you marry me?"

Willa's heart surged. Never in a thousand years could she have expected Burk to propose, but now that he had, she felt a version of happiness she'd never known before.

This was where she was meant to be. With Burk Olmstead, in this house. Forever.

"Yes," she whispered, tears coursing down her cheeks, "of course."

He stood and crushed her to him, sealing her answer with a kiss that left her weightless. "My love," he whispered over and over. "My Willa."

When they were finally able to get their wits about them again, Burk took her hand. "I have to show you the upstairs."

"Now?" Willa asked, dazed.

"Now," Burk said, a dark intensity in his expression that she immediately understood.

She was guessing there was still a bed upstairs. Somewhere.

Which, in fact, turned out to be true. Willa's room had been torn apart and put back together again—with soft, cream-colored walls and warm recessed lights—but the old brass bed was still there. "You needed a place to sleep," Burk said, motioning to it, "if you were going to stay."

Willa placed her palms on his broad chest, grinning up at him. "I think you had ulterior motives."

"I think you're right," he said, kissing her lips, her neck, her ears. "But I'm not going to get in this bed with you until I've had a shower."

"Your shower will be lukewarm," Willa teased. "I hear this place needs a new water heater."

She followed him into the bathroom. "Let me help you undress." He groaned softly as she pulled off his pants, then ran her fingers up his bare chest, helping lift off his shirt. As he stood naked in front of her, she found her lungs unable to draw enough air, her throat thick with emotion. *He was so handsome.*

His thick shaft stood erect with desire, the hair all around it dark and glossy. His muscles were taut as she studied him. The dust clung to the soft down on his forearms, and the white Spackle stood out on his golden skin. His pulse beat visibly in his strong neck. Willa stepped forward to place her fingertips gently on him. "You are so incredible," she breathed, running her fingers down his chest, to his penis. He hissed in a breath as she played with the tip and the softness underneath.

With her free hand, Willa reached over to the showerhead and turned on the water. "You're coming in with me, you know," Burk said, peeling off Willa's clothes in quick succession. When she was fully naked in front of him, he lowered his head to her breasts, nuzzling the cove between them, and kissing the delicate flesh that pebbled at his touch.

She tilted her head back to give him access to her long, white neck. He kissed her soft skin, pulling her closer to him with his strong workman's hands. She could feel the hard length of him pressed between their two bodies.

Finally, they stepped into the shower, glistening and wet under the spray. Reaching for her soap, she lathered her hands and ran them across Burk's broad chest, down his flat, muscled stomach and to his penis. She lingered on his hardness with soapy strokes that had him growling in the back of his throat.

"Careful, love," he said, staying her hands after a few moments. "If you keep going, I won't be able to do all the things I want to do to you. And that would be a shame." Quickly rinsing the soap from his member, he turned

Willa around in the small space, and pulled her toward his chest. Her spine fit against his abdomen; his penis pressed against the backs of her thighs. Water rained down on her skin in stark contrast to the shivery thrill she felt inside as he reached a hand between her legs. From behind, he gently parted her folds—a delicate touch that had her reaching out to the tiled walls for support.

Burk kissed her neck, nibbled her lobe, murmured into her ears as the water splashed. Slowly, he slid a finger inside her aching depths. She arched away from him, but he brought her back with his free arm, anchoring her to him. "Stay with me, my love," he whispered above the sound of the spray. Expertly he stroked inside her, plunging and pulsing with one finger, then two, then three, until she thought she would faint from the perfect movement. He drew her toward the edge of pleasure.

Placing his free hand on her stomach, he ran his fingers down, down the front of her until he discovered her center, warmer than the water that sprayed around them. He touched the swollen tip and she cried out. His penis pressed harder against her, his fingers slid deeper. "My Willa," he said, his voice impossibly deep, "tell me what you want. Tell me and I'll give it to you."

"There," she begged as his fingers swirled on her clitoris. "Oh, Burk, just like that. *Just like that.*"

He pulled her toward him, pushing his fingers deeper, and she broke in his arms, her pleasure raining down around him like the water in the shower. She arched and cried out, rivulets of wetness coursing down her neck and down the slick folds of her sex.

He held her as she shattered, his muscled arms supporting her, his lips speaking tender endearments. She whimpered, limp with spent pleasure under the soothing water.

"We get to do this forever, you know," he said. Willa could feel a smile on his lips as he kissed her damp neck. He turned her around gently to face him, freeing his fingers as he did so. She ached at the lack of him, but he shook his head, as if reading her thoughts. "Don't worry, there's more where that came from." Shampooing his hair quickly, he rinsed off and Willa did the same. Within minutes, they were wrapped up in towels, padding down the hallway to Willa's room.

As he dimmed the new recessed lights, Willa pulled back her old bedspread and dropped her towel. "My God, you are so beautiful," he said, his eyes raking over her body in the room's soft glow. For the first time in a long time, Willa felt as if that was really true. She ran her hands down her sides, up her stomach, feeling the divine fullness of her own breasts, the dewy softness of her skin, the hardness of the muscles underneath. Burk watched her, a hunger building behind his eyes.

Climbing into bed, Willa parted her own legs, touched her own center. She sighed at the delicate pleasure that tingled through every nerve. Across the room, Burk dropped his towel and came to the bed. "I can't watch you do that for very long," he said, his hands cupping one breast, then the other. He climbed on top of her, settling between her parted legs.

"You should never have to touch yourself," he murmured, the tip of his penis pressing against her. "Never again. Not as long as I'm around."

Willa smiled. "I don't mind," she said, "especially now that I know how much it gets you off."

"Not as much as me touching you, though," he countered, and slid inside her in one smooth stroke.

Willa gasped as he filled her up, the connection between them overpowering her senses. This was the man she loved. This was the man she would marry. She circled her arms around him.

"I need you so much," she whispered, twining her fingers through his glossy black hair. "I have always needed you."

"I'm here now," he answered, pressing against her until all of him was buried—until nothing more of their parts could be connected because they'd opened themselves so totally to each other. Willa arched her hips, and Burk grasped her rounded bottom in his hands, thrusting inside her. He swore softly as she writhed against him, struggling to be closer still.

She wrapped her legs around his flesh desperately. "I don't ever want to be away from this. From you," she breathed. He responded by kissing her deeply, hungrily, his tongue filling her mouth the same way his penis filled her core.

He brought her to the edge of ecstasy again. The headboard slammed into the freshly painted walls. Willa's hands gripped his shoulders as he drove her headlong into wave after wave of pleasure. Her innermost muscles contracted around him, coaxing him into his own overpowering orgasm. Together, they both cried out, calling each other's names, their physical bliss filling up the empty halls and rooms.

The whole house shook with the force of their lovemaking, the structure impacted and changed as they shook beams and rattled plaster and clattered windowpanes.

When it was all over with—as Burk and Willa tumbled, exhausted, into each other's arms—the house seemed to sigh as well.

The home settled around them, creaking and satisfied.

It was exactly as it was meant to be.

CHAPTER TWENTY-NINE

One year later
Saturday, September 14, 3:49 p.m.

The living room was filled with arrangements of sunflowers, chrysanthemums, sage, goldenrod, daisies, and burnt orange calla lilies. Willa fingered the baby-soft petal of a daisy, admiring how the bright flowers complemented the rich woodwork of the floors, not to mention the custom cream silk curtains that Betty had helped cut and sew a few months prior.

She inhaled the sweet, heady scent of all the flowers and smiled to herself. The house was perfect. The day was perfect. And this wedding was going to be perfect as well.

She hummed as she walked to the kitchen, the late-afternoon sun streaming into the bright white space through new windows. Outside, the crisp blue sky contrasted with the rust and gold leaves of the trees, which had just started to turn.

As she was reaching out to taste some of the salmon

mousse the caterer had left, hands grasped her from behind. She squealed and turned to face Burk.

"You'll give me a heart attack," she said, swatting him playfully, "and then who will make sure this wedding comes off without a hitch?" Burk's enormous hands grasped either side of her face and pulled her into a kiss that left her breathless.

"Forget the wedding," he said, his voice rumbling when their lips finally broke apart. "I want you. Let's head out and go somewhere. Just the two of us."

"And leave all these guests in the lurch?" Willa laughed. "I don't think so."

Burk studied her with amusement crinkling the sides of his ocean blue eyes. "You're more nervous about this wedding than you were about ours. How is that possible?"

Willa studied her husband and felt a jolt of emotion. They'd been married last winter, but it still felt like they were on their honeymoon. Every day with Burk was better than the last. And now, she felt a twinge of excitement that it was Betty's turn to discover the joys of matrimony—with Pastor Sondheim.

"I am scared to death that Betty won't like something and will yell at me in front of everyone," Willa confessed. "The minute she said she wanted to get married here, I knew it had to be perfect."

"And it is. You're doing a great job. The bed-and-breakfast is full of guests who couldn't be happier. Now will you please celebrate and stop worrying?"

"If it's not this business, it's the other," she teased. This past year, in addition to running the B and B, she and Burk had added an interior decorating arm to B.C.'s Contracting. That made it one-stop shopping for people who needed a new kitchen, for example, and also wondered how to decorate the new space. Many of the clients also wanted Willa's custom furniture in their spaces—a side of the business that Stephanie was managing now that the twins were in school full-time.

Everyone was getting used to the new arrangement, which was a far cry from where Willa had been just a few months prior. So much had changed over the past year. She still marveled at the notion that she and Burk were *married*. This man was hers. She reached out and placed a hand on the arm of his pressed suit jacket.

"I love you," she whispered to him as caterers came inside the sliding-glass door to grab trays of hors d'oeuvres for the guests out back. He pulled her to him, the tulle and silk of her bridesmaid dress rustling as he pressed her close.

"This whole day makes me want to marry you all over again," he murmured into her hair, which was pulled back into a loose chignon. "I love you, too, and I always will."

He'd barely grazed her lips in a delicate kiss when a streak of white and yellow dashed around them. "Burby!" Juniper cried, streaking through caterers' legs and nearly toppling a stacked tier of gourmet cupcakes.

Burk and Willa shared an amused look before Burk gave chase. "Come on, little bug," he cried, rushing outside in hopes that Juniper would follow, "let's play horsey in the yard."

Willa followed at a more leisurely pace. Her heels clacked gently on the refinished wood of the back deck. All around were ceramic pots filled with more flowers. In the middle of the yard was a white tent with white lights strung along the edges. When the sun set, it would light up like a fairyland.

A few rows of white chairs dotted the expanse of green backyard. Betty's wedding was smallish—around fifty guests—but Willa wanted to make sure no detail was overlooked.

She glanced over to the refinished garage, near which Pastor Sondheim was standing, sweating underneath the bright fall sun. His cheeks were pink, his brown hair slicked back. Willa grabbed a bottle of cool water on her way over to talk with him, which he accepted gratefully.

"Breathe," she whispered to him, patting his arm reassuringly. He nodded and gulped the liquid, as if his throat were on fire.

"Just a few more minutes," Willa said, glancing at her cell phone. She had a new text from Betty.

Let's get this party started.

"I'll start rounding up the guests. You'd better take your place by the pastor, Pastor."

Sondheim nodded, and headed to the trellis staged in front of all the folding chairs. Pastor Bjornson from the Lutheran church down in New Prave was already in place, ready to conduct the ceremony. Next to Pastor Bjornson was Pastor Sondheim's best man, his brother Gus Sondheim, who worked as a cardiologist down at the Mayo Clinic in Rochester. Willa gave them all a thumbs-up, then gently urged people into their seats, just as the small three-piece orchestra started up.

Seeing Audrey motioning for her from the sliding-glass door, Willa dashed up the back steps and inside to join the other bridesmaids. Audrey, Anna, and Stephanie all stood just inside the door. Each of them wore the same plum-colored dress that Willa sported. Betty was the beautiful anomaly in her long, white silk dress, her curly blond hair piled on top of her head in beautiful tendrils that were held in place with a delicate veil.

"Oh," Willa breathed, "you look stunning."

"I hope the photographer does his job," Betty said, barely holding back an eye roll. "Because I am never wearing this much makeup ever again."

Musical notes floated up to them from the yard. It was the bridal march.

It was time.

"Just like in rehearsal?" Audrey asked. "Two on each side?"

"If my dad were still alive, I know he'd approve of you girls walking me down the aisle," Betty said, her eyes shining uncharacteristically. "But even if he didn't, I wouldn't have it any other way."

Grinning at each other, the four women walked their friend across the deck and into the yard. After they handed off the bride to her new groom, Willa found her seat in the front row next to Burk. He laced his fingers through hers for the whole of the ceremony, his firm grasp a reminder that he was hers. Forever. Occasionally he caught her eye, and she read in his expression the same, steady message of love that coursed through her own heart.

When Betty and Randall had exchanged their *I do*'s and were pronounced husband and wife, the little backyard party stood and applauded.

"By the way, what did you choose on the menu option?" Willa asked as Betty walked back down the grassy aisle. Her face was light and glowing, her white silk train rippling behind her like pearled water. "Chicken, steak, or hot dish?"

Burk grinned. "I chose the one that will always remind me of you."

"Chicken?" Willa asked playfully.

"Hardly. You know it's hot dish. A blend of all the things you never knew could go together, but somehow work in perfect unison."

"Don't forget the heaps of cheese to tie it all together," Willa said, her hands playing with the platinum band on his left hand. "There's always lots of cheese with hot dish."

"Am I the cheese in this scenario?" Burk asked as the waiters began to circulate crisp, bubbling champagne to all the guests.

Willa smiled up at him, his handsome face making her heart race. "You're ... a Gouda guy."

"I'm cheddar than nothing."

"You'll Brie right back?"

Burk laughed and kissed her. "Good one. But I'm not going anywhere."

Willa returned the kiss with blissful abandon, while the smell of baking hot dish trailed out from the house and over the guests—and into her heart.

Willa Masterson's
Spice-It-Up Hot Dish

From the kitchen of the White Pine Bed-and-Breakfast.

Ingredients

- 2 pounds ground beef
- 1 sweet onion, diced
- 1½ tablespoons Worcestershire sauce
- 1 teaspoon salt
- ½ teaspoon black pepper
- 2 (10.75-ounce) cans condensed cream of mushroom soup
- 1 (16-ounce) package frozen spinach, thawed and drained
- 8 slices pepper jack cheese
- 1 jalapeño, deseeded, sliced crosswise into thin rings
- 1 package frozen potato rounds (Tater Tots)

Directions

Preheat the oven to 350°F.

Crumble the ground beef into a large skillet over medium-high heat. When it starts to release some juices, add the onion. Season with the Worcestershire sauce, salt, and pepper. Cook until fully browned and the onions are soft. Drain off any excess grease, and stir in the cream of mushroom soup and spinach.

Transfer the beef mixture to a 9-by-3-inch baking dish.

Top with slices of pepper jack cheese. Layer the jalapeños over of the cheese, then neatly layer the potato rounds over the top of the entire casserole.

Bake for 45 to 60 minutes in the preheated oven, until the potato rounds are toasted.

Serve and enjoy with friends.

Five years ago, Audrey Tanner thought that Kieran Callaghan was The One...until he suddenly left town and disappeared from her life. Now Kieran is back— hotter than ever—and determined to win her back.

But this time, Audrey's calling the shots. He broke her heart once, and she won't give in without a fight...

And Then He Kissed Me

A preview follows.

CHAPTER ONE

Audrey Tanner could feel her underwear riding up her backside. Sweat was trickling down her thighs in rivulets. Skin-tight jeans were nearly cutting off her circulation, and leather chaps on top of the denim were raising her core body temperature enough to make her light-headed. In that moment, she realized that a girl could be uncomfortable or embarrassed, but to be both at the same time was a special kind of torture.

One she'd signed up for.

If her denim had had enough flexibility, she might have tried to kick herself. As it stood, she was practically immobile from the waist down, so she figured the only thing to do was to try not to fall over in her stilettos.

She placed her hands on her hips and attempted to look *alluring* just like the sales manager had asked. Leather fringe on her cufflinks fluttered like strips of ribbon in the wind. Standing next to the Harley-Davidson motorcycle in the showroom, she wondered what, exactly, alluring was. Track coaches didn't get much practice with things like that.

Former track coaches, that is.

A sharp pain pierced the tender place just behind her breastbone. She gritted her teeth. *Smile more, think less.*

The murmurs of the customers filled her ears. People swarmed amid the shiny chrome and sleek black lines of the motorcycles lining the floor all around her. The machines were sleeping monsters that roared to life whenever the ignition fired. All day, drivers had been thundering up and down the road just beyond the towering showroom windows, like cowboys riding handlebarred horses.

The noise from the engines was so loud sometimes she could hardly think. Which may have been a good thing, considering the only thing her brain wanted to focus on was the question of what in the heck she was doing here.

"Audrey?"

She turned. It must have been the sixth or seventh time she'd heard the question since she started her shift, the vowels and consonants of her name laced with disbelief.

This time, it was Red Updike. He'd sold her grass-fed beef from his farm for years, and had been a friend of her dad's. He stared at her, flannel shirt tucked into his well-worn Levi's, his mouth pulled slightly downward.

Leave it to the people of White Pine, Audrey thought, to stare at her like she was an alien with three heads just because she put on makeup and some tight clothes. She imagined tongues were already wagging down at the Paul Bunyan Diner about her change in "status."

"Hello, Mr. Updike," Audrey said as professionally as she could, "are you looking for a Harley today?"

He shifted. Right then, the only thing he was looking at was *her*. And no wonder, she thought. With her wild hair, dark makeup, and stilettos as sharp and long as steak knives, Audrey knew she appeared nothing like the respectable track coach and physical education teacher she'd been just a few weeks prior.

Before she'd been let go thanks to district downsizing, that is, and had taken the first job that would help her pay the rent.

"This, uh…" Red seemed to be searching for a question that didn't involve a query about what she was wearing. His head, more square than round, tilted to the side.

Audrey had to fight off an eye roll. She almost liked it better when strangers from Marston or New Prave or Faldet or any of the surrounding towns would give her a once-over and a low wolf-whistle. It might be chauvinistic and objectifying, but at least their jaws didn't go slack and their eyes round with bewilderment. For crying out loud, she thought, was it really so impossible that she could work her…assets a bit?

Red cleared his throat. "What's the, ah, front-tire speed rating on this hog?"

Audrey flashed the smile she'd taught herself at the beginning of the day when it dawned on her that she'd be spending her time in a Harley-Davidson dealership, and she knew nothing about motorcycles. It wasn't her fault that she thought the job advertising "showroom spokesperson" meant she could wear her best suit and sell quality transportation to the good people in her hometown. Could anyone really blame her for assuming the position came with some training, when instead it came with a makeup artist and leather?

"You'll have to do," the sales manager, Fletch Knudson, had said when she'd walked into the dealership that morning. He'd given her a quick once-over and pulled her into the offices behind the showroom, where the new-paint smell of the freshly built building still lingered. Audrey had protested—she'd just been dropping off her résumé, she'd left clothes in the dryer at home, she hadn't been prepared to work today—but Fletch had motorcycles to sell.

"Look, we filled this job days ago," he explained hurriedly, riffling through a closet behind one of the new steel desks, "but the girl we had lined up quit. Literally just walked out the door."

"Literally?" Audrey had asked. "Because a lot of people misuse that wor—"

"She's *gone*," Fletch had interrupted, his dark brows pinched together with frustration, "and you're about her size. With some help, you might do. The makeup artist is here now, she'll teach you what you need to know. After today, you're on your own so listen to her. The gig is Monday through Friday, ten to four. Stand there, look pretty, sell some hogs. You want it or not?"

Audrey had hesitated until he'd told her it paid thirty dollars per hour. Beggars couldn't be choosers, it's true, but at that rate she wouldn't be a beggar for long.

Back in the showroom, Audrey raised her chin slightly. Fletch had told her to "get customers interested in the motorcycle that's closest to your ass." She was determined to see the task through, even if it was Red Updike and even if she was clueless about most things on two wheels.

"I can find out about that tire rating for you, Red. In

the meantime, can I show you some of the features of this one right here?"

She had no idea what any of the mechanics were on the Harley Street Glide she was pointing to, other than it was a beautiful, inky black that reminded her of a moonless night, and the seat was a scoop of leather deep enough to throw on a horse and call a saddle.

"These are the...handlebars," Audrey said, tottering over to the front of the motorcycle in her heels and wishing momentarily for her sensible running shoes. "This is where you steer."

The lines on Red's forehead deepened in a confused crinkle. Audrey was never going to be any kind of help to the dealership if she kept up this crap. She straightened, and looked Red square on.

"Honestly, I never would have guessed that a Harley was your kind of ride. Tell me what you like about them."

Red relaxed a little. He stared at the bike. "Oh, well, you know. Machine like this is quality, a real piece of craftsmanship. And—a fella can dream, I suppose."

Just goes to show how little I know, Audrey thought.

She never would have figured a Harley store in a small town like White Pine could make it. After all, her community comprised everyday folks who were farmers and teachers and small-business owners. But White Pine Harley had been open for a few weeks now, and it seemed to be doing fine. Today, there had been a constant, steady trickle of people in the showroom. And more sales than she'd expected. Ben Howell, her dentist, had bought a three-wheeled Electra Glide. And Lester Lawsick, the local large-animal vet, had bought a used machine off the back lot.

I may have been wrong about everything, Audrey realized suddenly, wondering how well she really knew her hometown. If the community could fire her from her dream job and support a Harley dealership, what was next?

"They've got used ones, too, if you're interested," she said, trying to help Red think about his options, if price was an issue.

"I suppose I'm just browsing," Red replied, "though I do like the idea of change. Riding this around instead of my old truck. Can you imagine?"

Audrey felt herself smile—this time for real. Part of her *could* imagine Red whipping along White Pine's back roads, the rumble of the Harley echoing over the hills, the smell of hay and grass on the wind as he sped past fence posts and freshly painted barns.

"We all need a little change," Audrey agreed, speaking the words for her sake as much as Red's. A few short weeks ago, she'd been coaching long-legged girls over hurdles to get the whole team to the state finals. As a PE teacher, she'd been teaching volleyball and softball and lacrosse. Then, the principal had told her that the district had eliminated PE from the curriculum due to emergency budget cuts that would avoid a district shutdown. Paul Frace, the bearded English teacher, would be taking over coaching duties. She didn't even get to finish out the remainder of the school year.

"No child left without a huge behind," she'd quipped to some colleagues about the disbanded PE program as she packed up her things. It was either joke—or bawl.

And now here she was, standing next to a motorcycle thanks to the fact that she'd been a runner, an *athlete*, and she could look good in some chaps.

She caught a glimpse of her body in the showroom's large, floor-to-ceiling mirrors. Every curve of her was pressed against leather and denim; every inch of her face was covered in bronzed makeup that gave her a sun-kissed glow; every piece of her glossy auburn hair had been sprayed to tousled perfection.

She looked good.

No, not just good, she looked hot. *Melt-your-butter hot*, as her sister, Casey, used to say. That is, before Casey locked away the lip gloss and blush and told Audrey that working hard and studying hard were her only priorities.

The result, Audrey realized, was that she had spent most of her life either too mousy, or too practical.

She smoothed the front of her leather bustier, wondering if she should have been strutting around Harleys all along. She figured she would have at least had more fun.

"You have a good day now," Red said, jolting Audrey back to the here and now. She blinked, worried she'd missed conversation with him while staring at herself. But Red had been looking at the motorcycle and was probably lost in his own fantasy, too.

He walked away, his workman's boots clomping on the white-tiled floor. That left Audrey alone for the moment. She lifted her face to the afternoon light that slanted into the showroom. It sparkled on chrome fenders and warmed the buttery black leather of the motorcycle seat enough to make her want to lie down and nap. Not that she was going to do any sleeping anywhere in her current attire. But she *could* sit for a while.

Grasping the motorcycle's handlebars and pitching herself forward, she scooted and shimmied until one leg was over the seat. It wasn't graceful, and she was pretty sure there were titters coming from customers in the showroom, but at least she was off her feet in those ridiculous heels.

She readjusted herself on her machine, trying to ignore the pinch of jeans on her flesh. She'd just gotten comfortable when she heard her name again, spoken from behind.

"Audrey."

This time, it wasn't a question.

A shiver ran through her, as if the air conditioners had suddenly kicked in and icy gusts were coursing through the room. Beneath the bustier, her heart began to pound so hard she worried for a moment that the stays might not hold, and she'd come toppling out of the whole contraption.

Her nerves tightened with adrenaline, both hopeful and fearful at the same time.

"*Audrey.*"

She struggled to breathe. Steadying herself as best she could, she turned and stared into the pale green eyes of Kieran Callaghan.

Her whole body swayed. If she hadn't been sitting down, she would have certainly fallen like a sawed-off oak in the middle of a clear-cut.

Kieran Callaghan.

Dear *God*.

He was wearing a dark leather jacket and jeans, standing with both hands in his back pockets as if he were reclining on life itself. His eyes were the color of new blades of grass reaching toward the spring sun. They searched her face as he likely tried to figure out what in the world she was doing in front of him, butt cheeks on a Harley.

With every ounce of composure she could muster, Audrey straightened her spine. She tried not to focus too much on the cleft in his chin, or how the afternoon light ignited hints of gold in his dark red hair.

She spoke the first three words that came to mind: "You're an *asshole*."

Kieran raised a brow at her. He opened his mouth, but she didn't let him get a word in. "I've been waiting five years to tell you that. And I have no idea what you're doing back in town, but you should leave this store. Right. *Now.*"

Kieran's wide mouth twitched. Audrey tried not to stare at the movement, tried not to think about how much she'd loved that mouth. She'd left a steady boyfriend who'd been good to her for that mouth.

She narrowed her eyes. "Well? What do you have to say for yourself?"

Kieran grinned—a goofy, toothy motion that had her insides fluttering.

"Well, since you're asking," he said, his eyes traveling slowly along her body from head to toe, assessing her curves and attire like *she* was what he wanted to ride, "I suppose I should tell you that I'm your boss."

Audrey stared. "Excuse me?"

"And as of right now, you're fired."

Fall in Love with Forever Romance

A HOPE REMEMBERED
by Stacy Henrie

The final book in Stacy Henrie's sweeping Of Love and War trilogy brings to life the drama of WWI England with emotion and romance. As the Great War comes to a close, American Nora Lewis finds herself starting over on an English estate. But it's the battle-scarred British pilot Colin Ashby she meets there who might just be able to convince her to believe in love again.

SCANDALOUSLY YOURS
by Cara Elliott

Secret passions are wont to lead a lady into trouble... Meet the rebellious Sloane sisters in the first book of the Hellions of High Street series from bestselling author Cara Elliott.

Fall in Love with Forever Romance

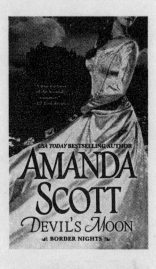

DEVIL'S MOON
by Amanda Scott

In a flawless blend of history and romance, *USA Today* bestselling author Amanda Scott transports readers again to the Scottish Borders with the second book in her Border Nights series.

THE SCANDALOUS SECRET OF ABIGAIL MacGREGOR
by Paula Quinn

Abigail MacGregor has a secret: her mother is the true heir to the English crown. But if the wrong people find out, it will mean war for her beloved Scotland. There's only one way to keep the peace—journey to London, escorted by her enemy, the wickedly handsome Captain Daniel Marlow. Fans of Karen Hawkins and Monica McCarty will love this book!

Fall in Love with Forever Romance

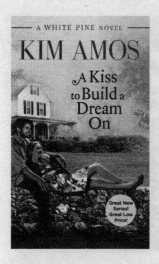

A KISS TO BUILD
A DREAM ON
by Kim Amos

Spoiled and headstrong, Willa Masterson left her hometown—and her first love, Burk Olmstead—in the rearview twelve years ago. But the woman who returns is determined to rebuild: first her family house, then her relationships with everyone in town... starting with a certain tall, dark, and sexy contractor. Fans of Kristan Higgins, Jill Shalvis, and Lori Wilde will flip for Kim Amos's Forever debut!

IT'S ALWAYS BEEN YOU
by Jessica Scott

Captain Ben Teague is mad as hell when his trusted mentor is brought up on charges that can't possibly be true. And the lawyer leading the charge, Major Olivia Hale, drives him crazy. But something is simmering beneath her icy reserve—and Ben can't resist turning up the heat! Fans of Robyn Carr and JoAnn Ross will love this poignant and emotional military romance.

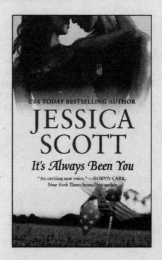

Fall in Love with Forever Romance

TOTAL SURRENDER
by Rebecca Zanetti

Piper Oliver knows she can't trust tall, dark, and sexy black-ops soldier Jory Dean. All she has to do, though, is save his life and he'll be gone for good. But something isn't adding up...and she won't rest until she uncovers the truth—even if it's buried in his dangerous kiss. Fans of Maya Banks and Lora Leigh will love this last book in Rebecca Zanetti's Sin Brothers series!